# masked

## HONOR BOUND: BOOK SEVEN

# ANGEL PAYNE

# masked

**HONOR BOUND: BOOK SEVEN**

## ANGEL PAYNE

WATERHOUSE PRESS

*For my Thomas...who loves my dark side.*

# CHAPTER ONE

It was going to be a breathtaking fall sunset in Red Rock Canyon. The birds still sang in a cloudless sky. Awakened by recent rains, the wind was still redolent with desert lilies, poppies, agave, and cholla blossoms. The air was cool but not cold. On a ranch in the valley below, a band played "Can't Help Falling in Love" for the crowd at a wedding reception in full swing. Appropriate, given that the lights of the Las Vegas Strip had just started to glitter in the distance.

"Good night to be alive. But an even better one to be dead, I reckon."

Daniel Colton glanced toward the source of the comment. His buddy, Special Ops Master Sergeant Tait Bommer, added a cheerful whistle to it while sharpening a wicked battle knife. The last rays of the day's sun glinted off the steel as Bommer checked the blade, flashing the dying rays of the sun into the eyes of the man who was bound and gagged in the dirt at their feet.

Dan grunted. "Wouldn't know the difference."

Tait nodded. Though he added a quick frown, he kept the expression to himself. Dan didn't need the guy's goddamn empathy, pity, attempt at understanding, or whatever the fuck they wanted to call it. His face was a freak show, end of discussion. He refused to process anything further than that. Didn't want to rehash the mission in which he'd "selflessly saved a woman's life" in a fire that should've killed her *and* him. Didn't want to talk about the months of burn therapy that made him wish he really *had* died—or the face that caused most people to think he was already half a corpse.

Best to just keep putting one foot in front of the other.

And looking forward to moments like this.

The sole advantage to being half Freddy Krueger was that a guy could go anywhere he wanted and do even more. Eyeballs on the guest roster at a Mexican Riviera resort known for its high security? No problem. The Ken doll side of his face, flashed at the right angle, charmed the front desk agent enough to turn it over. Getting past the guards at Cameron Stock's suite? *Presto magico.* Out came the burned monster, long enough to remind the assholes what they'd look like as worm food, allowing him to slip in with two hired goons and make off with Stock before anyone noticed.

By the time Stock's henchmen realized their boss was gone, Dan had the ass-wad drugged, tied, and loaded onto a private transport helo, charted for a direct flight here. The timing was advantageous. Tait was already out in the canyon, playing best man at his brother Shay's wedding at Spring Mountain Ranch. Dan threw a stare over at the lights of the celebration, where the Elvis tune was followed by the "Cha Cha Slide." He imagined the faces of so many friends in that glow, happy and smiling—and very relieved they didn't have to look at him, the burned husk serving as a reminder of the off-books operation that had nearly killed them all.

Due in part to the man now whimpering at Tait's feet.

"You ready to do this, spook man?"

Dan bristled. The nickname irked. He hadn't been a real spook for a while. Though he was still on the CIA's payroll, his indefinite medical leave wouldn't be lifted until he received clearance from one of their "approved" head shrinks—and he'd be damned if anyone was going to crack open his psyche for a guided tour anytime soon. Nevertheless, he let the label slide. There was more important work to focus on.

"You know it," he uttered back.

"Music to my ears." Tait chuckled while watching Stock's eyes widen before the man trickled a scream past the edges of a dirty cloth gag. "But that doesn't suck either, Stock. You sing all you want, because I've been waiting a long damn time for this—namely, from the moment I had to bury the woman I loved thanks to your terrorism." He ran the knife over the sharpening stone again. "Learning that you extorted my mom for years, keeping her from my brother and me, really wasn't helpful to your case either, man. And oh yeah...the bit about my sweet little old lady neighbor secretly being your minion, assigned to kill Shay and me if Mom ever tried to contact us? So a big winner in the karma department." He grunted. "Guess it's a good thing you got some points back when Shay and I found Mom last year."

Dan pivoted and planted a boot on Stock's chest, his face directly in Stock's line of vision. "Let's not forget his unique monster-making talent, either. Maybe I'll just stand here and remind you, asshole."

"Fan-fucking-tastic idea," Tait growled. "Nice little preview of hell."

"Bingo."

"You're so damn sweet, Colton."

"Right? That's me. Mr. Giver."

"That frees me up to be Mr. Karma." The tension rolled thicker off Tait, pretty much as Dan expected—but he still slid a questioning stare at his friend. Something was suddenly off about the guy. Tait had anticipated this day for a long damn time, twice as long as Dan. So why was there a palpable conflict in the man?

"Well?" Dan demanded. "You ready?"

Tait rolled his shoulders then nodded. "Yeah. Okay." But after he took two steps over, he paused—then returned Dan's stare with just as much determination. "No, Dan." He shook his head. "Not okay. Damn it, I'm sorry, but..."

Dan glared. Let his jaw plummet. "You're...*what*?"

A corner of his mouth jerked up. "Dude, sometimes...you just have to let love win."

"You have to do *what*?"

"I know, I know. Sounds like a sappy song, right?"

"No, goddamnit. Sounds like pussy-whipped walking."

"Maybe." Tait tossed the knife to the ground and then rolled his shoulders again. "Okay, probably."

Dan glared at the weapon. Again at his friend. "Are you fucking kidding me?"

"I'm sorry. I'm not. This time, love's the winner for me, man. The lightning bolt that just keeps hitting. I watched my brother declare the same truth for his life today. My mom was on one side of me, Lani on the other...lightning bolts number two and three, the loves I never thought life would give me, let alone in such abundance. And I've got a feeling that Lani, Kell, and I will be working on number four in a while too. Life is good, and I'm not going to blow it this time."

Rage pounded Dan's chest. Every mottled inch of skin on the right side of his face burned with it too. Logically, he knew the pain was only memory. Didn't matter when memories were as true as reality. And sure as *hell* didn't matter when the fury seeped so deep, he longed to strangle Tait before driving the knife into Stock.

*Life is good?*

*Love's the winner?*

What. The. Fuck?

"Well, isn't that the most precious thing?" He couldn't spit it viciously enough. "So glad to know things worked out for you, dude. That traveling all the way to Mexico, finding this ass-nozzle, flying him out, and bringing him right to your feet was so worth my fucking time!"

Tait's face—still so surfer-god attractive, he'd left at least a dozen women panting in his wake during Shay's bachelor party at Gilley's the other night—tightened. "Calm the hell down. Nobody asked you to play Dog the Bounty Hunter and traipse down to Mexico on a vendetta."

"Shut up," Dan snarled. He grabbed the knife and stomped over, thrusting the handle back out at the guy. "Shut the *fuck* up, Tait, and send this bastard to his maker now—or I will!"

★ ★ ★ ★ ★

"We're really going to hell for this." Tait's hands were matching loops of white around the steering wheel of his rented Escalade, even in the fading twilight. "You know that, right?"

A groan came from the back seat, laced with rickety agony—sounding a lot like a bastard with a knife in his scrotum. Dan glanced over his shoulder at Stock's prone form in the back seat. Well, imagine that. The guy *did* have a Bowie Hilt hard-on. The sack they'd tossed over Stock's head in Mexico now made for an improvised dressing around the wound, and a heap of hotel towels—God knew why Tait had the things in the car—were swaddled around the bastard, warding off a little of the encroaching shock. Even so, Stock's continued consciousness was surprising. He was either one of the most tenacious scumbags Dan had ever encountered or he'd really made a deal with the devil—a pact Dan would already be delivering on right now, if Bommer the magical Hallmark card hadn't stopped him.

Damn it.

At least he'd gotten in the satisfaction of going Benihana on the dickwad's scrotum. And yeah, he hated admitting it, but watching Stock in agony was maybe a bit more fun than gazing at his corpse. Now, he was determined to enjoy every moment of the show.

"Awww, Cameron," he drawled. "Is that a knife in your balls, or are you just happy to see me?"

"Fuh you!"

He snorted Tait's way. "Funny how that one always translates."

Tait added his glower to the mix. "You heard what *I* said, right? We're dragging that asshole, bleeding crotch and all, back to my little brother's *wedding reception.*"

"And that's my fault...why?"

Tait huffed. "Did you stop to think about the *date* of your little toodle-loo South of the Border, billionaire boy? You RSVP'd to the wedding too."

"No. Brynn RSVP'd for both of us."

"Because the woman's good that way. Really good. You know she's probably the best thing that ever happened to you, including your pre-asshole days, right?"

"You mean pre-Quasimodo days?"

"I mean pre-*asshole.*"

"Sheez. I sent Zo and Shay a present."

"You sent them a whole game room."

"They didn't like it?"

The guy stabbed a hand through hair that resembled a tsunami, due to all the product coating the strands. "For a second, just one, try to wrap your mind around how stressed we all were today. About *you*. When you didn't show up at the church, we all thought—" He stopped, clearly editing himself, though the damage was already done. Dan knew damn well what they'd all thought. "Well, we were worried. So when you texted in the middle of dinner with that *urgent, you gotta come now* shit..."

"Sorry to have disappointed," Dan drawled. "I know hand-delivering Stock wasn't as exciting as talking me down off the top of the Cosmopolitan. Shit, we could've topped off the night with foo-foo drinks in the Chandelier Bar too. What *was* I thinking?"

Bommer shook his head. "You know, asshole, I'm five seconds away from taking out your teeth with my fist. You want to devalue *your* life like that, I'm past fighting the issue. But stop dragging the rest of us into your goddamn hole."

Silence was the best response to that one. Even rounding the corner on his twenty-sixth sleepless hour, jacked on fury and adrenaline, the wisdom prevailed. Wouldn't do him any good to point out the "hole" wasn't his to begin with, dug deeper by the *two* off-books ops that the band of merry men known to the outside world as Operational Detachment Alpha, First Special Forces Group, had gotten themselves into. Wouldn't be a valid point, anyway. He'd been a willing accomplice to both the wild boys on both rides, including his decision to dive into that burning building in the north Nevada wilderness.

In the doing, he'd saved a nurse's life and lived through the ordeal himself, a miracle that should've brought more comfort than it did. But that was the thing about monkeys on a guy's back, especially the species known as bitterness—*especially* if it lived in the eyes of the mangled man in the mirror.

These days, it was simply easier to match the inside to the outside.

"Fuck," Tait groused. "I've been gone an hour and a half."

"Boohoo," Dan volleyed. "I'm sure Lani and Kell kept your seat warm." In more interesting ways than he wanted to imagine.

"You remember I'm the best man at this thing, right? The first toast guy? The keep-everything-moving guy?"

"And you would've been back to your duties much sooner than this, if—"

"Yeah, yeah. I know. If I'd let you go hara-kiri on fuckhead?"

"Technically, hari-kari is an act of suicide, but I'll let it slide. You've been under some stress."

Tait snorted. "Well, shit. You *are* Mr. Giver."

"Not too late for me to take your place as Mr. Karma." He glanced again at Stock, whose eyes widened in understanding of the intent. "Knife's still in the perfect position, man. More or less."

"No."

"Well, you're no fucking fun."

"And *you're* no fucking—" Tait gripped the wheel harder. "I really don't know how to finish that." The air in the car filled with the smoky edge of twilight before he murmured, "What the hell happened to you, Colton?"

Best to let that one descend into a long silence. Maybe

another. "That was rhetorical, right?"

Another question that provided its own answer. As if Bommer were serious about a single damn word. As if Dan didn't have the right rearview mirror to remind him of it. One glance that way, into the slab of mottled flesh from his temple to chin and cheekbone to ear, was proof enough of exactly what had "happened" to him.

"What's rhetoric got to do with this?" Tait snapped. "And stop answering me by moping at yourself in the mirror. You think anyone notices that shit but you?"

"Says one of the guys who used to call me *CIA Ken* because of *this shit*?"

"Yeah. So? We also called you Woofie the magical G-dog."

"The fuck?"

"Own it, man. If Uncle Sam threw a Frisbee, you'd kill yourself to catch it." A knowing smirk twisted Tait's lips. "Now you just have the badge of honor to prove it. On the books or off, you were always the get-it-right guy."

Dan's fingers dug into the dust coating the vehicle's roof. Beat the hell out of pulling his hand back inside, where it would've driven into the bastard's face. *Badge of honor?* Was he kidding? "Not amusing, Bommer. Not in anyone's fucking universe. *That*"—he jabbed his chin at the burn scar on the inside of Tait's right arm—"isn't your permission slip to spout about *this*." Flicking a finger at his face took care of that obviousness.

"Right. Because *you* don't let it define every damn move you make, right?"

"Fuck off."

Who the hell did Bommer think he was? Tait's burn could be easily hidden by a long-sleeved shirt, but even without the cover, somebody would have to be looking to see his "badge." Big fucking difference between that and walking around like something out of a circus sideshow. Bommer had no damn idea what this was like. None of them did.

"Fine," Tait finally muttered. "I'll give you the point. But do you really think any of us defined your work—which was damn good shit, by the way—based on your looking like a plastic doll minus the good parts?"

"Were you paying that much attention to my 'good parts'?"

"Says the guy who just got his rocks off by digging a blade into Stock's scrotum?"

"Says the guy who now shares a bed with his sniper partner?"

"*And* the hottest *wahine* in all the Hawaiian islands?"

Damn it. Fucker had a point. Tait and Kellan's unique relationship with their woman—yes, *their* woman, as in sharing the wealth in all ways imaginable—wasn't one Dan easily understood, though it was far from his place to point judgmental fingers. The three of them were obviously past the point of happy about the arrangement, and Tait deserved the joy after everything Stock and his partner, Ephraim Lor, took from the man.

And didn't that bring everything full circle once again?

Tait Bommer, the one guy on the planet who'd been craving Stock's head on a platter more than Dan, was now the guy who'd turned peace, love, and Ed Sheeran on him to all the sickest degrees—an anomaly so insane, it was a see-it-to-believe-it thing. Okay, so it had been over a year since Luna died because of Stock and Lor's terrorist plot. And, by all accounts, Lani Kail was even better for Tait than Luna was, a truth even Luna herself "agreed" with, Bommer had revealed with a cryptic smile.

Fuck.

IIe was actually using words like "cryptic" in the same sentence as Tait Bommer.

And maybe the earth was flat now too. And aliens were lurking in the stratosphere, ready to probe everyone like extraterrestrial kinksters.

But the cosmic issues had to go on hold for now. *Shitstorm ahead. Brace for impact.*

The second Tait hooked the car off Highway 159 and onto the access road to the ranch, the glow from hundreds of white party lights nearly made it possible for Tait to cut the car's headlights. The bulbs hung were suspended across one of the ranch's rustic picnic groves, with smaller lights wound around the supporting tree trunks. Old-fashioned oil lanterns rested on the banquet tables, which surrounded a wooden dance floor accented by big barrels brimming with sunflowers and wedding-type foof. It was a Wild West-themed wedding with all the gussy extras, and even from here, laughter filtered out from it on the wind.

There was a day, not too long ago, when Dan would've found such a sight enchanting. Hell, he'd probably have even conjured wistful thoughts of what his own wedding reception would be like. Now, the extra light was just an aid for illuminating his phone screen.

"I've got cell reception again," he told Tait. "But I really want to lie to you about that."

Tait cocked a brow. "You only gotta dial three little numbers, dude. Nine, one, and one."

"Fuck."

"That's not one of the numbers." His jaw clenched as Dan

snorted. "Okay, do you really want to go there, man? To know his blood is on your hands—for the rest of your life? Before you give me the *amen, brother* on that, listen to the guy who lines up sniper shots for a living." He exhaled through his nose and shook his head. "That crap sticks to your soul, Colton. It follows you—and not in the good ways."

Dan gripped the roof harder before retorting, "Right. Because I wouldn't know anything about 'crap' that follows a guy around." *Like half a face full of burn scars.*

"Just make the call, dickhead," Bommer growled.

As he guided the Escalade toward a spot at the back of the parking lot, a voice crackled through in Dan's ear.

"Nine-one-one. What is your emergency?"

He peeked once more at Stock. The guy drooped his pasty, sweaty face. *Now you know what it's like to wish you were already in hell, motherfucker.*

"Hello? Hello? Do you have an emergency?"

"How about a sack of shit who won't die?"

Tait swore under his breath before demanding, "Give me that, goddamnit."

As he yanked the phone away to give the operator *real* instructions, a commotion erupted at the other end of the parking lot. Okay, maybe not a "commotion"—but enough of a stir to lift even Stock's head for a second. That was the kind of effect Shay Bommer had on the air, anywhere he went. To be fair, he couldn't help it. Shay was an actual force of nature, genetically altered as a child by one of Stock's many "business partners," so his "animal side" *was* his animal side. As the guy stalked across the pavement, his massive body strained at the confines of his white shirt, ivory tuxedo vest, and tailored dress denims. His new bride was just a few steps behind, cobalt boots kicking from beneath her lacy wedding gown.

Dan exited the car and then leaned against the hood. Might as well act relaxed, even if his bloodstream wasn't in sync. "Congratulations, you two. Sorry I had to borrow your best man for a while—but I've returned him with a gift."

Tait jerked up his head, shooting over a fresh glower. "*E kala mai ia'u,*" he muttered into the phone. "Just one moment, my friend." He looked fast to Shay. "It's *not* a gift, brother. Stay back, and for fuck's sake, keep Zoe away. She's in no condition to see this."

Dan tossed his head back, barking a laugh. "Really, man? You don't know your own sister-in-law better?"

"Keep me away from what?" Sure enough, Zoe Chestain-Bommer bolted forward like Tait had lassoed her. "And what do you mean, 'no condition'? I'm pregnant, not schizo."

"Don't go near that one," Dan warned Tait. "Not with a hundred-foot pole."

Fortunately, it took three of Zoe's steps to match one of Shay's. "No way, dancer." He caught her by the elbow in time, tucking her behind him. "Not until I've played the full shell game on this first."

"*Qué?*" The little Latina's eyebrows arched. Technically, the word was a question. Not-so-technically, she'd told her new husband *oh no, you didn't.*

Shay received backup in the form of his groomsmen, consisting of Rhett Lange and Rebel Stafford, both still serving with the First SFG and instrumental in saving Shay's ass on that last off-books mission. They were joined by Ghid Preston, the walking rhino of a man who was passionately devoted to Shay and Tait's mother, Melody Bommer. It actually surprised Dan that Melody wasn't right behind—

MASKED

*Ding, ding, ding.* Two seconds later, Melody Bommer appeared, as elegant as Ghid was rough in a figure-flattering dress that matched Zoe's blue boots. Behind her was Zoe's sister, Ava, who'd gotten hitched last New Year's to one of the finest SFG operators Dan knew, Ethan Archer. Too bad Archer wasn't hanging with her now. Though the man's temper took longer to flare than most of the guys Shay hung with, he'd also be the kind not to fling fault for running a basic off-the-books revenge fantasy, given the means and the money for it. Dan needed such an advocate about now.

Instead, Ava's companion was one of Zoe's best friends, El Browning, who'd switched out her long red hair for a blond, wedding-appropriate updo. The look was good for her, but that didn't stop Dan's gut from twisting at her arrival.

Where El went, Brynn usually followed.

Brynn. Who'd been there through so much of the last eleven months. Who'd tolerated his bitterness and anger and impatience. Who'd sneaked him fast food in the hospital, sat with him through countless old war movies, and even taken him on his first trip in public after the scars had healed—as much as they would. And yes, she'd even been there when he needed to relieve his tension...in other ways.

Who deserved so much more than he'd given her in return—but had staunchly refused to acknowledge that fact.

Until now.

As the woman walked up behind her two friends, looking as gorgeous as a princess in the cobalt satin fitted perfectly to her lithe figure, one distinct message was written across her face.

She'd finally seen the light.

Had realized just how fucked up he really was.

Ohhh, yeah. Her glare told him everything. Disbelief, disappointment, and hurt raced across her lips and tightened the corners of her eyes. Tension clamped her bare shoulders and made its way down to both clenched fists.

"Hey there, gorgeous." It was his regular greeting. When he coupled it with what he could muster of a smile, the woman usually dissolved like butter in a sauce pan.

Not tonight.

"You're here."

Her tone conveyed what the words didn't. *You're here—but were supposed to be four hours ago. You're here—dressed in field mission gear that's splattered with blood instead of the tuxedo I bought for you on my dancer's salary. You're here—after letting all my calls and texts go unanswered for two days.*

"I am." *Lame. Ass.* But what the hell else made sense?

"Why?" Once more, tone that implied meaning. *Why did you even bother?*

"My question exactly." As Zoe stomped her foot, the asymmetrical angles of her foofy skirts swayed, hiding the slight baby bump beneath. "Dan the Man claims there's a present involved, but Tait the wuss says I'm too delicate to see it."

Tait jutted his chin away from the phone. "The wuss who's now your brother-in-law—which means you're as delicate as I say, damn it."

"That so?" Her dark-blue nails stood out against the cream lace as she cocked both hands to her hips. "News flash, *cabrón.* You're not in the islands anymore. And *I'm* not—"

"Zoe," Shay warned.

"Do. Not. 'Zoe.' Me. We stood in front of that minister and agreed we wouldn't hold any secrets from each other. That we would share everything. You need a refresher course on the definition of sharing now, Mr. Bommer? Because it sure as hell does *not* inclu—"

"Holy fuck." Shay's utterance sliced her short. He peered again inside the Escalade and then lurched back, a guy who'd just seen a ghost. And a zombie too. "What the hell? *How* the hell?" He hammered a frown at Tait and then Dan. "This had to be off-books. And *not* cheap."

Everyone's gaze reflected the same curiosity—except for Tait's. He scowled, seeming to anticipate what Dan was about to say.

"Colton Steel's been doing well this year." Dan smirked and crossed his ankles. "And let's just say this was a hell of a lot more fun than buying another Lambo."

Shay shook his head. "I don't know whether to shoot you or kiss you, spook man."

Tait grimaced. "There's a visual I never needed."

"*You* never needed?" Dan rejoined.

The guy-bonding respite was enjoyed for two more seconds. His gut was shoved back into the meat grinder as Brynn stepped around, approaching him with tight lips and folded arms. Her raspy whisper was just as much a spleen-twister. "Where have you been, Dan?"

He met her gaze directly. It wasn't easy, knowing exactly what she was forced to take in as he did—but at this point, he at least owed her his honesty. "In a lot of places I couldn't answer the phone. A lot of places you probably shouldn't know about, sweetheart."

Her forehead furrowed. Her eyes went dark. "You don't say."

The gut grinder cranked higher. Who knew it had a *mince*

setting?

*Damn it.*

It had never been his intention to hurt her like this—especially not to drag her this far into his darkness. When they'd first met all those months ago in Zoe's living room, the attraction had been instant—but they'd also been living in a bubble. They'd thought they could go after the bad guys and emerge unscathed. They'd thought they were superheroes in plain clothes, invincible and unstoppable. And after the fire, Brynn had just kept thinking the same thing. She agreed to ignore his monster face...if he ignored the dark preferences of his sexuality.

Like the messed-up shit he was, he'd agreed. Had even accepted the distortion of his face as karmic payback for the dark desires of his mind and body, indulged over the years in select BDSM dungeons, and now maybe the universe was realigned in that regard too. Maybe now he wouldn't crave the high of taking a woman to the edge of her limits, physically and psychologically. Maybe now he'd look like a monster but have the sexual needs of a normal man. And maybe, one day far away, he'd be able to settle down with a normal woman, just like Brynn. Maybe *she'd* be that woman.

But that had been an illusion too. His sorry dick still wanted what it did, and Brynn had made it clear she wasn't wired that way.

So maybe he was just a depraved fuck who deserved what fate had dished out.

Yeah, even the woman who edged away from him, shaking her head slowly. "You don't say," Brynn repeated, as if hoping to gain strength from it. That in itself was wrong. So wrong. *He* should be her strength. That so wasn't happening either. And likely never would.

He was still a messed-up shit. Only now, without any bubble.

Shay, still gaping in shock, was distracted long enough for Zoe to race forward. Tait's protesting bellow, as well as her husband's attempt to hold her back, were too late. The little brunette jerked open the Escalade's door.

"*Caramba!*" she shrieked.

"Holy crap!" El seconded.

Brynn joined her friends but didn't say a word. She stared, still tucked in against herself, as Stock let out a loud grunt. From his position at the front of the car, Dan couldn't tell if the guy was terrified, pissed, or both. Not that it mattered. Not that the shreds of his gut would magically heal, even if he strutted back and really finished flaying the asshole—a craving he fought harder with every passing minute.

A reward for the self-control came in the oddest form he could imagine.

Again, before anyone could hold her back, Zoe stomped forward. Grabbed the frame of the car door opening in order to balance herself—as she rammed the heel of one cobalt cowboy boot into the bridge of Stock's nose.

"*Woooo.*" El pumped a fist. "Oh, my God, Zo. Awesome! I heard his bones crunch and everything!"

"Shit," Tait muttered.

"Fuck." Shay pinched his nose.

"Damn." Dan snickered. Not even a censuring glare from Brynn quelled him. Why fight for a sinking ship? Tait was right; the woman was one of the best things that had come along in his life—but maybe he simply wasn't meant to have nice things. It was a damn idiot's game to continue thinking otherwise.

"Oops." Zoe swung a wide, innocent gaze at her husband. "Look, *papi*. The *desgraciado* fell down, right on his face. What a shame."

Melody high-fived her for that—on *her* way to the opening. "I'm next."

"No, you're not." Ghid roped a burly arm around her waist and dragged her six feet backward.

"Goddamnit!" She beat at his meaty chest. "Don't you dare deprive me of this, Ghid. That monster has to pay for the evil he dragged into my life. Into *yours*." She drove a glare at Shay and Tait. "And *yours*!"

"And we've all overcome it." Ghid braced her shoulders, making the order beneath his words clear. "Become better for it, even with all our battle wounds." Logical progression after that was a traded stare with Shay. Nobody in the circle needed interpretation. They all knew about the heinous "experiments" Ghid and Shay had endured at the hands of Stock's business partner, Homer Adler—and the incision scars that riddled both their bodies because of them. "Today isn't a day for killing—"

"Killing?" Zoe's head jerked up. She whipped her gaze, now sapphire bright, back to her husband. "Could we get away with that? Seriously? If we were quick about it—"

"No!" Shay shouted it along with Tait, Ghid, Rhett, and Rebel. Dan was the only abstention.

"Are you crazy?" The concurring growl came from Brynn, who whirled from Dan to advance on her friend. "Zo, would you listen to yourself?"

"She's sorta right, honey," El said. "It *is* your wedding day."

"And you have a condition." Tait stabbed a finger in the direction of Zoe's belly.

"*Ay*. All right, all right!" As Zoe barked it, sirens wailed across the valley. Red-and-white lights careened off a pair of emergency vehicles, closing in on the ranch at a NASCAR pace.

"Thank fuck for small miracles." Rebel hiked up his shirtsleeves, exposing his exotically tattooed forearms. He stepped over, roping Shay under one arm and Zoe under the other. "All right, you two, a few hundred people are over there because of you. Go forth and be charming. Rhett and I have this covered." He nodded toward Tait. "That goes for you too, T-Bomb. Stop moping. That's Colton's job now."

Tait clawed a hand through his hair. "I need a fucking beer. And a dance with my woman."

"Just a dance?" Shay waggled his brows at his brother but reached for Zoe.

"Easy, *papi*." Zoe giggled, though the sound was still strained. "It's not time for the honeymoon yet."

"It is when you get all feisty and want to kill people."

His stab at make-love-not-war was lost on his bride, who gazed longingly at the car once more. "It's a hell of a lot more than 'want.'"

"Zoe." He coupled the warning with a jerk at the small of her back. "Let it go, tiny dancer. Please."

"Because *you* have?"

He huffed. "Do we have to do this right—"

"Because you don't still wake up in sweats from the nightmares of what that *hijueputa* did to you? Because *I'll* never forget walking into that room in Adler's lab and seeing him standing next to the bed they'd strapped you to, locking you down like the breeding stud they'd reduced you to? Because it tore my soul apart to see you drugged, cut up, and—"

Shay cupped her face in both hands. "It's behind us now,

baby girl. Don't sacrifice our joy on the altar of hating him."

"Great minds." Tait jerked a thumb toward Dan. "Same logic I tried on the spook earlier."

Shay snorted. "I see how well that went."

"Stock's intestines aren't decorating the back seat, are they?"

Shay's brows jumped. "Point taken."

Dan's gaze was snagged by the approving slant of Zoe's lips. "You simply pulled the wrong member of the wedding party away, Colton. I would've gladly helped you turn that *cabrón's* guts into vulture food."

"*Enough.*"

Shay snarled it before smacking Zoe's backside with so much force, there was no doubt about his intent. *Obi-Wan, the Dom is strong in this one.* Dan had known that much about Shay for a while, though it was clear Tait hadn't. The guy gawked at his brother with new awareness. Shay flared a glare in return before pivoting back to his bride, who'd turned the texture of putty. They all watched as Zoe stood on tiptoe to whisper something in Shay's ear. He nodded and murmured, "Of course you may. But make it fast."

Dan leaned against the car again, grinning. Whatever Shay had just given Zoe permission for, it ought to be a good show. He hoped it involved something like freeing more little swimmers from Stock's balls or finishing the nose job she'd started.

But the little dancer didn't go near the car. She skipped over to *him*. Before he could recover from the switch-up, Zoe threw her arms around his neck—and landed a solid kiss on his cheek.

He froze.

Rhett and Rebel whooped. El joined them. Everyone else clapped. Even Brynn, who still looked like his *cojones* on a platter would suit her just fine.

"You were right, spook man," Zoe drawled. "*That* was a kick-ass wedding gift." She kissed his other cheek, using it as an excuse to murmur into his ear, "But next time, we'll just kill the *chingado*, okay?"

# CHAPTER TWO

"She actually said that?"

Tess Lesange laughed her way through the question. Number one, the reaction made sense. Number two, it beat having to hide how badly she wanted to jump the bones—and anything else—of the man who dwarfed the little table they shared for a last-minute lunch at Mundo.

Though they'd agreed to meet only an hour ago, Dan had arrived early enough to snag the table's location, in a corner deep enough to cloak the right side of his face from the room. As usual, he'd dressed like every other "power government" guy in the place—a concerted effort on his part to blend in as much as possible—though she didn't have the heart to tell him that would never be possible. The man would command the space around him even if he'd arrived in a gunnysack. But take that natural aura of power, leadership, and animal-attraction sensuality, then slide it all into a charcoal suit, pinstriped shirt, trendy tie, and polished Ferragamos...

No damn way was this man going to "just blend" in *any* room.

Or make her yearn any less to help him dirty it all up.

She forced herself not to fixate on the poetry of his long fingers, swirling their way around the rim of his beer mug. It was another effort altogether to ignore the glances he got from women at other tables, openly betraying how they'd let their bodies trade places with that mug in an instant.

Like she was any better than them.

Not by a single damn iota.

*Friend zone, Tess. You're solidly there, and you'll never be anyplace else. Get it through your thick, overstyled head. The man likes little, cute, curvy show dancers, not tall, gawky, a-little-too-weird intel analysts.*

Though she sure couldn't tell that right now.

Damn. The man had a gift, a potent one, for making a girl feel like the object of his sole attention, despite the lunch-hour chaos in one of downtown's hottest restaurants. She might be the one with the office nickname of "the laser," but she'd never felt like the entire world just went away unless she was with Dan. Though she'd never been in the field a day in her life, she imagined his intense focus was his hugest strength during the life-and-death ops he often regaled her with.

Never could she have guessed that his friend's wedding would be added to that list.

"Yeah." Dan smirked fully enough to tug at his scar tissue. "Word for word. That's really what she said."

She scooped a chip into the bowl of guacamole between them. "I think I like this Zoe person." She took a bite out of the bright-green smoodge of heaven. Holy hell, this place made *bueno guac.*

Dan chuckled. "She's a scrappy one, all right."

"You tell her that to her face?"

"You think I'm that dumb? She wanted to put a bullet in Stock's brain worse than me. 'Scrappy' wouldn't be jamming a bee under her bonnet. It'd stir the whole hive."

She flashed a bigger smile. "You were both right not to kill him. He's under max security watch now. As soon as his... errr...injury heals, he'll be processed and then prosecuted with anything we can throw at him. Cameron Stock and his empty nut sack will never see the sky free of barbed wire again."

Dan returned the grin. "It'll be good news to tell her after the honeymoon. She and Ironman are honeymooning on Kauai so he can spend a little time with T-Bomb during the trip."

Tess pretended to be picky about her next chip, disguising her nervousness about the question she couldn't evade any longer. "Brynn was there too, right?"

It was impossible not to notice how his fingers whitened against his mug.

"Yeah. She was."

"So what was her take on things? Did you let her know what you were up to in advance?"

"Of course not."

"Damn."

"Yeah. Damn." He glanced up, almost bashful about it, giving her a glimpse of his piercing blue eyes. *Gut flip number ten thousand*—for today alone. Those twin blues could sear her like the purest heart of a flame, meaning her system didn't know whether to shiver or overheat. Screw it. She went for both.

"Oh, dear," she muttered. *Liar.* Thank God for the chips. Something for the hands to do besides betray her schism of excitement. "Trouble in paradise?"

She could only hope.

No. *No*, she couldn't.

*Therese Odette Lesange, you are going to hell. In handcuffs. And flip-flops. Ugly ones, like the kind they sell at the hotel pools. The disgrace of plastic flowers and cheap rhinestones shall follow you throughout eternity.*

"You could say that." Dan didn't look comfortable about the admission. Nor did he look heartbroken. "She pulled the plug."

Yesssssss.

*Straight. To. Hell.*

"Pulled the plug? In what way?" Wow. She had no idea she could play this stupid. It was sort of scary.

"As in, pulled the plug," Dan reiterated. "Broke it off."

Ohhhhh, yesssss.

*In crappy flip-flops.*

"Oh, my God."

He cocked his head, going into let-me-see-if-I-can-freak-you-out-with-the-scars mode. "Oh, come on. You're not *that* shocked, Ruby, and we both know it."

Tess grinned. Sneaky charmer had her at the nickname. He was the only one who called her that—whom she *let* call her that—and since it was the deepest intimacy she'd ever share with him, it was special.

"Fine. I'm not rushing to catch the Twitter feed on it, okay?"

There was a great follow-up to that, wasn't there? She couldn't remember—not after he retaliated by softly tugging on one of her dark-red curls. She'd gone for a new shade yesterday, *Rose Temptation*, which was darker than the usual tint that simply enhanced her natural color. The result was more startling than she thought, and she'd expected Dan to pop a joke involving Strawberry Shortcake, Jessica Rabbit, or both. Instead, he'd been pretty fascinated, an energy she didn't remember from the other times she'd opted for the retro, tube-curl hairstyle.

And maybe she was reading too much into everything

he said and did now. Because hell, *that* had never happened before.

"But..." He canted his head the other way. "You're still surprised, aren't you? Really surprised?"

She let out a careful breath. "I suppose I am."

"Why?"

Shit. Did the man have to punctuate everything by yanking on her curls? As he did it again, his knuckles grazed the side of her neck. Heat radiated from the contact, permeating her with a thousand sparks, forcing her to lick her lips before concentrating on coherence.

"I guess...well...the two of you have been at it for a while. I assumed everything was going great."

And because it was easier than contemplating any different. Dan in a relationship was much less painful to think about than the Dan of a year ago, dating a different woman every month, none of whom had been her. Of course, a year ago, they'd also been work pals who barely spoke. Hadn't stopped her nonstop fantasies about the man. The fire and his disfigurement had changed everything between them—for the better *and* the worse.

The better? Dan talked to her about everything now.

The worse? Dan talked to her about everything now.

Including the one big "everything" she'd suspected almost from the day she'd met him—that he was a lifestyle Dominant, as dark and kinky as desert summer days were long.

Like he hadn't given her enough to envision already.

Like she hadn't dreamed of giving herself over to a man in the exact same way, in the exact same scenarios he described— which had become only memories to him since the accident and his recovery. She'd always listened eagerly, eventually slipping in enough questions that Dan must know she was curious about this stuff. But by the time they'd arrived at that level of disclosure, he was hot and heavy with Brynn Monet—meaning lunches like this usually ended with her driving back to the office with a racing mind and soaked panties.

*Yay.*

Dan's snort brought her back to today's daily dole-out of frustration. "'Going great'?" That's really what you thought, eh?" He grunted hard. "Guess that depends on your idea of great."

She leaned in, resting an elbow on the table. The move was for caution, not flirtation. *Sure, honey. You just go ahead and keep believing that—especially with what you're about to let slide from your "virginal" little lips.*

"You already know what my idea of 'great' is."

He tilted his head again, as if he'd yanked the cord on the lightbulb inside it. "Yeah," he said slowly, "I suppose I do."

"Then why do you sound so stunned?"

"Do I?"

His head dipped lower as his grin inched higher. The little-boy-bashful look was one of his hottest moves before the burns. Now, he used it to hide those scars—like Tess even remembered they were there by this point.

"Okay," he declared, "so now that we've gone there with the conversation... How *are* things going with the FetLife guy?"

The question affected her like a physical shove. She returned to her original posture, grabbing the chance to regain her composure.

She'd walked right into this one, hadn't she? That was what she got for meeting the man for lunch, knowing he'd wear a suit, which would in turn make her forget her own damn name, let alone that if she went for the subject of kink, he'd bring up the lifestylers' version of Facebook, which replaced prompts like "mood of the day" and "favorite movies" with "favorite fetishes" and "hard limits." Dan had encouraged her to form an FL profile about two months ago, after she'd finally confessed that a lot of reading, research, and soul searching had led to the conclusion of wanting to explore the Dominant/submissive lifestyle more deeply.

She remembered the day he'd made the recommendation to her. He'd seemed wistful—and that wasn't a surprise. By that point, she'd known he hadn't stepped foot into a BDSM dungeon in over a year and that Brynn was digging her heels in about ever giving it a try.

The situation had never met Tess's approval. To be more accurate, she was incensed. But some of that was due to her baggage, not Dan's—shit that would likely take her a lifetime to figure out. From the outside, life in the Lesange household made Mattie, Viv, and her the envy of all their schoolmates, raised in an atmosphere that appeared the epitome of "Parisian hip"—though in reality, was a gilded cage of limits and bigotries. It was all so insidious, she'd never seen any of it clearly until a few years ago. Who the hell had the right to throw sludge on another person's choices, unless it was dangerous or stupid? And going priss-prude on a man like Dan Colton, who offered to be a patient guide into the subtleties of the D/s dynamic? Instant induction into the *stupid* column. When she'd said as much, Dan had chuckled and called her "cute."

Cute.

Brynn was giving the man vanilla sex in a handful of positions, and Tess got "cute."

*You need to be grateful for what you* do *have with him—a*

*hell of a lot more than what you dreamed of having in the first place, right? Don't mess with the goodness, Tess. Not now.*

It was the same reasoning she'd used to finally open the FetLife page—but so far, with the results she now relayed to Dan. "Honestly, they're going nowhere," she muttered, though managed a laugh to set up her next revelation. "I'm not sure why the guy called himself a Dom. Every time he loaded a new profile photo, he'd message to ask me if his butt looked big." She giggled as Dan nearly spat out his beer. "Sorry. Should've warned you that was coming."

He shot up a brow. "Euphemism intended?"

"Probably."

The brow descended. "Fuck. Sorry about that, Ruby."

She shrugged and smiled as the waiter delivered their lunch. Beef enchiladas for him, Ensenada chicken for her. "Well, don't cry me a river," she quipped, spooning some sauce from her plate to the ridge of the big flour tortilla. "A wise man, who happens to like a little food with his salsa"—she eyed the three salsa dishes mounted next to his plate—"once told me this process might take a while."

"Sounds like the idiot didn't know what he was talking about."

"Oh, sure he did."

"Oh, *no*, he didn't."

Whoa. *Commander Colton is in the house.* Only she couldn't figure out why. When his direct order of a statement came accompanied by an incisive gaze, she gulped down some more tea. Cleared her throat. Drank again. Yet he still stared. What the hell was going on? Or was *nothing* going on? Wouldn't be the first time she'd read too much into his actions just because she longed for it to be so.

"Errrm...I'm lost." At least it was the truth.

Dan didn't let up on the stare. *Not helping*, screamed her frazzled nerves.

"Men can be idiots, Ruby."

*That* was what she got worked up about? She made up for it with a hard snort. "You said it, not me."

He loaded up his fork but didn't bite. Instead, after blowing out more air through his nostrils, he stated, "That 'wise man' told you it would 'take a while' because he didn't think you were completely serious about finding a Dom."

She felt her brows reach for her hairline. "Is that so?"

"Yeah. That's so."

Forget frazzled. She was miffed. "What? Because he thinks he knows me?"

"Well, yeah. Probably a little more than most people."

"Well, screw that." She stabbed into her own food. "And screw you." *Oh, how you once wished. Thank God for the friend zone now.* "I appreciate all the things we've talked about, okay? But I meant it when I said I've been reading about the lifestyle on my own. Believe it or not, 'Laser' Lesange knows how to apply herself to more than spreadsheets, satellite shots, and classified intel."

"Okay, okay." He reached over, grabbing her hand before she could think to yank away. "Men? Idiots? Remember?"

*Damn.* Was she really just thanking God for the friend zone? She took it back. Immediately.

Skin-to-skin, the man was even harder to view on a platonic plane. His hand surrounded hers in heat, strength, and command. She looked at their entwined fingers before lifting her stare back up to his face. God had given the man an incredible face. If he'd been born fifty years ago, his long-lashed eyes, aquiline nose, and forceful jaw would've been splashed across movie screens from beneath a white Stetson, chasing bad guys alongside John Wayne and Clint Eastwood. Every time she saw him again, even just a half hour ago in front of the restaurant, her breath caught and her heart stopped.

And yeah, that was even with the scars.

Who the hell was she kidding? The scars were just another giant crank on her libido. The mottled strip of skin was like Wayne's strut and Eastwood's cigar, a signature symbol that proclaimed much deeper waters than the surface—a much more dangerous message than the placid outside. *You really want to fuck with me, man, after seeing what I've taken already?*

Shit. What were they talking about again?

"Idiots." She grabbed onto the one word she remembered before her logic had decided to feed itself to her lust. "Yeah, well...that might be an exaggeration. At least sometimes."

"Well, not this time," he said, humble and soft. "Put that together with a guy who's been in the lifestyle for six years and seen more than my fair share of subbies who dive into it for all the wrong reasons, and you end up with a guy who looks at things cynically."

She took a bite—using her other hand. She was going to enjoy the crap out of the physical connection to him, even if it was only from wrist to fingertips. "That's understandable," she conceded. "Kind of like bringing in civilian consultants on cases, who then think we're all Sydney Bristow and Jason Bourne."

"Wait." His forehead crunched. "I'm *not* Jason Bourne?"

"Smartass."

They laughed together. And that, she concluded, was the end of that—

Until he squeezed her fingers tighter.

*The ruby has officially melted.* The second grasp confirmed what the first couldn't. He hadn't reached for her just to prove a point. He *wanted* to be holding her like this.

*Dry out your panties, girl. Holding hands in a public restaurant is a long way from stepping into a play room together. Would you really let the man tie your ass down to a spanking bench right now—after he admitted to privately bankrolling an off-books op to catch a bastard before nearly flaying the man open for the Red Rock vultures?*

Her heart answered that before her head could. And that answer was no relief for her dilemma.

*I'd trust him with my life right now if I had to.*

So letting him work some Dominant magic on her bare ass? There was a no-brainer.

As she allowed her mind to rev with that daydream, she was conscious of wetting her lips again—but very little else. Even Dan's voice was dim and distant until he all but yelled her name.

"Huh?" she stammered. She took in his face, still filled with rugged intensity, and gave up on walking out of here with anything less than a soaked pussy. *Juuust great.* "What?" she snapped.

His tawny brows settled harder over his piercing blues. "Where the hell did you just go?"

She managed another shrug. "Doesn't matter." It *couldn't* matter. Not where he was concerned.

"Unless you were strolling through the mental weapons room, contemplating which one to use on me."

A laugh spurted. "Shut up. I'm over it."

"And I'm sorry."

"What?" Her confusion was genuine. She was used to chip-on-the-shoulder Dan, not this new, different gentleman Dan. It was weird—and seriously messed with her dungeon fantasies of him. Swiftly, she demanded, "Why?"

"For lumping you into the wannabe subbie box."

"*Pssshh.*" She took another bite to smooth the moment. Apologies from him were like straight talk from back-channel radio chatter: weird and unnatural. "You explained that reasoning. Made sense. Water under the bridge. Can we move on?"

"Right after I tell you that you're going to make some Dom the luckiest guy on the planet."

So much for smoothing things out. Hell. He'd never spoken words that affected her so deeply. They warmed her in depths she never imagined him reaching—but brought an arctic freeze in their wake.

*I don't want* some *Dom.*

*I want you.*

And he was going to know that...how? The question made a ton of sense—and brought a truckload of hope. Every book she'd devoured about BDSM stressed the importance of communicating one's needs, even if it wasn't comfortable. Doms weren't gods, psychics, or mind readers. They were simply men who did their best with what their subbies gave them. With being entrusted with the truth.

Maybe it was time for her to heed that advice.

*Suck it up, Lesange. You've tracked terrorists and human traffickers and drug kingpins. So just apply the laser to your own damn insecurities.*

"Well..." Shit. This felt like the first step off the high dive board. Now she was committed to the plummet. "I just heard one of the hottest Doms in town is newly available."

Dan's fork fell out of his hand. Clattered to his plate.

Salsa and cheese spattered, dripping down the salt and pepper shakers like blood and guts.

Tess set down her fork and gulped again—this time hoping the heat across her face didn't look as mortifying as it felt. "Well. Who's sorry now?"

"Tess—"

"Don't." She yanked her hand free from his. "Just...don't, okay?" The last thing she needed was some excuse about how this "had nothing to do with her" and how he just "wasn't ready" to go there with anyone right now—when they both knew he'd been damn ready for at least the last six months.

Silence stretched. The most uncomfortable minute of her life.

"Tess. Listen."

"No."

"*Yes.*" He pulled her hand back in. She yanked back. He held fast. "You are so goddamn beautiful. And stunning. And smart. Everything a Dom could ever dream of—"

"Except a Dom like you."

Deliberate pause. Determined stare. "Yeah. We might as well drill that one in. Except a Dom like me."

"Because you like it rough?"

He blew out a tight huff. "Darlin', 'rough' is just the tip of my whip, okay?"

"Oooooh. And that's supposed to make me scared?"

"Damn it, Tess. Look—"

"'Listen.' 'Look.' 'Drill that in.' Awfully bossy words from a guy who doesn't want to be my Dom."

He reared back. Narrowed the corners of both eyes. If

he was still going for scary, it wasn't working. Even the guy's ticked-off look stopped her heart on every track it possessed. "Is that what you think?"

She rolled her eyes. "Oh, here it comes."

"Here what comes?"

"The big lecture."

Tighter eyes. Blue steel irises. Anger and power that turned her panties from moist to soaked. *Damn him.* "What 'big lecture' would that be?"

"The one when *I play too hard for your virginal ass* isn't working. The one about how you're too fucked up right now to even think about training a submissive—and about how I'd be better off with a guy who better knows where his life is at, what the hell he's doing, and how to treat a *gift* like me. Hmmm. I'm sure I'm leaving something out. Give me a second..."

As she tapped at her jaw, his tightened to the texture of canyon cliffs. Right before he yanked out his wallet, tossed some twenties on the table, and swept a hand out to jerk her to her feet. Okay, so the commander was back—but Tess wasn't sure she dug the pissy upgrades. At *all.*

"Dan! Sheez!"

"Grab your phone and purse," he ordered from locked teeth.

"What the—"

He didn't wait any longer. Instead, he snatched up her phone and dropped it into her purse before wrapping the pocketbook's straps in a fist. Hell. She'd have to pull everything out to find the device again. But there wasn't time for fuming. There wasn't time for anything except fighting to keep up with Dan's long strides out of the restaurant.

The midday sun hit them at full blast. It wasn't blistering

hot, but that didn't make a difference at this end of town, with no skyscraper hotels to block the rays. If anything, the effect was intensified by the Cleveland Center across the street, its "collapsed" aluminum heights throwing back the light at crazy angles.

Before Tess could shield her eyes, Dan yanked her back into the shade. Inside seconds, he had her pressed to the concrete wall, where he loomed with a stance as furious as his grip. Though she knew he'd let her up if she so much as whispered such a demand, her nervous system didn't know the difference. He was huge and overpowering, even a little daunting. Maybe a lot daunting.

*Note to self: you really like daunting.*

For a moment, just one, she imagined they were in the shadows of a dungeon together instead. Maybe she'd just mouthed off at him and he stared down, contemplating what discipline she deserved for it. Would he spank her bare ass? Flog her nude body? Oh God, would he whip her trembling thighs? How much would she take from him? How much *could* she take?

Damn it, how she burned to know those answers.

Damn it, how she wished he'd read her mind right now.

Damn it, how it looked like he did.

Her breath ached as their gazes locked. As he inhaled, his face hardened into new angles. He was beautiful. Even his scars were stunning, betraying rolling tides of intense emotions.

But what emotions were they? Why had he hauled her out here?

"New lecture," he finally grated. "And this time, you *will* listen."

"Yes, Sir."

She smiled, letting him know how freely she gave the words.

Dan's eyes slid shut. His lips flattened.

*Was that good? Bad?*

"I value you," he muttered at last. "I value...this. Us. I've never been able to have this with a woman, besides Devyn, in my entire life. I'm pretty sure she's disqualified by default. So maybe...you came along to show me I could." His breath left him in a significant rush. "I only know it's too important to fuck up. If gaining you as a submissive meant losing you as a friend..." He shook his head just before Tess dipped hers. "I don't know what I'd do, okay?"

She jerked out a nod. And didn't mean a damn moment of it. Not when her vision was consumed by the proximity of his legs to hers, braced and long and commanding. She wanted to slide her ankles up those legs—on her way to wrapping them around his waist. Begging him to fill her body with his...

"Tess?"

"Yeah," she blurted. "Okay, okay." But it wasn't. He'd not only mushed her back into the friend zone like so much Play-Doh in a can but slammed the lid shut by notching her next to his sister on the priority list.

His sister.

Crap. Just crap.

*You really need to peel back the cloud, damn it. The silver lining here is pretty damn good. You're practically on the same pedestal as Devyn.*

Comforting enough for her head. Shallow solace for her heart. Her body. Her soul. Which, she now realized, had been suspended in *her* version of a limbo...waiting for this day. Hoping Dan would be free to return to kink one day—and that she'd be by his side for that journey.

Now, one look back up told her all she needed to know. The little smile on Dan's face, tender and respectful, was a beacon of confirmation.

She'd waited for nothing.

The finality of it settled over her like mourning shrouds.

They burned away the very next second. The flare of new realization could do that sometimes—thank God.

She didn't have to wait anymore.

If Dan refused to take her down this path...she was now free to find someone who would.

The epiphany twitched a grin across her own lips now. Dan peered at it with curiosity but clearly misinterpreted the end result. "So, we're okay, then?"

Tess pulled him into a tight hug. And this time, meant it. "Never been better, my friend. Never been better."

# CHAPTER THREE

Dan contemplated the pads of his fingertips through the dark amber liquid in his glass. The Scotch glimmered, reflecting the ambient lighting that made the huge bar he sat at appear a little more intimate.

When a BDSM club was named Catacomb, it needed all the cozy touches it could get. Not that the name didn't fit. The subterranean space, located half a mile off the highway between Vegas and Lake Mead, was originally hollowed out as a nuclear fallout shelter for a paranoid mob boss plus his wife, mistress, six kids, and four grandchildren. Half the rooms never made it to the steel reinforcement phase, leaving many of the rooms as rock-walled tributes to something between a Moroccan palace and a desert prison.

Only a year ago, Max Brickham had scooped up the space for a song when visiting down here after the "mission from hell." Dan remembered the day Brick practically danced into the burn center to tell all of them about his purchase, proclaiming he'd found the perfect place to open his second alternative-lifestyle club. His first, Bastille, was a glam fortress in Seattle's warehouse district and was practically a second home for many of the guys on the team. Heading that list was John Franzen, the battalion's CO, as equal a best buddy to Max as he was to Dan—which was why he led the group in calling Max a complete loon about the purchase.

Funny thing about Brick. He had a lonnnng memory.

Validation of that came from the man himself, folding his massive arms and surveying the bustling main room. The fucker was cockier than Starlord with a new mix tape. "So what was that you all were saying...about renaming me Sir Loon and all that shit?"

"Yeah, yeah." Franzen, seated next to Dan, muttered it into his own Scotch. "You want me to eat my hat or something? Because I'm sure as fuck not gonna kneel and kiss your feet."

"Hey." The protest was as soft and sweet as the petite woman who nudged her ink-black hair against Max's shoulder. "That's *my* job, mister."

"Thank fuck," Franz muttered.

Max growled with pleasure, hooking a finger into the ring that dangled from the woman's diamond-studded collar. "Wouldn't have it any other way, *tamago gata no kao.*"

The Japanese endearment was his way of honoring her heritage and submissiveness, as well as her official name as his collared submissive, declared during a formal ceremony at Bastille six months back. Dan had missed the occasion due to continued surgeries and healing, thank fuck. Even being around Max and Megan now was difficult. They were the epitome of the D/s dream, an ideal he'd once looked forward to finding for himself, as well.

A fantasy he'd only be experiencing from the outside now.

"You two want to get a room?" Franz barked it when the pair behind the bar kept making out like porn stars. "Like your private one at the end of the hall?"

"Fuck off." Max broke away from his girl long enough to laugh it out. Two seconds later, his mouth was jammed harder to hers, his hands sliding greedily beneath her leather skirt.

"Shit," Franz groused.

"They just want us to start throwing twenties," Dan quipped.

"Like you'd notice." Franz glowered. "You seeing Jesus in the depths of that drink, ass munch? *You're* the one who wanted the *Catacomb experience* tonight, remember?"

Dan hunched his shoulders. Yeah. He remembered. How could he forget? Same way he couldn't forget much of anything about the last seven days. When the world hit midnight in an hour, it'd be the one-week anniversary of the moment he'd marched into a Mexican Riviera luxury suite and gotten his hands on Cameron Stock again. There, with Stock's terrified face filling his vision, he'd been truly complete—

For ten seconds.

After that, everything had reverted right back to normal. His scars were still there. The fury was still there. Frustration still clawed him like a demon, leaving charred trails everywhere it went in his psyche. Not even driving the Bowie into Stock's ball sack had relieved the agony.

Only seeing Tess had done that.

Until she'd brought a new torture of her own.

Making that coy little statement about him dominating her...that had changed everything.

For a few seconds, he'd actually thought she was kidding—until the glints in her eyes said she wasn't. Fuck. How had he not seen it before then? How had he not realized that the little torch she'd carried for him before the mission had somehow kindled into something more?

Easy answer.

Because it was impossible. She just didn't see it yet.

She was Rita Hayworth. He was Lon Chaney. She was Emma Stone. He was the Phantom of the Opera—without the let-me-fuck-you-and-get-away-with-it voice. She turned every head in rooms she entered. He made people avert their eyes. He'd told her all of that too—and meant every word. She deserved someone who could be with her anywhere, everywhere. A Dom who'd take her dancing in the sun as easily as he pulled her into the shadows. A man who'd never be ashamed to lead her anywhere.

She'd finally understood, thank God. They'd hugged to affirm the new course of their friendship, righted on a fresh keel of honesty.

Then why hadn't his demon gone back into hibernation?

Why was he taking four days of radio silence from Tess into something more than they were? Why didn't he believe himself when rationalizing she'd likely just been thrown an intense case? Why was he so restless that he'd called Franz and suggested they go out?

Why was he so messed up, he'd thought a few hours in Catacomb would *calm* him? That all this would *help* with the images she'd evoked the other day? That he'd be able to banish the dream of her nudity as she stripped for him...and then the fantasy of her dark-red curls beneath his fingers as she knelt at his side? And the imagining of her lips, plump and red, wrapped around those same fingers as he slipped them inside her mouth. Then the words he'd murmur, telling her how good it would feel when he fed her his cock in the same way.

Shit.

*No more thinking of your best friend's mouth like that, damn it.*

Not even as Max slipped his fingers between his little *tamago*'s lips, damn near picking up where his fantasy left off.

Dan grimaced. "*Dude*. Want to show some mercy to the

hard-ups?"

"Speak for yourself," Franz snarled. "But *you*"—he speared a finger Max's way—"are still being cruel."

"*Pssshhh*," Max volleyed. "Cruel would be neglecting to tell you who just walked in the door." After Franz spun on his stool, eyed the cute blond Goth at the door, and then appeared to swallow his tongue, Max chuckled. "Yes, I called her when I knew you were coming. And yes, you're welcome."

The half Samoan swung his friend a pleading stare. "Tell me you reserved room five for us, and I'm naming my firstborn after you."

Max barked a laugh. "The thought of your progeny bearing my name is a terror I'd never unleash on the world."

"Whatever. Room five?"

"What's in room five?" Dan cut in.

"Not much." Max smirked. "No carpet, pillows, or cushions on the rack. Fairly primeval."

"Exactly what she begged for the last time we scened," Franz filled in.

"Damn." Dan smirked. "Dog face has found a soul mate."

"Right?"

"Just give me some advance notice for the wedding date. I lost my social coordinator a few days ago."

Franz glowered. "Mention the W-word again and you're castrated."

Outwardly, Dan chuckled. Inwardly, a different growl echoed. *Castration would be a mercy, my friend. At least my body won't remember what I'm missing.*

Max held out his hand to Franz. A medieval-looking key hung from his finger, engraved with a fancy number five. "All yours."

Franz's lips burst into a grin. "You're a god."

Tamago slapped his arm. "My line again!"

"Easy, baby." Brick's words were cute, but the tone was command. He stressed the point by tucking a hand beneath her corset and sharply pinching one nipple. After she grimaced, Tamago dipped her head Franz's way.

"Apologies for the outburst, Sir."

"Accepted, my girl." Franz threw a grin at Max. "Guess we'll both have our hands full tonight, buddy."

The pronouncement actually gusted Dan with relief. He'd bit off more than he could chew tonight. Mix, mingle, and make-nicey were normally smack-dab in his wheelhouse, but that was in another life lived by a Dan with another face. A guy who'd walk into a club like this and barely pause at the bar, let alone think of camping out at it all night nursing too much Scotch and Shazam-ing tunes from the stream of sensual EDM flowing from the speakers—or wondering why Max refilled *two* glasses from the bottle of Macallan now.

"Go have your fun, dude," the big guy told Franz. "I'll be pulling public duty for a few more hours tonight, at least."

"Huh?" Franz volleyed. "Why?"

"We have a new girl in the house."

Max nodded toward the second living room area that the bar overlooked. Both spaces were crowded tonight, lots of people hanging out in couples or small groups, chatting or snacking before deciding what playrooms they'd be going to. In general, the crowd struck Dan as experienced and informed— not that newbs had the word stamped on their forehead— but there *was* a nervous energy that first-timers to the scene usually gave off, especially women. It made them as detectable as cheese to rats—a perfect comparison, since that was usually how the Doms in the room behaved once the chase was on.

Dan gazed across both rooms again. No swarming rats yet, though there was a lone figure, sitting in a wingback chair, at the back of the second room. From here, she could only be viewed from midtorso down. And damn, what a torso it was. Even half her cleavage was a pleasure, imagining how high and pert her tits likely were, spilling from her red latex corset. Delicate tattoos feathered from her bare shoulders to just above her elbows. Her stiff forearms led to the tight clasp of her hands in her lap—perhaps because she knew that from there down, the ensemble needed an overhaul. As in, huge. Where the hell had she gotten that black lace skirt? Its layers looked more Dolly Parton than dolly kinky, stopping at the tops of lace-up boots that looked like she'd really tromped across the desert to get here tonight.

"What the hell?" Dan groused.

"Right?" It came from Tamago, who glanced up at Max for the clearance to say more. When he nodded, she went on, "After Master gave her the orientation three nights ago, I tried talking to her about the Little Match Girl look. She's been too nervous to give it up."

"Too *nervous*?" Dan echoed.

"She won't come out and *say* it." Tamago shrugged. "But a girl knows when another girl says she's *fine* and means it—and when she doesn't."

"Is she in the right place?" he inquired. "She had orientation *three* nights ago?"

"And keeps coming back," Max filled in. "And just sitting in that same chair."

"And not a single Dom's requested her?"

Tamago offered, "Well, she also insists on the mask."

"The—" Dan couldn't help his double take. "There's a *mask* involved too?

"Well, it's a super *pretty* mask."

"Pretty or not, she's a bank of virgin snow at this." Which had its own set of plusses and minuses, though the mask clearly belonged in the latter column. "How's a Dom supposed to read her if she's wearing a damn mask?"

Max spoke for everyone with his weighted exhalation. "Now you know why I'm a little uppity."

"Uppity?" Franz grunted. "You did not just say 'uppity.'"

Max rolled his eyes. "Don't you have a subbie to flog?"

Franz's lips lifted again. "Now that you mention it..." He shoved to his feet. "You all know where I'll be. Knock on the door only if there's really a nuclear apocalypse. Wait. No. Only if there's a *zombie* apocalypse."

Apocalypses. Zombies. World destruction. All the connections were too easy—and cruel—to reach, as Franz stepped away, just as the woman across the room fully rose from her chair fortress.

And the bottom fell out of Dan's gut.

Yep. There was the mask, easily covering half her face—its strings tied beneath a waterfall of brilliant red curls.

*Rose Temptation.*

The color he hadn't been able to forget for four damn days.

Framing the face that had clung even tighter to his mind.

The proud carriage of her neck. The determination beneath her heart-shaped chin. The high, sweeping cheekbones. And damn—*damn*—that perfect pinup girl's mouth, defined by her favorite cherry-red lip stain, glistening anew as she swiped her tongue nervously between the curved surfaces...

"Fuck," Dan grated. He spun back around on his bar stool as her gaze circled toward them. Ducked his head, leaning it into his right hand.

*What the hell?* Why was he hiding from her? Wouldn't be like she'd be stunned to see him here. She knew all about his dark side. Probably too much.

*But you told her anyway. You told her more because she always begged to know—and that felt good. Damn good. Better therapy than what the "assigned" shrinks had done for you. Because that was something you were* ever *going to bring up to a person who could decide if you got your job back, right?*

There was that.

Which didn't do shit for *this.* All the craziness in his nervous system, still breaking down the fact that Tess stood across the room, looking like *that.* That she was so determined to find a Dom, she'd come to the most hardcore club in the city by herself, for the third night in a row—

Where she eventually *would* find that Dom.

The guy who would be good to her. Would be good *for* her. Every Dom and Domme in this place had to pass Max's rigorous evaluation process first. They'd been studied, screened, and tested. They were men and women damn good at what they did, serious about their responsibilities to the people who knelt and served them.

She'd asked *him* to be that guy.

He'd turned her down.

Karma's teeth did *not* feel good in his ass.

"Dan?" Max's query was low with concern. "You chill, man? You look like you just saw a ghost."

He forced a nod while sneaking another glance at Tess.

"Maybe I'd have preferred one." God*damn*. One of the overhead lights caught the top of her head. Her hair was like fire, her skin toasted cream. He didn't even dwell on her mouth. Hard-ons were tough to hide once they busted past a guy's fly.

Max didn't miss a nuance of his movement. "Now you know why I'm 'uppity' about her." The guy cocked his skull-cut head while bracing his arms to the bar. "Though my screening process is rigid, I'm tweaked that some guy is going to hear *new* and think *open to anything*."

"Fuck," Dan snarled. "You're right." Everything about Tess's wide stare, nervous gulps, and lost-lamb stance was like an open gate for a Dom who wanted fresh ground to churn with dark fantasies. But that was the trouble with plowing fertile soil. If tilled too deeply, it was ruined for any growth.

"Last couple of nights haven't been a huge concern," Max went on. "Midweek without a huge convention in town, we usually see only regulars and their bottoms. But it's Friday now. I can already see a few of the weekend guys considering a reset of their radars in her direction."

"Who? Where?"

"Whoa. Easy there, Dothraki."

"*Where?*"

"Snarls don't earn you cookies. Or answers. What the hell, Colton? Do you know her or something?"

He wanted to lie, but karma had it too bad for him as it was. "Yeah," he muttered. "In a way." Max's snicker whipped his head up. "What the fuck's so funny?"

"'In a way'?" Max taunted. "Dude, I've never seen you like this."

"Like what?" he snapped. "Breathing? Sitting? Enjoying my drink?"

"Gawking? Scowling?" The guy chuckled again. "And sure as hell not 'enjoying' yourself." He suddenly frowned. "Don't tell me you've played with her before."

"No." He had no idea why the clarification felt so important. "Fuck, no."

Max settled in lower, meaning he leaned closer. Nearly beneath his breath, he murmured, "So do it now."

"*Fuck* no."

"You want to, Colton. Don't tell me you don't."

He jerked up his head. "You know what I was doing one week ago tonight, don't you? Looking at these hands as they shook, Brick. *Shook* because I didn't know if I could hold myself back from killing Cameron Stock before we flew his sorry ass back to the States."

"But you didn't." Max notched his stance one degree closer. "And I'll bet, my friend, that you need to shut off the world as badly as she does. So maybe this is what *you* need too."

He hated how much that made sense. How much he couldn't retort that hooking him up with Tess would mean the monkey was off Max's back. Max was a lifestyle purist who actually liked the monkeys, so that argument had no teeth.

What was he supposed to do now? Stride over and inform Tess that—*ta-da*—here he was, and he'd changed his mind? That getting a good look at her in latex had reformed him about getting into a play room with her? It'd be a lie. She could've worn a damn potato sack, and watching her walk off with *any* man would mangle him worse than a totaled semi.

Who was he kidding? He'd already been tossed into the scrap heap, damn it—and now glared hopelessly at the two metal plates about to crush him, one stamped with *Damned if you do* the other stamped with *Damned if you don't*.

"What I need is to get out of here," he finally growled. "Look, Brickham, if you can just call me a cab, then—"

He spoke to empty air. Max had gone ninja. Tamago didn't provide any clues as to where he'd disappeared either, having moved to the other end of the bar, absorbed in conversation with a newly arrived couple to the club.

"Shit." He fought a weird paralysis. He didn't dare look back to gauge where Tess had traveled in the room. Did it matter? He could pretend not to notice her, that her mask was meeting its purpose, that her hair hadn't already given her away like a signal flare.

Or he could really just get the hell out of here.

Just as he pulled out his phone and punched in a search string for reputable cab companies, a text blazed across his screen—from ninja boy.

*:: I have an idea. Meet me in the storeroom behind the bar. ::*

"Shit," he repeated. "The last time I bought into one of your 'ideas,' Brickham..."

Was all too recently. Tait's bachelor party, at Gilley's two weeks ago. Everyone had gotten blotto except him. Not one of the most memorable nights of his life, probably because he *could* remember it.

But going to the storeroom meant he wasn't sitting out here, waiting for Tess to spot him like a fly on a pest strip.

He walked into the storage area to find his friend wearing a cocky smile. Hanging from one of Max's massive hands was a half-face mask, decorated with very little except some silver filigree at the outside edges. In the palm of his other hand was a black disk about the size of a quarter.

Before Dan could say anything, Max drawled, "If you can't beat her, join her, buddy."

"The hell?"

Max shoved the mask at him. "Try it on."

He stepped back. "No."

"Shut up and try it on, you wuss." He slammed the thing into Dan's chest. "It got the Phantom of the Opera some tail, right?"

"The fuck it did."

"You want to tell me he took that hot chorus girl down to his grotto and didn't take advantage of the setting?" Brick leaned against the cooler door. "We've even got a grotto here, you know. It's fed by underground hot springs. Ideal for aftercare...and other things."

With visions of "other things" parading through his head, Dan growled at his friend—and tied the damn thing on.

Hmmm. Not bad. Actually...kind of cool. The mask was made out of reinforced velvet, making it form to his face without constricting too much. The cover extended all the way over his nose and also shielded a lot of his cheeks.

Max pointed to a small mirror mounted on the back of the stockroom's door. Dan peeked cautiously—then grunted in shock. Because he hadn't shaved in the last four days, the bottom half of his face was transformed, too. A person would have to be looking really hard to discern his scars...

A person would be looking even less if she was blindfolded.

Just the thought of cinching a blindfold over Tess's face made his dick jump to life again. He jerked back from the force of it, shaking his head. This was *still* a crazy—

"Now stick this against the base of your throat." Max jammed the small disk at him. Dan shot another glare but complied, peeling back the coating on the disk's strip of sticky tape. No use protesting at this point.

He pushed the circle to his skin, just beneath his Adam's apple, and huffed. At least that was his intention. What the hell?

"Brickham." He stopped, too astounded to punch his friend for snickering at him. "What the fuck have you done to my voice?"

People always told him he sounded like Clint Eastwood crossed with a good ol' Atlanta boy. Now, his voice was like Vin Diesel after a pack of smokes—and a good ol' Atlanta boy. It was freaky but kind of cool.

"Pretty dope, eh? We offer it as part of a few role-playing kits. Subbies love it because it turns their Top into any number of slathering beasts. The disk is like a high-end voice box. It adds artificial resonance to your throat. If you want, we can go deeper with the tone."

"No." Damn. *Weird.* "Not sure I'll get used to *this.*"

"Sure you will." Max raised a hand, his *voilà* implied. "Good thing is, between this and the mask, she'll never know it's you."

It came around to this again.

Another moment of truth.

Another invitation to forge trails he hadn't traversed in a long damn time. A *long* damn time. Since before the fire...

"Man...I appreciate this, I really do." The voice discrepancy was a little less unsettling. "But it's been over a year since I last scened. I don't know—"

Max dug both hands into his shoulders. They felt like eagle talons. "Colton, I've seen a lot of Dominants in my time. Some have been coerced into it. Some have been lured into it.

Some have been attracted to it and can learn it. But the good ones...they're born for it. And that's you."

Dan grunted. "You're not going to give me a Mr. Miyagi speech, are you?"

"Shut up." He gave a hard jerk. "And listen. You *get* this, okay? The exchange—taking what a submissive gives you and processing it into all the things she not only wants but needs... It's not something you get an instruction sheet for. But a Dominant with his—or her—heart in the right place, who intrinsically realizes dominance is just as much about service as submissiveness...well, that's exceptional. And rare."

Dan stepped back. Rolled his shoulders. "You ever consider that the mask and magic voice box were already enough for the ol' self-consciousness meter?"

"Fine." Brick pulled his hands back. "I get it. Getting back on the bike is hard, even if you were an expert rider. Don't stress. Like I said, it's Friday. I'm sure somebody will come in who's just right for our little red rose."

Max pegged the color right. It was the perfect theme for the moment, considering how it blazed through Dan's vision. The rage even blasted in beneath the mask, making him burn to rip the thing off—while vowing to keep it on. Some crazy logic dictated that if the cover stayed, he could ward off the images, so vivid and merciless, of Tess giving her submission to another man.

*Just what you told her to do, asshole.*

Kneeling for him.

*Because that's better than her doing it for you, right? You're still too fucked up to handle it. To even* consider *handling it.*

Undressing for him...

The sound that emanated up his gut and out his throat

seemed more beast than man, even pushing Max back by two steps. That was just fucking fine. Took away the hassle of having to slam Brick against the employee lockers as he retied the mask, double-knotting it this time, and then whipped off his leather jacket and T-shirt.

"The rose is going to be fine." He embedded his ownership on every word. As each syllable growled out of him, he wasn't surprised to watch a slow, knowing grin grow across Max's lips. Or to receive his buddy's respectful utterance in response.

"Understood completely, Sir Daniel."

# CHAPTER FOUR

"Little rose."

Tess jumped out of her chair. Literally. Not that it had been a particularly comfortable chair. She'd found another wingback in the second of Catacomb's living-room areas, hoping she'd have better results in here with the whole calm-down-and-talk-to-somebody-damn-it efforts.

*And how did all that go for you, missy? Did changing rooms help you escape one drop of the feeling that you've shown up at prom without a date, three damn nights in a row?*

She'd given herself until eleven o'clock to get the stick out of her ass and strike up a conversation with somebody or just leave. No use sticking around until midnight when she didn't even have mice, a pumpkin, and glass slippers to worry about.

All of a sudden, her fairy godmother of BDSM got a huge damn clue.

And delivered a prince who defied her wildest, kinkiest dreams.

And *not* because he instantly reminded her of Dan.

*Get off the Colton crazy train! Especially now!*

It was his hair. It looked so much like Dan's dark-blond waves, she was initially captivated—though her perception was undoubtedly hindered by the thick velvet strings from his mask, tossing all kinds of shadows through his thick style.

About that mask...

*Dear God.*

Sometimes great minds really did think alike. Though it covered half his face and transformed his eyes into daunting mysteries, she tilted a little smile. She was *looking* for daunting, right?

She'd just had no idea how much. And one look at this man, powerful and beautiful and looming before her in nothing but his huge black boots, faded jeans, and that mask, revealed he probably had a doctorate in daunting.

She'd only concentrated on his covered parts so far too. The face she couldn't quite decipher. The legs, endless and powerful, converging at a bulge beneath his zipper that stripped the moisture from her throat. But everything else was...

*Dear God.*

It bore repeating. Probably out loud. If she could only figure out where the hell all her air had gone.

He was beautiful. Almost unreal. She'd only had this sensation a few times in her whole life, like the moment she'd gazed at her first Michelangelo statue in Rome or gasped at a *Cirque* performer who supported three others in his palm. His lean but rock-hard build emphasized every captivating striation of his muscles: the hard ropes of his neck, the shoulders and arms that rivaled the ridges of Red Rock, the abdomen that was another mountain range all its own as well. He moved closer to her with grace that reminded her of an eagle's flight, deadly force honed for efficiency and grace.

Was he even real?

She yearned to reach out and learn that answer for herself. She'd never been more afraid to move in her life.

She cleared her throat. Tried to straighten her stance but wondered if she should lower her head instead. Or bow. Or curtsy? Or shake his hand? *Hell.* She was the girl who'd read every research book on dungeon etiquette, right? But now she really did feel like the girl at the prom with toilet paper attached to her heel.

"Hi," she finally managed. "I...I mean hello. Hello, *Sir*. I...I mean..."

If she really had something to say after that, it would've disappeared as soon as he lifted her hand between both of his. *Shivers*. Everywhere. Her blood. Her skin. And yes, even in the deepest parts of her most intimate tunnel. His skin was so firm and warm, his grip a steady command, his eyes still impossible to read. That fact alone brought even more of the illicit tremors...

He stepped closer, peering at her harder, as if trying to figure her out more fully. "Ssshhh. Breathe, red."

*Red*. Though she liked playing up the unique color of her hair, she always cringed when someone used the too-typical nickname. But on his lips, it was transformed into something new. Magical.

"Breathe. Right. Okay...*right*. God. I am so sorry. You must think I'm so—" She injected a weak laugh. "I'm normally better at the whole conversation thing, I promise."

Why was she blowing this so badly? And why did he make it worse with his disarming grin and his tightening hold? And the intensity of his nearness. And the potency of his scent. How could the combination of Scotch and dust suddenly smell so incredible?

"Why are you sorry? I'm the one who intruded."

"Oh, yeah. 'Intruded.'" She blew a pseudo-raspberry. "Because there was *so* much going on here in my corner to intrude on."

"There would've been."

ANGEL PAYNE

His mutter edged close to an animal's timbre, making her shiver. Tess had heard enough radio spy chatter over the years to know the small disk on his neck was a voice distorter of some sort—but instead of raising her wariness, it only added to his allure. A lot.

*Too much.*

The conflict hastened her reckless heartbeat, especially as he repeated, "Oh, yeah. You were going to have a waiting line tonight, I can guarantee it. Then I would've had to bounce a few skulls together."

"Why?" She knew how stupid it sounded. The possessive snarl beneath his words spoke enough meaning for anyone to figure out—except, perhaps, her. The protective thing was usually *her* gig, a default when one was looking out for sisters who were "the pretty one" and "the smartass." Grasping the concept that anyone wanted to look after her in the same way...

Weird. Very weird.

But nice.

*Really* nice.

Still, she braced herself for his teasing chuckle. Maybe some sarcastic quip at what a "silly subbie" she was for not comprehending his intent.

Once more, the man turned her expectations sideways. No. Fully upside down. Her senses careened as he released a hand, lifting it to her jaw, yanking up her face to the focus of his fathomless gaze. "Why?" he repeated. "Because I'm pretty well set on having you all to myself tonight, rose." His fingers pressed in. "Unless you aren't interested in what you see?"

She laughed. She couldn't help herself. "You're kidding, right?"

"At the risk of being trite, do I look like I'm kidding?"

"At the risk of being obnoxious, do I look like a nun? Because that's the only situation where I can imagine you being turned down, Sir Sexy."

Air pushed past his smirk. His thick stubble disguised the exact edges of his lips, but the flash of his teeth briefly showed her they were curved and lush...and maybe a little wicked.

Wicked. Right behind daunting on what she'd come here looking for.

"I ought to stamp your ass with my palm for that cheek, little rose. But I don't even know your name yet."

She couldn't help grinning. If "cheek" earned her comments like that, she was tempted to change her name to *Cheeky*.

"Odette." She supplied the name she'd used with Master Max when turning in her application. If Sir Sexy had asked about her before coming over here—and something told her he had—then it was best to be consistent. "And *you* are...?"

"Interested." His lips tugged up again. "And intrigued. And fully cleared by Max, if you'd like to ask him about me. He and I have been friends for a while."

She looked toward the bar, where Max was waiting with a reassuring nod. It reinforced the security she already felt with Sexy—but also the apprehension, delicious and decadent, that inched its way into more of the sensitive skin between her thighs.

Hell.

She was really stepping down the rabbit hole this time, wasn't she?

With a Dom she couldn't stop staring at.

Who hadn't stopped staring at her either.

Who turned her bloodstream to mush because of it.

"You're good," she finally blurted. "I-I mean, *it's* good. I like it...that you're interested."

"And intrigued," he prompted.

"Same difference," she volleyed. "Right?"

"Not necessarily."

She swallowed. How had he pressed at least six inches closer without her noticing? "Your semantics are certainly curious."

His kiss, soft yet sure, was the last response she expected— yet the perfect pin in her careful composure. Pin? Try a full arrow, piercing to her very core...a wound that felt so damn good. She moaned and then inhaled, ordering her brain to locate its *This End Up* sign. This was the craziest opener to a date she'd ever had—if this could even be qualified as a "date."

Damn good point. What the hell *was* this? Maybe they needed to talk about that. Set some parameters. Lay down ground rules for next steps, and—

Thoughts that flew from her mind the moment Sexy kissed her again. Longer. Deeper. Pushing her mouth open this time, coaxing her tongue against his, all but dictating her to kiss him in return—like she'd resist a single moment of this heat and fire and pleasure. He turned her into a firework. And like the song said, she was ready to let her colors burst.

*Don't stop. This is so good. You feel so good...*

But he did, all too soon, dragging away despite how she grabbed his shoulders to stay upright. His muscles felt even better than they looked, solid boulders beneath her fingers. *Wow.*

"Odette?" he murmured.

"Hmmm?" she managed.

"You still with me?"

She blinked, struggling through a dreamy fog. "If I said no, would you kiss me again?"

His laugh was a gentle rumble. "No." He compounded her dismay by stepping out of her reach, steadying her with his hands instead of his body. "I want more than just your mouth, little rose."

She gave him a half-drunk smile. "Like what?"

She barely comprehended his hand lifting to her face. But oh, how she felt it when he grazed his fingers along her cheek, against her temple, into her hair. "Like what's in here."

She scowled. "*Not* the answer I was going for."

He tightened his grip on her scalp. "But this is where it begins." For a moment, he dipped a heated gaze down the length of her body. "As much as I long to discover all of this...it doesn't happen until I learn more of this." Then he was back to focusing on her face, as if committing her features to memory. Tess swayed toward him, a flower straining for the sun, needing more exposure. *More...*

"Then learn me."

He sucked in a deep breath, almost as if her words had become his air. As he released it, he snarled. "Damn it."

"What?" Her gaze snapped wide. "What's wrong? Did I mess up?"

He chuckled. Oh, yes. *Chuckled*. What the hell? Being with him felt like riding a rubber band. Dark mask but gleaming eyes. Hot kisses and then chaste clinches. Snarls and then chuckles.

"That wasn't messing up, red. Not one damn bit. You're just so new. *So* new. And open, and willing, and..."

"And what?" Her whisper didn't surprise her. She was amazed it had volume at all, considering how deeply his words tore at her. He sounded like he was in pain.

Yep. Rubber band. Wasn't he Mr. Interested and Intrigued just a minute ago? Hadn't he kissed her like it?

"And...well...I'm not new," he finally answered her. "And I don't know how to do this in your kind of way. And *my* kind of way is..."

He trailed into such a thick, dark growl, Tess wondered if she'd sprung a crimson cloak on her shoulders to match the forest in her imagination, looming around the path she had to take to "Grandma's house." Only, she *wanted* the big bad wolf to devour her—in any way he could imagine. But how to prove it to him?

The answer blared at her like a shaft of light in that forest.

And was as easy as tugging the ribbon that secured her own mask.

She let the covering fall all the way to the floor. Then tilted her bare face up at Sir Sexy, letting him see the surrender in her gaze.

"Your kind of way is what I came here to find," she confessed. "So show it to me...please?"

# CHAPTER FIVE

She swallowed. Then again. Both struck Dan as the world's hugest jokes. *He* was the one suddenly out of moisture in his throat, air in his lungs, and sense in his head—though he turned and filled her a cup from one of the water coolers positioned around the club before ordering, "Drink."

She flung up a hand. "Nice try, but you're not deflecting me again."

"*Drink*, damn it." He shoved the cup into her hands. "This isn't negotiable. My plans require that you be fully hydrated."

Her eyes popped wide. She lifted the cup and started to gulp.

Thank fuck she comprehended the implication of his statement. But of course she did. She was Tess Lesange, one of the most astute and perceptive women he knew—a fact he'd almost been able to forget with the mask layering her identity. With the lacy black cover in place, he could turn her into another person, a saucy little rose he'd planned on bringing to full bloom, spreading her wide before going at her pussy with a vibe wand until she dissolved beneath him. She'd be properly initiated into BDSM but still easy to separate from his lunch buddy and confidante.

Impossible now.

Completely, damnably impossible.

Everything changed the moment she'd resorted to that beautiful display of trust—an exposure that meant a thousand times more than taking off everything below her neck. Ironically, she'd made him damn sure that was going to be next. And very doubtful he'd only be going at her with a wand now.

Fuck.

*It's your own fault, ass face.* He'd practically threatened Max with castration if anyone else went near her. What the hell had come over him—other than feeling like a fire-breathing dragon at his first sight of her? Had his "sabbatical" from dungeon life turned him into an A-class jerk at his first whiff of submissive pheromones?

*Fuck.*

That was exactly the case, wasn't it?

Luckily, there was an easy solution here. He'd simply have to follow through—but keep all emotion out of the picture. *Cake walk.* He'd done it before and could do it again, especially now. Beneath that I-am-subbie-hear-me-roar ensemble, Tess had a body worth zeroing in on, as her tailored office outfits had shown him on numerous occasions. So he'd become her Dominant dream for a night, satisfying what they both needed, restoring the proper balance of nature, and leaving nobody the worse for wear. She'd go home high on endorphins, sighing from memories of her first night beneath a Dom's rule. He'd be on a cloud pretty close to hers, mind cleared of cobwebs, cock cleared of pressure. Win-win for all.

Tess's groan broke into his speculation. "Okay, my eyeballs are floating," she decreed, setting the cup down. "Happy now, Sir Griffin?" When he gave her a double take, she curled a serene smile. "Don't glare. My first choice was Hawkface."

*"Hawkface?"*

"What? You've never been told you can eye a subbie like

she's your exclusive prey?"

*Not in a very long time, Ruby. But you make it sound so damn good again.*

Not that the saucy thing needed to know that. Or that her little gibes and jests already stirred heat through his blood and fire through his mind, considering all the interesting methods he could use to tame her "cute" little tongue...

Or that she'd helped Max Brickham perform one hell of a kinky miracle tonight.

The bastard had known damn well what he was doing, hadn't he? *Colton, you were made for this. You get this.* With that kind of affirmation, was it surprising he'd approached Tess? Now with her standing beside him, so trusting and gorgeous and excited, anticipation surged him as it hadn't in over a year—transforming Brick's words to the truth.

What was the other thing the guy had said? Something about getting back on the bike? More truth—which Dan acknowledged with a provocative growl.

His eruption flared Tess's eyes. It prompted his savoring smile in return, giving her about two seconds to comprehend his intent before he acted. A gasp burst from her, high and shaky, as he whirled her around, slamming her back against his body. Another groan rumbled through him in return. *Holy fuck.* Her ass fit perfectly against his shaft. His cock swelled, pushing at her body, already knowing what it craved.

This was amazing. *She* was amazing. So much more than he'd anticipated. A hundred times softer. A thousand times more fragrant. A million times more supple...a billion times more submissive.

"Good girl," he grated into her ear. "So damn good."

Yeah, yeah; he heard the blares of logic from his brain,

blustering that the reaction was just long-overdue Dom space, but he didn't listen. Right now, the world was his little rose, his perfect ruby—and the submission he'd been a fucking idiot to turn aside. A mistake he wasn't about to make again. Not tonight.

"Thank you, Sir." Her breathy response made him smile. How quickly she'd dropped the griffin and hawk jokes...and embraced her submissiveness. He'd sure as hell pegged it wrong when doubting she'd be happy with all this. There were more layers in Tess Lesange than he ever thought possible, even as her friend. Now, he was so eager to learn those answers...and more.

"Come," he said, grasping her hand. Without stopping, he guided her down the corridor toward the private rooms, walking past portals that had been textured to blend with the stone walls. Every door had an Egyptian-themed emblem carved into it, enforcing the sensation of walking through an ancient desert crypt. He guided her past an ankh, a cobra, and an ibis on the left, then a scythe and a pair of jackals on the right. Sounds filtered from behind a few of them. The crack of a whip. The moan of a climax. A merciless bellow. *Kneel, boy! Now!*

Tess's fingers trembled a little.

He tightened his hold—as his cock jerked tighter.

He stopped in front of the next door on the right. It bore three stars that cradled a half-moon, poetic deceptions for what the room undoubtedly possessed. Without ceremony, he turned to face Tess, dropping her hand in order to brush knuckles across her cheek.

She shivered again.

He turned his hand over, flattened it to her nape. "Scared?"

Her lips parted. Pressed back together. Fell open again. "Yes."

"You know that only makes me hotter."

"Then that makes two of us."

*Christ.*

His fingers clamped harder, digging into the bottom of her scalp. When she sighed and then gasped, arching and showing him the tops of her nipples, he groaned to keep from kissing her again. Couldn't happen, not out here. When he took her mouth once more, it wasn't something he wanted everyone in the hall watching.

Getting the key out of his pocket was torture now that his erection was part of the picture. Once the heavy piece was out, he reached around her and shoved it into the dark hole beneath the wrought-iron handle. But he didn't turn it. Instead, he lifted *her* hand to it, curling her fingers around the protruding iron.

They still shook beneath his touch.

He got even harder.

"Open it."

Her breath, which had been coming in little spurts, stopped. She couldn't have given him a better reaction. It relayed that she got it—that she understood it wasn't just her obedience he demanded but her permission. That by twisting that key, she was acknowledging her consent to step with him farther down into the pyramid—into a dungeon that definitely hadn't been designed for casual lifestyle dabblers.

The room they entered was obscenely faithful to that promise.

An ethereal soundtrack played from hidden speakers, a perfect match to the sepulcher feel. In the center of the room, an altar of sorts was highlighted, ensuring one could see the many chains that hung from rings at its edges. Several chains hung from the ceiling over the round platform as well. To the side, a multi-tiered rack held a dozen melted candles, next to a padded bench rigged with an adjustable spreader. While Tess stopped, transfixed by that, Dan circled his gaze across other equipment—a coffin with creative bondage points, a pair of skeletal gargoyles holding a custom fucking swing, a "mausoleum" that housed at least a hundred implements to make a subbie beg for her punishment—

Or in this case, more of her truth.

*Ding ding ding.*

"Yes," he murmured. "Perfect."

"What?" She was adorable, jumping a little from his savage underline but getting little goosebumps at the same time. That was just the start of how alluring she was, gawking at everything in the room like a child who'd never seen candy before. She wanted it all but wondered which sampling would give her the biggest stomachache. "Wh-What's perfect?"

"You." It sounded glib, but oh hell, did he mean it. He stepped toward her again, jerking her face up with one hand, tugging her closer by her chin. "Oh, yes." It was deep and animalistic, grated into the inches remaining between his mouth and hers. "So perfect."

He kissed her with meaning too. Not that he hadn't before—but now, he could do it with all the plunging, thorough possessiveness he wanted, slanting his mouth and stabbing his tongue, yanking her hair until she moaned from the pressure of his grip—guaranteeing that when he released her several minutes later, she gasped for every breath—

And reached for the edge of his mask.

Dan swung his head and caught her fingers between his

teeth.

She hissed. Jabbed him with a glare. "Why?"

Dan didn't set her free. He wrapped a hand around her wrist, positioning his bite marks for soothing with languorous licks. Between the ministrations, he murmured, "Because I'm in charge. That's why."

"I want to see your eyes."

"Will you trust me any more if you do?"

Her lips flattened. It was a one-way street of a question, but he'd known that in the asking. By walking in here with him, she'd implied her trust, mask or not. On top of that, Max had personally endorsed him. There was also the small camera dome mounted in the corner near the door, ensuring their session would end if he violated any of the hard limits listed on her submissive's agreement—which they *were* going to discuss, once she got over her latest bout of topping from the bottom.

"What about mutual needs?" She hitched out a hip in defiance. "Come on, Griffin. I showed you mine. Now how about reciprocation?"

Dan folded his arms. "What about it's not up for discussion?"

"Is this a deal breaker?"

"You tell me."

"I'm not the one still hiding."

He couldn't help his bark of laughter. And his sweeping glance from her head to her toes—though that sure as hell might've been a mistake. Even in her strange cross between kinky and gypsy, she was so damn delectable. "Now *that's* up for discussion, girl."

"What?" She dipped her head defensively. "You dissin' my threads now?"

"Not if they hit the floor inside the next two minutes."

So much for defenses. Her head jerked back up, just as he'd hoped, eyes full of riotous green reckoning. "E-Everything?" she stammered.

"Hmmm. Valid question." He stepped back, appraising her again. "We do still have business to attend. Craving to fuck you won't be a welcome distraction."

She beamed another saucy grin. "Depends on your point of view."

He flung back half of a smirk. "Down to your corset and panties, red. You have a minute and a half."

The smirk was a stupid move. She caught it and took advantage right away, taking her very sweet time unlacing her boots. The little brat lingered even longer on the thigh-highs beneath, languorously rolling them down the sleek curves of her legs. As Dan wet his lips in anticipation of the skirt following next, she instead went for the pins in her hair, maddeningly slow about shaking out the long cherry curls.

He almost growled—but was damn glad he didn't. Just when he debated stepping forward and ripping the lacy layers away himself, she moved her hands to the garment's waistband. But when she stopped, trembling a little, he stepped forward and charged, "Take it off or *I* will, little rose."

Inside of five seconds, the skirt was a puddle at her feet. Producing the most exquisite phoenix he'd ever seen.

"Fuck. Me." Dan didn't hide the readjustment he gave to his hard-on, right through his jeans. What was he supposed to do when her nudity slammed him like a masterpiece in the Louvre, all creamy skin and curves, with an ass that made the line of her thong a nuisance instead of an enhancement? His palms burned, needing to cup it. How was he going to get through all the "first session fine print" with her, with those incredible spheres taunting him?

*"First session fine print?"*

*What happened to "only scene fine print?"*

*You get to do this once with her, asshole, remember? Once, just to get her out of your goddamn system, and then you're setting her free for a Dom who can treat her right—someone who won't fuck with her the way you just did Brynn. So get the hell on with it.*

"What's wrong?" She glanced down, thinking his profanity had been a bite of displeasure. She was batshit crazy for it, but that was his gray line to clear up, not hers.

"Not a thing." He reclaimed the two steps between them in order to stroke his hands down her shoulders, her arms, and then around over her ass for one perfectly awesome moment. God*damn*. How would one night be enough to explore that backside in all the ways he wanted? "Not a single thing," he emphasized, pulling back up to lift her onto the raised dais with the dangling chains. "Settle in here," he instructed. "On your back, arms stretched out."

Energy thrummed off her body and glittered in her eyes. She smiled and murmured, "Yes, Sir. And what about my legs?"

He smiled back and kissed her softly. "That's for me to worry about."

As soon as she was in position as he instructed, Dan circled around the platform, locating the chains that had leather wrist cuffs attached. Fast adjustments to the hooks on the cuffs secured the bindings around her wrists.

It was time for his plans for her legs.

A quick trip to the mausoleum supply cabinet, and he returned with the medieval-looking spreader bar that was as heavy and noisy as he'd anticipated when first eyeing it. As he secured her ankles into another pair of cuffs and then clamped the cuffs into opposing sides of the bar, he watched a corresponding pair of shivers run up her legs. Her calves clenched, followed by her knees and thighs. He slid his hands the same direction, focusing on exhaling through the motions, wordlessly bidding her to relax. Watching his touch have a ripple effect across her skin, making her tremble and writhe... It was fucking intoxicating.

He spread his hands, kneading the beautiful curves of her thighs, both outside and in—until his thumbs joined together atop the triangle of fabric covering the hottest part of her body. She jerked as he stroked her there, her pussy instantly moistening the satin beneath his fingers.

"Oh!" she cried out.

"Damn," he murmured back. "You're drenched already, little rose."

"Yes." It spilled out, nearly all breath, despite the frustrated whimper that followed. With her legs tethered to the spreader, she could only open so far for him. Not far enough, if he properly interpreted her urgent little squirms.

He leaned over, taking her mouth in another commanding kiss. "Patience, little girl. We'll get there."

"When?" She bucked harder, arching toward him.

"Soon. After I discover a few more things about you."

"L-Like what?"

"Like a safe word?"

"Oh. That." She giggled a little, tempting him even more to loosen her corset and set her tits free. But her open sensuality had already injected its way into his cock, forming an erection he fought like hell to ignore. If the rest of her breasts were as gorgeous as the crests he'd already glimpsed, that battle would be lost—and none of the important stuff would be covered. Not an option. When one already had a woman chained to a dais, even fourteen months of absence from the lifestyle didn't excuse a Dom from paying attention to the important stuff.

With gritted discipline, he slid away from her. Made a full circle around the altar to observe her extremities for circulation and her bindings for comfort. During the circuit, he glanced several times at her face, captivated by how she looked left, then right, and then back again, past the lacy ink defining the muscles of her shoulders, smiling every time she got to the sight of her bound wrists.

"Comfy, little rose?"

She emitted a dreamy hum and nodded. "Oh yes, Sir."

"And what's the word you'll use with me if you aren't?"

She tilted her neck, trying to look at him once more, but he'd deliberately stopped behind her. Mask or not, the less she viewed him straight on, the better.

Wouldn't be an issue for much longer. On his way to retrieve the spreader bar, he'd passed a tiered rack displaying a variety of blindfolds. One in particular had caught his gaze, a black leather cover rimmed with golden studs, a perfect accompaniment for her gleaming red curls.

He stepped over and pushed the blindfold onto the top of her head. Her breath caught, but he didn't lower the covering all the way. "Safe word, Odette. This goes no further without it."

She wrinkled her nose. "Can't we just green-yellow-red light it?"

Her flippant use of the "dungeon standards" sounded instant alarms for him. Clearly, she'd *not* thought about the matter, a common error for fresh submissives. So eager to know the D/s dream, they blithely back-burnered safe words, thinking they could handle anything a Dom dished out.

Well, if she wouldn't think about it, he sure as hell would. "How about taffy?" he suggested, predicting her reaction before the words were finished.

"*Taffy?* That stuff will tear your fillings out. I hate it!"

He barely hid his knowing smirk. *No kidding.* "That just means you won't forget the word."

She snorted. "I'm not going to need the word."

He snorted as well, harder and harder, before lowering the blindfold fully over her eyes. "The safe word is taffy, sweet girl. It belongs to you now. Use it if you need to." While trailing his fingers lower, over the soft planes of her cheeks and then down the sides of her neck, he went on, "But remember this: the rest of your words are mine. You'll give them to me without hesitation, with full honesty."

At first, her answer was nothing but a long sigh—but that was partly his fault. He couldn't resist sliding his fingertips along her collarbones before spreading out, following the intricate curls of her tattoos. "Yes, Sir," she finally whispered.

He let her hear his approving rumble. Her trust, so pure and earnest, aroused him as nothing had in a long time...such a *long* damn time.

And yeah, it scared him.

A little.

Maybe a lot.

What if he hadn't ended up as the man in here with her tonight? What if she lay here, freely giving herself to someone who didn't care for her as he did? All right, so Max's screening process was too good for that, requiring all Doms to go through background screenings, but the thought of any other man stroking her as he did now, subjecting her to his mercy, in charge of absolutely everything she felt...

Rage, as illogical as it was indisputable, fired his veins.

*Back burner, asshole. As far back as you can shove it. You only get this much. You can't handle more than this much. Stop pouting like a pussy, and get the fuck on with it.*

"Tell me about these." He fanned his fingers along all her ink, inciting more shivers through her body. Or maybe it was the new timbre of his voice, dipped even lower than Vin status now, a sexed-starved Darth Vader. He wasn't about to alter it, though. He could tell she enjoyed it.

"Not much to tell," she murmured. "They've been there for a few years. I was going through a strange adjustment period and needed to do something beautiful for myself."

"'Strange adjustment period,'" he echoed. "That sounds like shorthand for something else."

Her lips pursed. "It was."

"Or some*one* else?"

He didn't want to admit how good it felt when she broke into a dismissive laugh. "If it had only been that easy." Her sad murmur canceled the effect. "But men have always been one of the easier parts of life for me."

He cocked his head, wondering briefly if it added to the gentle prod of his tone. "By your choice?"

She laughed softly again. "That obvious?"

"Only to someone who's been there before." He skimmed his fingers back up, dipping them into her brilliant hair. "Someone who settled for vanilla and simple instead of having to explain my kink."

"There's nothing wrong with that."

"Until there's everything wrong with it."

His truth slipped her into silence. Him, too. He knew she felt the change in the air, too...the sudden tension twisting between them. But while unexpected, it wasn't unwelcome. The moment reminded him of skydiving: of how time seemed to stop before taking the plunge. It was always a fusion of terror and excitement, a deep and visceral connection to life.

But this time, it was even better—because the link was to her.

*With* her.

He waited through another moment, absorbing the warmth that flowed through Tess's skin...praying like hell that she felt every zap of his energy in return. When her whole body trembled and her muscles undulated, a victorious grin split his lips.

So this was what it felt like to be the grand wizard.

It was damn nice—yet the most humbling experience of his life. Like many D/s lifestylers, he'd flippantly tossed around the words "Power Exchange" but never comprehended the term as deeply as he did now. Or had so much respect for it. Or been so in awe of it.

Or wanted even more of it.

The conclusion turned his next question into a possessive growl, but he was beyond caring. "So you've never explored something like this with any of your partners?"

"No, Sir."

His pulse jacked. His arousal rocketed. But he still had to know more.

"Why?"

She breathed in and out, her chest shaking. "I was afraid of it, I guess. I always thought I was a deviant, having fantasies of men restraining me, ordering me to their sexual will...but when you're the good little rule follower of the family, even a little experimentation feels like mortal sin."

Dan felt a frown furrow his brow. The statement was given as straightforward fact. It occurred to him that though she always spoke lovingly about her family, she didn't mention them often. "So you were brought up with lots of religion?"

"No. Lots of structure. My dad and mom worked hard to support the three of us. With my older sister unable to resist boys and my younger the ultimate anarchist, I learned fast to become the peace-keeper."

"You mean become invisible."

"I'm not sure that's—"

"The rock that caused no ripples?" he persisted. "The wheel without the squeak? The one who blended just to makes things easier?"

Pain marred her face, betraying his bull's-eye. Accurate or not, he hated being the one who wielded her grief.

"Sweet little rose." He raised his hands to frame her face again. "No wonder all of this beckoned to you."

She sighed in bliss but questioned in a whisper, "Sir?"

He brushed his lips over her forehead, down her nose, across her mouth. Breathed in her beautiful scent, like fresh-plucked roses dusted with cinnamon, before murmuring, "I see you, woman. All of you." Pulled his hands back into her hair again, kneading her with yearning possession. "I see you."

"Oh..."

Her mouth opened as if to say more, but all that came out was another sigh. She swallowed hard, clearly fighting back tears. Every Dominant bone in Dan's body wanted to call her on that shit, to demand she not hold the reaction back, but the friend in him overrode the Dom. He really understood the pride beneath her battle. No wonder she'd always been the "level-headed" one at the office, earning her nickname through countless trials of staying the course when everyone else wigged out. Shouldering the burden, even when national security was at stake, came naturally to her—

And was the first thing she wanted to lose when getting naked for a man.

Too bad none of her other lovers had gotten the clue.

No, not really.

Those bozos might be crying about their loss—which didn't stop him from rejoicing about it. And from taking a stronger lead now, combing his fingers deeper against her scalp. "Sssshh," he soothed. "Take a minute and regroup."

She was so gorgeous, expelling a long breath before he twisted his fingers a little at the end of a stroke, delivering enough pain to keep her alert and connected to him. "Th-Thank you."

He did it again. Then again. A few more times, simply for the pleasure of watching her sexy little gasps, before prompting, "So what finally led you here? Coaxed you across from good little peacemaker to sexy little subbie?"

The edges of her lips inched up. "Sexy? Errr...really?"

Dan groaned. "Little girl, you have *no* idea."

After smiling wider, she confessed, "It was a friend. A colleague. At work." To his curiosity, a blush suffused everything between her face and breasts. "Okay, he's not really at work anymore, but he was. He got badly hurt, so he's been on leave."

"Hurt?" He echoed the word because only then did it crack his thick skull that she might be talking about...

*Holy fuck.*

"Yeah. Burned. On his face. Not a lot of it, but the damage was deep enough to leave deep scars, and he's been a tad aggro about it. He saved a woman's life, though."

"Holy shit." Thank fuck he didn't have to squelch it. Didn't know if he could.

"No kidding. He's a hero but doesn't recognize it, though the rest of us do." Her head dipped to the side, as if she didn't want to keep talking. But she inhaled and continued anyway. "I'm going to go to hell for saying this, but I'm...well, I'm kind of grateful for what happened to him. Before the accident, I was smack-dab in the middle of his *work buddy* space. Not a prayer for escaping the friend zone. Major problem, since *he* was pretty much just my ultimate fantasy fuck."

"Your *what?*" He managed not to choke on it.

She giggled. "You heard me. And don't play prissy, *Sir*. You have a few too. I'd bet solid money on it. A subbie you've been eyeing around here? Girl at the day job you've stolen an extra peek or two at?"

Dan grunted. "So what's this guy to you now?" Shit. He had to go there, didn't he? No matter how she answered, it was bound to mess with his brain. He didn't care. The opportunity was too ripe not to be plucked—and yeah, her answer meant too much now. "You still want to *fantasy fuck* him?" He pressed his hands to the dais on either side of her head and leaned low over her face. "Are you thinking of him right now, girl?"

She managed to look indignant, even with his position— and hers. "Of course I am—but only because you brought it up!"

He ignored her huffy finish. "Did you ask him to do this with you first?" he growled. "To bring you someplace like this and dominate you?"

He sensed she wouldn't lie about it—but also didn't anticipate the speed of her honesty. "Yes," she declared. "I did. I'm not an idiot. Dan's a great guy, and fucking gorg—well, he's nice-looking, we'll leave it at that. So of course I tried. And for the record, he turned me down."

"For the record, then, *he's* the idiot." He meant it—now more than ever.

"Probably." She stunned him again with her soft laugh. "But that doesn't diminish my gratitude to him for all this. Without his openness about BDSM and his encouragement that I be open about it as well, I'd never have come this far. It's a gift I'll never thank him for enough."

Well, shit.

*You asked.*

That didn't ease the constriction in his chest. Or that the follow-up question to that was more obvious than the shine on her corset—as well as the last thing he wanted to speak. But avoiding it was even less an option. This would be his only chance to learn her complete truth.

"So that's why you asked him to do this with you? Because of gratitude?"

"Uh-uh." She jerked her chin up. "I asked him because I wanted him. And before you ask, I wanted him in any way I could get him, especially between my legs. If that makes things weird now, you just say the word."

Dan barely suppressed his laugh—and his whoop. Both temptations grew the next moment, as the weight on his chest transformed from lead to feathers.

*Weird?*

Okay, he saw how her logic went there, especially since

she was so brand-new to all this—but his little ruby still had no concept of what a gift she'd given him, in more ways than one. The man inside him preened, floored by the idolatry she'd nourished even after half his face had turned into a burned omelet. The Dom in him glowed, proud of her for embracing honesty that most *seasoned* submissives wouldn't possess in her present position.

She amazed him.

Humbled him.

Hardened him.

To an intensity he hadn't experienced in a long damn time.

"My brilliant little rose." He pressed a kiss into the curve of her neck. "You have no idea how *un*weird this make things." He suckled and nipped his way to the other side of her neck. "How perfect it makes everything."

As he expected—and hoped—his sensual abuse made her whimper. "Th-Thank you, Sir."

He flattened both hands, sliding palms down her sternum, over the swells of her breasts. As he slipped his fingers beneath her corset, Tess moaned. As he found her erect peaks, she gasped. As he squeezed those gorgeous nipples, she yelped.

"Damn," he grated. She was so responsive. So ready. So open. So submissive.

*Ohhh, fuck.*

*Ohhh, yeah.*

Despite the torture of his zipper along his cock and his heartbeat against his ribs, this was going to be fun. A *hell* of a lot of fun.

# CHAPTER SIX

*This is going to be fun.*

The man's savoring growl all but said the words for him. The sound curled through Tess like incense, dark and exotic, aiding the fantasy that she was a sheikh's plaything for the night, brought to his desert dungeon to be spread for him, awaiting her role in his pleasure.

The thoughts brought on a hard shiver. Dread, joy, and anticipation coursed through her veins...and moistened the crevices between her thighs. She breathed in, forcing herself to absorb that this *wasn't* a dream but truly happening. It still felt too huge to comprehend, almost too much to bear. How long had she dreamed of this, longed for it? And now that she was really living it, would all her expectations be fulfilled? What if this wasn't as amazing as she'd hoped? What if she did something wrong and let this incredible man down in some way?

So far, thank God, that didn't seem to be the case. A pleased rumble rolled out of him as he pinched her nipples again, tighter than before. Tess cried out, sharp and high, turning his growl into an illicit chuckle. Almost instantly, she felt her pussy grow wetter. Hell. She was all kinds of messed up, with her arousal tied so closely to the man's sadism, but hearing the pleasure she brought him was the most potent aphrodisiac she'd ever experienced.

She lifted her chest, desperately hoping he did it again.

And he did. Harder. Longer.

"Ohhhhh!" she screamed.

"Mmmm," he murmured. "So good, little girl."

"Yes," she rasped. "Oh, *yes*."

It almost came out as a question. How could it be that so much pain led to so much pleasure? In the wake of his abuse, her nipples tingled and warmed, developing into arrows of sensation with her sex as the target. When they struck, she moaned again.

"Well, well, well," he drawled. "My little rose has a penchant for thorns too."

"Yes, Sir." The sensation of his fingers on her flesh, intensified by the pressure from her corset, was erotic, exquisite, incredible. "Ohhhh. It's so good."

"And going to get even better. I promise."

He had a damn strange way of proving it. When he finished the vow by rising up and away from her, Tess whined in protest.

"Breathe, sweet one." Though underlined by gentleness, the words were nails of command. "And trust me."

He moved off toward her right with steps sure as a puma, making her head instinctually fall in that direction too. Nevertheless, Tess nodded and replied, "I trust you, Sir. I do."

His responding snarl pebbled her skin with fresh arousal. Then again as he uttered, "Perfect, little rose. So perfect."

The enjoyment was short-lived. As he slid a hand down her torso and across her waist, Tess fought not to tense up. Mattie and Viv had inherited Mom's cute, curvy build, but she'd gotten her body type from Dad, meaning her figure had the sex appeal of a tree. With every new inch Sexy glided over her nonexistent figure, she took another breath to combat the feeling that it wasn't enough. That *she* wasn't enough.

*Damn it.* Even here, even now, she wasn't free from it all, was she? At least, thank God, he'd let her keep the corset on. There was hope, if she could impart the illusion of a figure...

Until she couldn't.

"Wait." His mandate, sharp but flirty, preceded the tug he gave to the cords dangling between her breasts. The corset fell free from her torso, returning her breasts to their flimsy normality. "Okay," he growled, "*now* everything's perfect."

She bit back the craving to scream. Was the mask fucking up his vision that bad? She wasn't perfect. *This* wasn't perfect. Not anymore. Not when he was so masterful and powerful and captivating, and she was so...

Her.

Just her.

Not Odette the exotic, full of sex appeal and sass. Not even his cute little rose, witty and flirty, keeping things fun. Now that he'd stripped her bare, in more ways than the obvious, she didn't even have the potential of being a beautiful submissive. She was just pale and trembling and embarrassed, as useful for turning him on as a pool cue. The burn behind her eyes confirmed the fact.

"*Rose.*" His summons crashed into her mind, sounding like he'd issued it for the sixth time. He tweaked one of her nipples to emphasize it.

"*What?*" Pain yanked the word from her, full of irritability and tears. *Great. Barely into your first scene with a real Dom, and you hit him with* that *crap? Nice going. Real smooth. No wonder the world will never see you as anything more than the redheaded intel geek or the blank space of humanity between Mattie and Viv. You won't stand out any more here than you do anywhere else. You can't even get it right when there are clear-*

*cut rules involved in the equation.*

Bright side? She already knew the back way out of this place. And tonight when she left, it'd be for good.

Which couldn't happen soon enough.

"Shit," she blurted. "I'm...sorry. I'm mucking this all to hell. I'll just go. Just...just let me up." She wrestled against her cuffs, but the only thing that actually moved was her blindfold. She grimaced and blinked as Sexy Beast pushed the covering off her eyes. The lighting in the play room wasn't glaring, but it seemed that way after spending fifteen minutes in darkness. "Look," she bit out, "we tried, okay? And—"

And every thought in her head vanished as the sudden lighting change gave her a deeper look beyond his mask.

Straight into his eyes.

"Oh, my God."

How was his stare such an eerie match for Dan's too?

Okay, not an exact match. The color was a shade or two darker, but the staunch focus of those twin blues... It socked her in the middle of her chest, just as Dan's always did. And ohhhh, yes...clenched at her sex exactly the same way too.

"Oh, my G—" She couldn't hold back the repeat button—until something jabbed into her right wrist. She looked to see that she'd reacted on pure impulse, reaching to attempt unveiling him again. The wrist cuff, secured to the chain, stopped her. In the same moment, Sexy jerked backward, as if trying to rip the thought out of her head.

"I'm sorry," she stammered. "You just... It's just..."

"Just what?" Sexy fanned his fingers over her abdomen as he softly prompted it.

"Nothing," she defended. "Nothing. It was crazy." A breath whooshed out, thick with more tears. What the hell was wrong with her now? "Maybe this is all too crazy."

His fingers tightened. "Whoa. What?"

"I mean it," she stressed. "I'm not...just not..." Her eyes squeezed shut. Not having the help of her hands as a shield... it was scary. Intimidating. More unsettling than being naked. "Maybe...I shouldn't be here," she confessed. "Not tonight." *Not ever.* "I'm all over the place. My head feels like it's in a cloud."

There. Task surely accomplished now. It was lame enough to be sincere but still dumb enough to turn off any world-weary Dom wanting a drama-free play session.

Which apparently, he was *not.*

Well, *hell.*

Tess's chest flipped over as he lifted his other hand to her face, realigning her gaze with his. Other parts of her body took up the tumbling act. *Ohhh, God.* It was a replay of the first moment he'd approached her. Dizzy attraction. Swoony lust. Feeling small next to his bulk but huge at the same time, the sole center of his attention.

"Clouds?" he murmured then, his voice a strange ribbon of sensual promise. "Ohhh, little rose. You've barely touched the sky yet."

*Shit.*

She didn't know she'd given the word volume until her dry rattle hit the air. "Ugh," she followed in a murmur. "I'm real smooth now, right? Take foot, insert in mouth."

He shot out a gentle *tsk.* "Not on my watch, beautiful. I believe I have better plans for that mouth."

"Holy *shit.*" Forget blushing. Her face became a furnace. "Errr...for the record, that's all *good* 'shit,' okay?"

He chuckled. "You *did* sanctify it."

She shifted a little. Only a little. His fingers felt even better than his voice, so steady and warm against her skin. Letting her eyes slip shut again, she pushed her face closer toward his hand.

"Holy *fuck*." He gritted it while tucking his fingers into her hair, positioning her for his kiss. She let out a groan as soon as his mouth meshed with hers, and for good reason. It felt better, tasted better, resounded deeper than all his other kisses, searing her alive from the inside out. His tongue burned her like brandy. His moan turned her blood into mist. No. Into clouds. The clouds he promised to take her to...

He pulled away all too fast. A whine crawled up her throat, but she managed to rasp, "Does this mean you still want to do all this?"

He slid his hand from her hair, flattening it to the dais on the other side of her head. "Hmmm. What part of 'still want to' might you be referring to, sweet rose? The part about how I'm going to tear your panties from your incredible little body? Or the part about doing that just so I can stuff my fingers inside you, because getting inside your mind has made me need your body in the same way? Or the part about feeling your cunt soak my skin as I tell you it's been a long damn time since I've met a subbie like you?"

Shaky sigh. Searing lust. Both flamed through her nipples, her pussy, her toes, and beyond. Dear God, did the man know his way around pillow talk—and there wasn't even a damn pillow in sight.

"L-Like m-me?" she managed.

"Gorgeous," he clarified. "Fiery. Fascinating. Amazing."

"Can I pick the 'all of the above' option?"

He dipped his head, grazing his lips along her hairline.

"But you haven't heard *all* the options."

*Gaaahhh.* "All the...options?"

He pushed back a little, angling his head in contemplation. "*Option* may not have been the best word for it. Should've just used *commands.*"

"Commands for what?"

She didn't expect the extended pause before his reply. Or the long strokes of his hands inside her splayed corset, framing her body in pure heat before arriving at the apex of her thighs. With his thumbs denting her panties, he finally said, "For the part where I tell you to pick which toy to use on you tonight, to make you scream the loudest for me."

*Holy.*

*Shit.*

It deserved an encore.

"Oh," she squeaked. "Right." Only *that* part.

His burnished hair gleamed in the light as he ran his hands down her inner thighs and over her knees—before leaning back and yanking one of the pins out of the spreader bar. With an accomplished tug, he lengthened the bar. A high gasp escaped Tess as her legs jerked wider too. New parts of her pussy, now exposed to the air, zinged to life. Her thighs constricted. Her womb clenched. Her mind spun and whirled, almost disengaging from her body, flying higher...higher...

*Little girl...you've barely touched the sky yet.*

Was he kidding? How much better could this get?

"Well? Let's hear it." His charge was masterful, its gentle ribbon traded for a blade of demand. "Time to open up again, Odette." He splayed his hands to her inner thighs. Opening her more. Exposing her deepest, hottest vulnerability to him. "Talk to me."

She swallowed. Okay, he really *had* to be kidding. Talk to him, when he had her quivering and needy and mushy like this? When all she could think about was getting those fingers back on her pussy again?

"T-Talk? About what?"

He gave her another dark hum. "You know what. It's all inside you, aching to get out. It lives in the place where you hide all your deepest fantasies. Now open the door and tell me. In your most wicked dreams, the ones that fill your mind when you touch your pussy late at night...what's your Dom doing to you?"

"Besides what *you're* doing?" Like teasing his fingers along the inner seam of her thong. Like brushing his fingers across her skin, strings of erotic butterfly kisses, dancing his fingertips around the bloom of her sex, driving her to the brink of sanity...

Until delivering a swift smack to the tender triangle.

"Oh!" Tess cried. "What the—"

"*Tell me.*" Screw the blade. He lowered a full verbal scythe. "And don't gape at me like that. You didn't come here for the easy shit, girl. You could have bypassed Max's intake process for any of the happy-shiny BDSM circuses on the Strip." He cupped her now, smashing the fabric into her sex, making her moan from the illicit excitement. "You're soaked, little rose," he growled. "I feel this. Every drop of this. I smell it, too. You're in heat from just the idea of what I can do to you after a trip to that toy cabinet. So hear this: if you don't tell me what you want me to get when I'm there, I'll fill in the blanks with *my* preferences. How about clamps for your gorgeous tits? Yeah. That's a good place to start. I really like clamps... so maybe another set that's made to spread your pussy wider for me, so I can tease every inch of it just the way I like." His smile spread when her mouth dropped open. "Yes? Okay, both of those, then."

"Wait!"

She blurted it desperately but not reluctantly. There was no point arguing what his suggestions did to her, since his hand was still mashing her panties against her core, proving him completely right about her arousal. The sharp silk of it scented more of the air with every passing second—heightened by his nasty words, his feral grin, and the power beginning to pour off him in discernible waves.

Holy hell. A thousand *wows*. What he could do to her. What he *was* doing to her...

She tried to swallow. Yeah, *right*. Her body barely remembered to breathe, it was so amped and hot and pulsing and turned on.

She was either in for the biggest slice of heaven or the biggest splash to hell. And right now, the promise of the former far outshone the risk of the latter.

"Flogger," she exclaimed. "I mean...a flogger, please, Sir. That's...that's what I'd like you to use on me. Please. Oh, please."

He canted his head. "Beautiful, sweet rose." He scooted back again but not before tucking a pair of fingers into the top of her thong and twisting. As he left the dais, the garment followed. *Thwack.* It snapped off her body in one sharp instant.

Tess blinked, unable to hide her wonderment.

Sexy smirked, spreading what remained of the panties between his long fingers. "Liked that too, did you?"

Her jaw worked on air for a second. "That's only supposed to happen in movies."

"That so?" His twisting lips pulled his stubble into roguish angles.

She scraped her brain for something witty to fling back at that, but her brain stalled. What other explanation was there for the fact that he now stood at the end of the altar, braced legs positioned between hers, black leather flogger in hand—and a sinful smile on his lips?

"What movie am I from now?" He twirled the falls over her left foot. Tess shivered from the ticklish tease, wondering what he was thinking. Between the mask and his dark-gold scruff, he was unreadable—but utterly sensual. She was damn grateful he didn't slide the blindfold back down. Beholding him now, with his grin widening and his chest flexing, she really wondered if there were hidden cameras capturing every magical moment of his movements. Her pussy clenched all over again, thinking of someone watching the security feed from this play room, an envious voyeur to their exchange.

"Hmmm." She sighed as he brushed the leather over her right foot. "Good question. Hero in disguise. There's a lot to pick from there."

"Hero?" He glided the strands up her leg, stopping before they got to her trembling sex. "You sure about that?" Twirl. Twirl. The falls fanned out, brushing so close, making her tissues shiver...and moisten. "Maybe I'm the diabolical villain instead."

"Oh, Sir." She pushed up her hips as high as she could. "I can only hope."

He didn't twirl the flogger anymore. With a *whoosh*, the strands arced, gaining power before he brought them down across her upper thighs. Tess cried out but more in astonishment than pain. Every sensation was just as she'd imagined...and more. A slight sting followed by a subtle throb and then a suffusion of heat. Her muscles softened—just before he struck her again. And again. And again. Each time was as perfect as the last. Sting, throb, heat. Sting, throb, heat.

After half a dozen strokes, the *whoosh* became more pronounced.

He brought the flogger down. The leather smacked louder, harder on her legs.

*Fireworks.*

Tess moaned. Sexy emitted his most luscious growl yet.

"Damn. What a beautiful rose you really are." He reached down, petting the skin he'd just heated, moving in broad, strong sweeps. "Pink and tender, like petals folding back. And soon, I'll know the nectar of your pussy." He leaned in, fondling the lips that were now swollen and moist around her deepest core. "So sweet," he praised. "So glistening and ready for me. I want to see more of it, little one. Bear down for me. Convulse your cunt. Give me some more sweet cream."

She obeyed because she had no choice. Because with every sweep of that flogger, he'd sealed more cells of her body to his will—and now, with every syllable from his lips, he bent her mind deeper to his command. His magical mouth entranced her even more as he sucked on his fingers, growling from the taste of her sex on his skin. Tess fixated on his movements as she tightened her tunnel, clenching for him over and over, finally rewarded by the dark groan that escaped past his locked teeth.

"Fuck," he uttered. "*Yes.*"

An answering sound tumbled out of her, needy and wild, as he unbuckled her from the spreader bar. He didn't bother to free her ankles from the cuffs themselves. Instead, he gripped the pads as leverage, shoving her legs high, splaying her sex for him.

A higher cry burst off her lips. She'd never been on display like this for a man before, so wide and vulnerable, positioned for one purpose alone. As a result, every rational thought in her head was incinerated, replaced by hopes that became pure pleas.

*Take me. Use me. Fuck me.*

"So good." Her Dom bit his way along the inside of one thigh until he hungrily tongued her slit. "So damn good, rose."

"All...yours," she panted back. There was so much more to say. So much gratitude to convey. But right now, as he unraveled the last shreds of her sanity, it was excruciating to think of voicing anything except the purest intent of her soul. "All...yours...Sir."

"Yes." He confirmed it in the form of a dictate, claiming her with harsher need. As he sucked harder on her clit, exposing every damn nerve to his merciless desire, he snarled, "But I need more. *Yeah.* More."

His demand was her undoing. Eyes closing again, she nodded. Moaned. Reveled in the hot beat of her blood as his fingers pushed her folds wider—

Until the pressure became pain.

"Ahhhh!"

*What the hell?*

She glared down her body, into the griffin's smiling eyes— and the pair of diamond-topped clamps he'd just secured to her pussy lips. While her first instinct was a one-liner full of sassy profanity, not a single word manifested. Crazily, she was drawn to the sight of her most intimate body part, adorned that way for the first time in her life. It was exotic, even exciting. For a moment, she even forgot that the clamps hurt so much.

For a moment.

"Uh...ow?" she finally spat—earning her a burst of laughter from the masked sadist now resting on his muscular haunches.

"Breathe, beautiful," he exhorted. "It'll get easier if you focus on that."

"Says the bastard with his privates still all tucked in and safe."

"Says the *Dom*," he retorted, "with the dick that's been imprinted with my pants ever since I locked you to the spreader bar."

When her gaze impulsively dropped to his crotch, she expected his humor to reset. Instead, his demeanor hit the burners in the opposite direction, taking on a more ruthless veneer.

"Masks come in all forms, little girl. I know the pressure you feel. I've been forcing myself to wait for this moment"— his hands slid back up her thighs, now tough and possessive— "when I knew you'd be spread like this for me. Every time you've sighed or moaned, I've imagined what you'd sound like when I finally attached these—and these." His hands rose along her torso, now armed with another pair of clamps, attached via sparkling chains to the pair below. Before Tess could even gasp, he closed the two toys over her erect nipples.

"Ohhhhh!" she shrieked. "Are you freaking kidding—"

The bastard cut her short with the drive of his mouth on hers, plunging his tongue inside. He was so passionate now. So possessive. Moans climbed up her throat. Her mind spun. Wait—*what* mind? Primal didn't begin to describe this hot, throbbing mixture of paradise and purgatory. Her body, her mind, her pain, and her pleasure were thoroughly his to command.

It was wicked. Wild. Wonderful.

She moaned, deep and long.

He snarled, dark and satisfied.

Bastard. Did he think that fixed everything? Tess fought him, even maneuvering to bite his tongue, but it made no difference. He just growled harder before mashing their mouths tighter. Demanding even more...

*Yes.* The word flared through her mind with sudden, shocking brilliance. *More. Take more...*

No!

She yelled the word as soon as he set her mouth free. Her hard breaths framed it. Sexy's lungs pumped just as hard. His stare glittered like cobalt on fire as he pulled up, hitching to his elbows. "That's not your safe word, rose." His teeth bared a little. "But use the fucking thing now if you're going to, or *breathe* and accept my dominance, goddamnit."

She swallowed hard. Air rushed out of her when that was done, thick with conflict. She'd longed for this for so many years, even more acutely since getting to know Dan better. And here she was, living the Power Exchange dream, though unable to shirk her reality long enough to really surrender to it. To *become* it. To understand it was okay to give up Tess for a little bit and just be Sir Sexy's little red rose...trusting that with the pain, he'd bring ultimate pleasure...

*Taffy.*

If she uttered it now, it really would feel like losing half her fillings.

She swallowed again. Breathed in. Breathed out. Her breasts and her pussy still throbbed—but the agony was more acceptable now.

"I'm breathing," she whispered at last. "I'm...breathing."

The griffin brought his hands to her face. Fanned his strong, long fingers along her cheeks. "Yes, little girl, you are." Gave her tiny, hot nips of his confident, curved lips. "And it's fucking perfect." He readjusted his hips a little, settling the bulge beneath his fly along her distended clit. Ohhhh, *hell*. That was—

"Good." It burst from her on a little choke. "Oh, wow. Th- That's...good."

He licked his lips, thoroughly bacchanal about it, a demigod who knew exactly what he was doing with the quivering mortal girl. "And that's only the beginning."

"*Shit*."

They laughed together at her reprise. He skated his touch down to her breasts. Teased at the sides with searing circles of his fingertips. Extended his tongue between the tines of the nipple clamps, laving the buds trapped inside.

*Dear God.*

Her throat clutched. Her back arched. The motion increased the pressure on both sets of clamps. Pain coursed through her, jumbling with arousal in a dazzling mix before slamming down to the erect nub between her thighs. The sensations turned her feral, aching and unthinking, an animal enslaved to nothing but carnal needs.

The world careened again. Her focus flip-flopped. She could suddenly hear every note of the EDM-remixed Donna Summer song out in the bar, but the clanks of the chains that she tugged at, just inches away, seemed like they were miles gone.

So this was submission.

What a Dominant could do to a woman, if she gave him

her complete trust.

How he could consume her...

And consume he did. Burning her with his mouth, on her breasts and neck and face. Searing her with his hands, along her waist and hips and thighs. Skyrocketing her desire with the rub of his arousal against her swollen sex. Scrubbing her cognizance of time. Had a minute passed? An hour? Did she care? The world became sensation and sin and necessity and heat, honed on the space deep inside that screamed for one thing only...

"Please." She could barely infuse the word with volume. "Oh, please. I need it. I need you. I...I..." What? What did she need? She'd find the words in a second. She had to. She *had* to.

He kissed her again, mercifully ripping the responsibility of speech from her again. Tess whined in gratitude, accepting the dives of his tongue as a deeper baptism into his control, reveling in the rhythmic clanks of the chains at her wrists, timed with every passionate lunge he unleashed.

"Reach out with your fingers," he finally dictated, his voice practically sinister with authority. "Wrap them around the chains. You're going to need the extra strength."

"Y-Yes, Sir."

She knew he didn't need the affirmation—but she did. As her fingers closed around the thick steel links, she imagined his shoulders felt much the same way, as they coiled to jerk at his straining crotch. His teeth flashed, white and gritted, as he finally freed his erection from his jeans.

Her breath left her in a stunned rush. She couldn't see his cock but sure as *hell* felt it. He was magnificent. Hot. Swollen. Straining. The tip already dripped, so ready for her. After another frantic tug, one of his hands reappeared, foil flashing between his fingers and then his teeth. Once the condom was free, he rolled it on with an urgent push. She bit her lip, hating that he had to sheath himself but rejoicing in the hardness and heat she felt even through the latex. Her body matched the crucial energy from his. Her channel sluiced with new wetness. Her limbs softened, preparing for ultimate surrender. As he shuttled his cock upward, lubricating himself with her cream, she arched up. Her heart, already hammering from the "helpers" fixed to her labia and nipples, threatened to explode from her chest and scream at him in person.

*Need you. Need you. Need you!*

"I'm going to fuck you now, little girl. And I'm not going to be nice about it."

"Don't need nice," she rasped. "Just...need—"

Her high scream took the place of the rest. The griffin had saved a not-so-little surprise. The moment before he filled her tunnel with his sex, he flooded new blood back into her pussy, pulling off the clamps with two fast snaps.

Agony. Ecstasy. The rush of both was insane, incredible, unreal. As his cock ignited her core, pain rushed her tender lips. Her clit throbbed and raced, needing to explode.

"Oh, my God," she panted. "Oh...so...*good.*"

"Words out of my mouth." Her Dom dug his teeth back into her neck, his breaths fierce, his heat surrounding her. "Your body...your submission...my God...so much better than I ever dreamed..."

Tess gulped. Then again. Surely, she imagined the depths of intensity in his voice, especially as it trailed again into the dark huffs of his passion. Okay, he was a Dom, but he was also a *guy*, a member of the Mars brigade, biologically programmed to spill crazy things "in the moment" that they'd never cop to once the big head was doing the thinking again.

In short, it wasn't worth cataloging, let alone stressing over—especially because "in the moment" was like nothing *she'd* ever dreamed either. With every scalding thrust he delivered, she was stretched beyond comfort, filled beyond arousal. She reveled in every second. He surrounded her. Owned her. Possessed every whimper off her lips, sweat drop on her skin, sensation in her sex. He knew it too. Growled in dark, heavy pleasure because of it, as he fisted a hand into her hair, using her scalp as an anchor for his harder assault.

"Your cunt is so wet for me."

"Shit," she managed. "*Yes.*"

"Gripping me. So damn tight for me."

"Yes." It was slurred due to his hard bite on her neck, teeth nearly tearing at her like a vampire. "Yes. Yesssss."

"Is it going to come for me too? Convulse around my cock, begging my body to burst inside yours?"

"Yes, Sir. Ohhh yes, Sir..."

He changed his position, angling in deeper, ramming parts of her that were somehow more sensitive than before. Tess gasped. Every nerve in her body spiked to a spectral frequency, turning her into a creature of energy and ecstasy, of light and lust, of carbon colliding on itself, racing toward a completion so shattering but inevitable that she began to shake.

Overwhelmed. Decimated. Destroyed.

*Oh...God.*

Where the hell was her blissful mental mist? Her perfect, floating numbness? Why had it dissolved *now*? This was going to break her apart. *He* was going to break her apart.

"It's all right." His voice, though still a growl, was redolent with understanding. "It's all right, sweet girl. Let it happen. Let it come."

Heat stung the backs of her eyes. *How did he know?* And why did it matter? The only answer she could render was a tight sob, tumbling out as he slammed even deeper into her. Again. Again. Again. Smacking his body to hers. Driving his passion into her. Entwining his energy with hers. Roaring faster toward the explosion...

"I can't," she stammered. "It's...it's so much. Too much..."

"You can." Like the bastard he was, he flattened a hand between them again. Curled his fingers against the bundle of nerves that shivered so close to where his erection filled her. With every stroke of his hard column, he pressed deeper against her clit, quickly finding the spot that unfurled her from the inside out. "You can, little rose, and you will." He grunted as she shuddered. "Your cunt is going to come for me, and you're going to scream through every moment of it...starting now."

As if he was the damn president pushing the red bomb button, he tilted his thumb in...setting off the explosion.

She screamed.

Loud.

Hard.

Forever.

And then some more as he blasted her off a second time.

As the orgasm ripped her clear of any mental mooring, Tess clung even tighter to the chains. The griffin was a man of his word, ramping the cadence of his passion nearly to jackhammer speed. His shaft was a steel rod, his body channeling a power surge. His eyes were blue flames behind the mask. His teeth were gritted white beyond his lips. His shoulders were flexed into stark beauty as the fire in his body roared through more and more of him, building, climbing—

Then erupting.

"Fuck." He threw his head back, exposing his straining neck along with the disk that reddened his skin as its adhesive was tested, until he burst inside her with a long groan. "Oh. Fuck. Yes. Good girl. You're my good, tight little girl."

Tess arched and sighed as he kept up his pace, plunging hard and deep for several minutes, continuing his words of praise and completion and perfection. Gradually, he slowed his speed-metal pace to a slow rock beat. Despite that, his penis was still tight against her walls. Was he thinking of going for round two? She was up for it if he was.

Holy. Shit.

Correction. *Holy shit* was just the tip of the spear. Not even that. The words barely touched the magic of the sparks still zapping her veins, the tingles still roaming her skin, the thunder still ruling her heart.

"Wow," she finally rasped. No wonder Dan always sounded so wistful when he spoke of his lost dungeon days. Was this what it was like *all* the time? If so, then she only had one regret: that she hadn't given in and come here a lot sooner.

Sexy finally leaned out to release her wrists from the restraints. Tess almost threw him a disappointed pout, but the concern that radiated from him was a damn good deterrent. He carefully watched her while rubbing the circulation back into her arms. "Doing okay?" he asked, soft and gruff. After she nodded, he continued, "Good. Because you're not going to like me for this part."

Apparently, that was his idea of fair warning about removing the nipple clamps.

"Hoooo-leeee..." She never got to the rest of it. Shrieking oneself hoarse was a tougher gig than it appeared. Didn't stop her from thinking it. Shit, shit, *shit*, her breasts had never endured something like this. She'd even thought her research gave her a leg up on what to expect from the action, blood rushing back at the speed of light and all that hooey, but she was as prepared as Red Riding Hood in the woods—with her own golden, grinning, wicked wolf to show for it.

"Sorry." He gently kissed one bright-red peak and then the other.

"No, you're not."

He turned the kisses into silky licks. "That was supposed to happen at the same time you climaxed, but I couldn't rob a second of that orgasm from you." He raised his head a little, letting the light catch the intensity of his gaze. "Watching you come like that..." He shook his head. "That was something else, little rose. Thank you."

Just like that, her belly borrowed a few Cirque twists. There was no denying the amazement in his voice, but what did it really mean? *Something else.* What did that term entail to a Dom who'd clearly done this *a lot* before?

Tess raised a hand to his face. He flinched but didn't jerk all the way back. The moment, perhaps just five seconds long, was a gift as precious as the last hour with him. He trusted her not to go for his mask, clearly as indispensable as armor to him. And she wouldn't. With a little smile, she simply curled her fingertips into his tawny-colored stubble, needing to touch the man beneath, if only for a few moments.

"You stole my line, pal," she quipped. "Aren't you supposed to let me up now, so I can kneel and thank *you*?"

He slanted his head away with a scowl. "Don't buy into every line from those books, red."

"How do you know I've been reading books?"

"How do you know a kid's gotten into a pail of crayons?" He jogged a brow. "Scribbling's on the wall, babe."

She couldn't help giggling. When it escalated to a little snort, she slammed a hand over her mouth and nose. "Oh, my God. I'm sorry. I feel a little weird."

He exhaled, seeming amused and concerned at the same time. "Hazy? Kind of buzzed?"

"Yeah. Exactly."

A smiled breached his lips. "Then I've done my job."

"Did I...do my job, too?" She managed to string it all coherently as he pulled out and discarded the condom, though never fully left her side. Before he answered, Sexy left the dais, regained his footing, and then swept her into his arms in a traditional let's-play-wedding-night hold. The irony of it wasn't wasted on her, though she didn't dare indulge even a snicker as he solemnly carried her across the room, toward a little alcove containing a pallet-style bed, a washstand, and a wicker basket brimming with blankets.

Strangely, the sight of the basket made her shiver. When she tossed it off as coincidence, her body rebelled with another. Even nestled against the male muscles that were warm as sunbaked bricks, she couldn't fight off the tremors. They bristled at her very hair follicles and descended to the tips of her toes.

*Don't freak. This is normal.* Sometimes the scribbling from the books *was* right. The adrenaline from her orgasm and the endorphins from the pain play, mingling with the gauntlet of nerves, arousal, and excitement she'd just subjected her emotions to, collided like marbles in a giant jar. She just prayed like hell that her jar didn't break.

Thank God Sexy was on board with that comparison too.

While setting her down on the bed like she'd turned into spun glass, he reached for a blanket and then tucked it around her. In the same motion, he swung onto the cushion. After propping some pillows between his back and the wall, he reached for her, cradling her to him again. His muscled arms enveloped her. His heartbeat thudded between the planes of his chest, close and strong and reassuring.

She couldn't remember feeling safer in her life.

She felt a long sigh leave him before he finally murmured, "You did your job very well, little rose." His lips dipped against her temple. "I'm so damn proud of you."

She replied with an equally long sigh, infusing it with enough bliss that he couldn't mistake how happy she really was, before burrowing tighter against him.

Ohhh hell, this felt good. Too good. Between one blink and the next, exhaustion enveloped her. The man next to her was no help, starting to comb the hair off her face with spread fingers. It wasn't long before she succumbed to the pull of sleep, too exhausted to even wonder about his next words, whispered soft as wind, following her down to perfect darkness.

"My little Ruby. How truly beautiful you are..."

★ ★ ★ ★ ★

She woke up as if someone doused her with ice water. For a moment, Tess wondered if that was really the case. If it was time for school and she'd made the mistake of sleeping through her alarm again, she wouldn't put it past Viv or Mattie to resort to the tactic—not when Mom or Dad's anger would have been worse. They weren't paddle or belt kind of people, but the alternatives with Bob and Ann-Marie Lesange were just as debilitating.

"Shit!"

She forced herself to repeat it, using the mental force to wake her faster. At least one of her legs got the message, thank God, kicking the blankets off.

But as she jacked her head up and clawed a hand through her hair, she slowed. None of Mom's favorite French torch songs bled through the walls. Dad wasn't in the other room, browbeating Viv about how she'd be starving by twenty-five for not finishing last night's homework. All she heard was the sigh of wind through tunnels, along with someone humming softly. That wind brushed her face in the form of a warm breeze, wafting a combination of earth and sage, with a hint of fine Scotch...

Oh, God.

*Sir Sexy.*

She was still at Catacomb. Where she'd fallen asleep in his arms. And she was still mostly naked, on the cushy pallet in the aftercare nook.

Alone.

Where was he? How long had she slept? And was it weird that she wasn't mortified at all to be here?

On the little table next to the bed, propped up against a glass of water, a folded note caught her eye. Written on the front of it, in handwriting so bold it couldn't be ignored, was one distinct word.

*Odette*

She reached for the paper and then unfolded it.

*Little Rose,*

*I'm sorry my farewell has to be in this form, but you were sleeping so soundly and so beautifully, I admit that I fell prey to the dominance of you and couldn't find the strength to wake you up from a slumber you so well deserved.*

*I cannot help but think things are better this way, as well. I came to Catacomb as a onetime experience on a business trip, and work duties will call me away again in a few hours. If I awaken you, I'm completely sure I'll be tempted to shirk them before enticing you to stay locked in here with me for at least a few more days.*

*The memories of our experience will be often replayed in my mind for years to come, treasures I'll never take for granted.*

*It was my honor and pleasure to be the first man to witness the perfection of your submission. I am certain I won't be the last. The man who finally claims you with his collar will be the luckiest Dom on earth—and forever the target of my envy.*

*You are a gem among your kind, sweet girl. Do not ever forget that. Yes, that's an order.*

*~~Sir G*

Surely, he meant the initial to stand for Griffin. But it fit no other word right now except the one that tumbled from Tess's lips.

"Gone."

She clenched her teeth, but a grimace broke through

anyway. The words on the page jabbed at her like spikes, prodding her thoughts down a path of lonely finality. It wasn't a pretty trip. She felt like anything but a "gem."

*What the hell were you expecting, nimrod? White lace, promises, a diamond collar, and a promise of forever? They call it "playing" because it's supposed to be fun, and what man have you ever met who thought commitment was fun? Not Dad, that's damn clear. Not any of the guys at work, even Dan. Especially Dan. He gave up his kink for a commitment, and look where it got him in the end.*

Rereading his note wasn't a torment she could opt out of. Arm tense and fingers tight, she took in every word he'd written once more. His script was like his dominance: decisive, determined, without any fluff—or doubt.

She ached for him.

*Stop. It.*

With a heavy huff, she refolded the note—before ordering herself not to toss it into the wastebasket. One day, she'd thank herself for keeping it. She hoped.

"Well, hey there, gorgeous! You're awake."

She jumped a little at the voice, despite it being very comforting and very female. Instinctively, she reached again for the blanket. Clutched it against her body while one of the most stunning women she'd ever seen stepped in from the dungeon portion of the room. Luxurious red curls tumbled around the woman's huge green eyes, striking cheekbones, and full, smiling mouth. She walked like a queen, regal and proud in a black corset and skirt that showed off her beautiful curves. At the same time, warmth radiated from her, a natural glow from within.

Around her neck was a collar inlaid with stones that

matched her eyes.

As soon as Tess saw it, her chest flamed with jealousy.

*Damn it.*

This was so stupid. So illogical. And so damn impossible to dispel.

The woman settled to the mattress next to her. "How are you doing?" Tilted her head, peering more deeply. "It's Odette, right?"

She blinked, not understanding at first. She didn't want to be Odette right now. Or even Tess. She wanted to be Rose, fulfilling every carnal wish of the Dom who'd taken her to heaven just ten feet away.

"Oh," she finally blurted. "Right. Yeah. That's it."

"My name's Julianna—but in situations like this, I'm better known as Emerald. Use whichever one you prefer."

Tess smiled in spite of her stupid envy of the woman. The first name, probably her real one, fit the fact that she looked badass enough to take down the Lannisters by herself. The second, obviously in honor of her eyes, was a perfect lifestyle name. "They're both nice, but Emerald matches the accessories." She dipped her head toward the collar. "It's lovely."

Emerald fingered the collar with a soft smile. "Not as beautiful as the man it represents." She lowered her hand with a decisive breath. "But if we start talking about Mika, I'll keep you here until the sun rises and then goes back down again. Can't happen. We're only in town for a few days, on our way out to LA for a lifestyle convention. We promised Max we'd stop over during the trip. We run our own club, Genesis, and business has been booming, so Mika hasn't had a chance to catch up with Max lately."

"So they're friends?"

"Couple of pervs in a pod." The woman flashed a wry grin. "Sheez. I don't know a lot of guys *except* Max Brickham who'd look at an old bomb shelter and envision a desert kink den."

Tess found herself returning the smile. "Well, it's a damn nice kink den."

"Yeah? We were thinking of checking out some of the other places in town tomorrow night too—well, later on tonight— *after* Mika keeps his promise to do the Voodoo Zipline with me."

Shudder. "You two have fun with that." The sarcasm was an excellent excuse to avert her eyes, lest Emerald—who didn't seem to miss much—caught the sadness she hid with it. "What time is it, anyway?"

"About two a.m."

"Whoa." She sagged into the pillows. "I was out for a long time."

"You needed it, honey. According to your Dom, you were all about earning that shiny beginner's badge tonight. From the look on his face, you did just that. You made an impression on him, you know."

"Right." She couldn't hold back a snort. "Nothing says *you made an impression on me* like a note on the nightstand, right?"

Emerald winced. "He probably deserves that. But it ripped him apart like glass in a twister to leave you. I had to swear to him that you'd get everything you needed when you woke up. Speaking of which..." She scooted a little closer and then tugged gently at the blanket. "May I see?"

Heat trampled Tess's face and didn't stop there. *Dork.* For God's sake, she had two sisters. *And* walked around naked in the locker room at the gym. But pulling away the blanket for the woman, who'd shown her more maternal tenderness in the last five minutes than Mom had in the last year, was suddenly unnerving.

"Wow!" The exclamation, along with the open admiration on the woman's face, quickly banished the discomfort. "That is one pretty pair of nipples, babe. Hope you don't have plans requiring a bra for the next few days."

Tess laughed softly. If a flock of nuns traipsed in here, she was certain Emerald would have *them* at ease enough to flash tits too. "Guess I don't now."

"Here. Apply this cream a few times a day. It's got calendula in it. You'll want to apply ice to them every hour or so too. Same with the lady parts. You're probably a bit bruised, but because the skin is naturally darker on your nips and labia, it won't show as easily." She lowered the blanket farther, rushing cool air across Tess's legs. "Ooooohh. More pretties. Flogger, right?"

"Right."

"Bet it was heaven."

She blushed again, but it felt good this time. Like sharing a delicious secret with a friend. "Yeah," she murmured, "it was."

"These will heal faster. Looks like he just gave you a little taste this time."

She barely refrained from gaping. A *little* taste? She wondered what one of his "bigger bites" felt like—and if she'd ever have the chance to find out. Sure, she could come back here next weekend and have more confidence when it came to mingling with people, but the idea of surrendering to anyone other than Sir Sexy...

No. It felt wrong. All wrong. From the moment his eyes had first glittered at her from behind his mask, her body had retuned itself to a vibration with his name on it...

*A name you don't even know.*

*A man you don't even know.*

*A Dom who indulged you with a night of mutual pleasure and never promised anything more. Now deal with it, damn it.*

"Thank you," she finally said to the woman now softly cleaning her thighs with a cool, damp cloth. "For everything. You've been...very kind...and..."

And apparently "dealing with it" now included a burst of the most embarrassing, ugly sobs she could imagine. Hell. *Hell.*

"Ohhhh." Emerald shoved the cloth to the table and yanked her into a fierce embrace. "You sweet thing. There now, honey. Just spill it out."

"No." But just hearing the ragged gasp from her own lips was another defense buster. "Oh God, no!"

Like that was effective, especially as Emerald yanked the blanket back up, cradling her close and stroking her hair.

Exactly what Sexy had done just a few hours ago.

Yeeaahh, she was screwed. This shit was just going to happen. Right here, right now, with barely a shred of reasoning or an ounce of justification. Fighting it was like trying to tamp a stab wound with a Q-Tip.

"It's okay," Emerald soothed. "Perfectly okay, baby."

"No," Tess choked. "It's mortifying." She yanked a dozen tissues from the box the woman offered. "It wasn't like we blood bonded or anything. Last time I checked, I was calling him Hawkface, not Lestat."

"Hawkface!" Emerald laughed it out. "Not a stretch, is it? He does have that intensity..."

"*Who* has *what* intensity?"

The demand was issued from the archway by a voice like

high-end bourbon: robust, smooth, thoroughly masculine. Tess instinctively straightened as soon as she beheld a gaze of the same dark gold, matched by drop-dead gorgeous features covered in skin the color of luxury chocolate. The rest of the man was equally beautiful.

She knew exactly who he was. The transformation of the woman next to her spoke it clearly enough. Emerald turned an adoring smile up at the dark demigod.

"Master," she greeted. "This is Odette." She yanked on Tess's hand. "Odette, I am honored to introduce the first half of my world's center, Mika LaBrache."

"I am honored, Sir."

Mika gallantly bowed. "The honor is mine, sweet Odette. Lovely to meet you."

Tess threw her gaze between both of them while echoing, "The first half?"

The two linked hands, sharing soft smiles. "We have a little boy," Emerald explained. "His name is Tristan."

"And he's fucking awesome," Mika added. As Tess joined Emerald in a giggle, he continued, "And, according to his nanny, is starting to fuss a little for Mama." He wrapped a hand around his woman's shoulder and squeezed gently. "We should think about returning to Max's villa, pet."

"Of course," Emerald replied. "Though your eagerness wouldn't have a thing to do with the new three-sixty fucking swing in Max's home play room, would it, Master?"

The man narrowed his amber gaze, promising of a spanking or twelve—a look so intimidating, it was hot. But when Mika turned toward her, all Tess felt was the same warm comfort she'd received from Emerald.

Which was why the new boulder in her throat made

no damn sense. Nor the fresh tears that brimmed. No. They *did* make sense, but she was ashamed to confess it to these strangers who were sharing such kindness with her. In the middle of the night. When they had a *baby* waiting for them.

The truth? She was jealous as hell of them. Of the collar around Emerald's neck, outshone only by the devotion in Mika's eyes. Of their constant awareness of each other, as if bound by an unseen electrical field. Of the way they joked about fucking swings and spankings the way other couples joked about who got to pick the rental movie next and what direction the toilet paper should unroll.

With their truth, she grasped another piece of *her* truth.

She didn't just want a Dom.

She yearned for a Master.

Longed for him with a need that dug into her soul and hurt in her heart. Ached for him in the valley between despair and hope, unsure which one to pick. Somehow, Emerald saw all of that. The way the woman initiated a new hug, fierce and fervent, spoke the statement for her.

"I get it, doll. I really do."

Tess snorted. "Is that so?"

"You think I locked eyes with this luscious hunk of caramel on my first tango in the dungeon?" Her snort put Tess's to shame. "I had to chew a lot of bad candy first—and I made matters worse by being my own worst enemy. Even after the candy went rotten, I didn't toss the shit away like I should have. I let it muck up the floor all around me so that everywhere I stepped, the rotten experiences from my past glued me down. Until I scraped it all up and tossed it away, I wasn't free to see my value as a submissive or even a woman in a healthy relationship."

"So you're saying...that tonight...I did this to myself?"

"I'm saying this is a journey, not a ride on a bullet train. Sometimes it's magic and sometimes it's hell, but you don't know the difference between either unless you walk the path first. *You*, Odette, not anyone else. This is your story to discover, your gift to give, your happiness to embrace—and tonight was only chapter one. Regrettably, I don't know of any books that jump from chapter one to happily-ever-after."

"Says the girl who learned that lesson after vowing to become the wicked witch just so she could shove the broom up my ass."

Tess gasped, but Emerald laughed. "It's true. Every word." She elbowed her man's thigh. "But you loved every minute."

"Because I was already in love with *you*."

Tess curled her arms in and threw a scowl at the pair that only half teased. "Not helping."

"Bullshit," Mika growled.

She fumed but didn't argue again. Partly because the Dom still scared her. Mostly because he was right.

Emerald grabbed her hands and clenched her hard. "Listen to me, Tess. It'll happen, okay? I simply look at your face, into these beautiful eyes, and I see the journey you've taken just to get *here*. Celebrate *that* distance too, okay?"

Tess swallowed, ducked a fast nod, and mumbled, "Okay."

"*Do it*, baby. The journey ahead won't feel so much like the highway to nowhere."

She nodded again, with a little more conviction. And prayed like hell that the woman was right.

# CHAPTER SEVEN

"Sir? May I get you another beverage?"

Dan forced an indulgent smile at the little blonde who dropped gracefully to her knees in front of the chair he occupied, in the darkest corner of the club where he'd agreed to meet Franz tonight. The woman's breasts filled every inch of her corset, and her hips were lush beneath the schoolgirl uniform skirt beneath. She'd managed to let him know, through a series of equally practiced flounces, that she'd gotten rid of her panties about thirty minutes ago.

In short, kinky flying conditions were perfect. Clearly, masked men with thick scruff were her type. And hell if she wasn't completely *his* type.

Or *had* been.

What the *fuck* was wrong with him?

Three days. It had been three damn days since he left Tess's side, long enough to rinse her scent from his skin, her presence from his mind—and her effect from his cock. But while the first was easy to handle, the others were tenacious ghosts, badly in need of an exorcism—and damn it, he couldn't figure out why.

For the sake of his throbbing crotch, he prayed for the revelation soon.

The usual suspects, regret and guilt, had nothing to do with it.

He just had to keep telling himself that.

Over and over *and over.*

Wasted emotions, damn it. He didn't regret a second of what Tess and he had shared at Catacomb, nor did he coddle any guilt about how he'd concluded it. They'd both walked into that dungeon with clear heads and clearer expectations— which were *no* expectations, other than the pleasure that was mutually given and received, so...

*Mutual pleasure.*

Christ.

*That* was the trip-up, wasn't it?

Those words. Clinical, clean, polite—and a lie. *Pleasure* came nowhere near what he'd experienced in that room with Tess...or what he'd given her in return. Pleasure covered about their first five *minutes*—before the universe had imploded, morphing pleasure into things he'd never thought he'd find in a dungeon again. Awakening. Connection. Communication. Unity.

Magic.

The Dom space had been the best of his life—and fully reset his kink button. *He was back.* Master Dan had returned, new and improved, ready to flog some ecstatic subbie ass from one end of the valley to the next. All he had to do was wait a few days for Tess to clear out of his head, and...

And he'd been a goddamn idiot.

Three days, and she'd gone nowhere. Was still parked at the center of his frontal lobe. Still consuming the lock screen of his memory with her heart-shaped face and big, stunning eyes. Still teasing him with her impish gaze and taunting him with that sleek body...

"Sir? That drink?"

He looked up, stunned. The prompt no longer belonged

to the curvy schoolgirl. Instead, he stared into the remorseless smirk of one goofy half Samoan. Franz's huge shoulders shook with a laugh. The guy's teeth flashed against the contrast of his sienna skin.

Dan's ire jacked by another notch.

"Darling." He gestured to the blonde. She scooted in like a kinky roadrunner. "Thank you, really, for your service and your sweetness..."

"My pleasure, Sir. Completely."

"But I'm not going to be playing tonight."

"Oh." Her shoulders slumped. He felt like shit. She was gorgeous and knew her lifestyle protocols. For a fleeting moment, he wondered what she was doing in a mid-Strip, lookie-loo poser club like this.

Which begged a bigger question.

What the fuck was *he* doing here?

He already knew the answer. His clenching gut confirmed it. Catacomb was off-limits—also due to an answer he already had.

"Maybe some other time?" the schoolgirl offered. "Do you come here a lot?"

He pressed his fingers into her scalp, a kink version of a meaningful hand squeeze. "Perhaps some other time."

"Okay!"

"Go get yourself something at the bar. Put it on my tab."

She'd barely moved out of earshot before the Samoan shifted forward. "You're so full of shit."

He snorted. "Takes one to know one, Captain Franzen."

"Sperm to worm besties, Agent Colton."

"*Besties?*"

"Like it?"

"That does it. I'm wiping all the Broadway musicals off your Spotify."

"Not if *she* has anything to say about it."

He followed his "bestie's" gaze, to where a new arrival in the club had already garnered attention on her way over. The Goth princess from the other night at Catacomb, with her near-white hair, black lips, and slinky sepulcher fashion, slid onto Franz's lap.

"Greetings," she murmured to him.

"Greetings."

The second Franz echoed it, they went for it. As in, *went* for it. Tongues down throats, hands under clothes. Dan attempted to focus on his Scotch and the gyrating bodies across the dance floor, but Franz and his girl were a lot more captivating—and a lot less difficult to ignore once he started imagining how beautiful Tess had been beneath him, making so many of the same sounds.

*Fuck.*

By the time they pulled apart, Franz wore most of the black lipstick. Princess Goth ran a thumb across his lips, smearing the shit even more across his face. "There," she declared. "Perfect."

From hooded eyes, Franz growled, "Perfect for what?"

Dan coughed. Loud. "Okay. This is *really* the part where I tell you two to get a room."

"Don't mind if we do." Franz smiled. "By the way, man, this is Infinity."

"Of course it is."

Infinity laughed, making it harder to dislike her. "I wish I could say my parents were high, but they were just weird." She extended the hand not covered in black lipstick streaks. "Nice to meet you. Johnny's told me a lot of cool things about you."

Dan shot up both brows. "Johnny?"

"It works." Franz worked a hand around her nape. "*Outside* the play room, at least."

Infinity nudged Dan's foot with a pointy-toed boot. "Let it slide, and I won't make any funny mask jokes." To Franz, she cracked, "I had a few, but I'll save them."

Franz laughed and nudged her to her feet. "Better idea? Why don't you go and check on that room he told us to get?"

"*Excellent* idea," she returned. "Though you sure this place can handle us? Pretty sure the bouncer who let me in was dangling a *Target special* flogger off his belt."

"That's why I brought my own toy bag, beauty."

She nuzzled more black marks into his neck. "I get so wet when you say 'toy bag,' Sir."

"You can prove that in a few minutes, toy *girl.*"

He smacked her bottom playfully as she strutted toward the meathead in the corner playing the club's dungeon master. As he turned back to Dan, the pleasantry faded. "Wish I could send you the same promising juju for your night, but you already let that ship sail right out of the harbor."

"Thanks for the enlightenment." He matched his sneer to the one already flung at him. "But you forgot about the kittens I drowned and the angels I shot down while I was at it."

Franz spread his hands, emphasizing the expanse of his chest. "Doesn't matter to me if you let Kate Upton get up and walk out. Just need to be sure you're okay...okay?"

Dan chuckled. The mirth didn't come close to assuaging the unfinished business that still lurked with Tess, but it still felt good to smile in public. Why hadn't he thought of the mask thing earlier? It didn't exactly work for grocery-store trips, but during a night out in a place like this, where at least ten other guys in the place wore masks, it was serendipitous. "I'm fine, man. No secret flights scheduled for Mexico tonight."

"Good." His shoulders relaxed a little. "That's good."

"So you're saying it's good?"

The guy picked up a piece of snack mix from the glowing bowl on the table and lobbed it. "Cocky-ass spook."

"Paranoid soldier boy."

"Like you've given me reason not to be?"

He sipped more Scotch before conceding, "Fair enough."

"No shit, especially with the buzz that came down today from Langley. Figured that once you heard, you'd be in the mood to blow off some steam, and—"

He slammed his glass down so hard, the snack mix lurched. "*What* news that came down from Langley?"

Franz inhaled. "Shit."

"Shit *what?*" He leaned forward, ripping off his mask. Missing any nuance on the guy's face wasn't an option right now. "Christ, Franzen. If you tell me Stock was able to get a call out from the hospital and—"

He refused to finish it. If any of that was true—if Stock had bribed his way into getting even a single phone call, even in max security custody—he'd be able to buy his way out of the rest of it. The dick nozzle would once more hit the game reset button on them—only this time, he'd run a lot farther than Mexico.

"No," Franz insisted. "*No.* Stock is right where we left him, chained to a hospital gurney, staring at the prunes between his legs. This time, it's Newport."

Dan stiffened. *Newport.* As in General Kirk Newport, another member of Stock's groovy Scooby gang who were behind the freaky genetic alterations on Shay Bommer, Ghid

Preston, and at least a hundred more unwilling subjects, finally resulting in the men joining forces to hide the mutants—and the "experiments" that were nothing but sanctioned torture—in a top-secret "research facility" inside Area 51. After Shay went deep undercover to expose the operation, Newport was apprehended, jailed, and awaiting his due process by the military powers-that-be.

Or so they'd been led to believe.

With fury attacking his gut like a doomsday virus, Dan snarled, "What about him?"

Franz pulled in a measured breath. "Trivia tidbit. What other living general has more knowledge of Russian internal affairs than Kirk Newport?"

"Would that be the same zero as the one in front of his moral character rating?"

Franz scowled. Not just any scowl. Dan had only ever seen that look when the guy was in battle gear, getting ready to kick scumbag ass. "New math is going down, buddy. Zeros have no bearing. With things as tense as cock clamps between Moscow and Washington right now, the buzz says they're talking to Kirkie-poo about a downgrade on sentencing if he cooperates with sharing the intel in his head."

Dan swore under his breath. "So, a rabid wolf with a pile of new chew toys."

Franz nodded. "Let the carnage begin."

He downed the last of his drink. The bottom of his glass wasn't an encouraging sight. He was about to flag down a waitress for another but set down the tumbler and let out another string of profanity instead. Tying one on wasn't the magic bullet right now—not when *he* felt like the damn wolf, prowling and savage, yearning for a full moon to rise and morph him out of the skin he was stuck in.

Trouble was, that moon now bore a name.

A moon who hadn't returned his texts or phone calls in three damn days.

One more time. Maybe he'd try just one more time.

*Pathetic putz.*

So what? After Franz's bomb drop, a dip into the pond of pathetic didn't seem such a horrifying option.

"Hey." Franz's baritone yanked his head back up. "I can rain check things with Infinity, if you just want to sit here and get polluted."

He jammed up his middle finger, their way of expressing *thank you* and *fuck you* in one clean package. "Pollution's bad for the soul. And I'm going to be as much fun as an ex at a wedding. So *go*, damn it. You kids have fun."

At least *somebody* would tonight.

After "Johnny" cleared out to join his little Goth, Dan threw down some more bar mix, hoping the shit infused his gonads with enough steel to try punching Tess's number again. When he caught a trio of miniskirted girls eyeing the table, he rose and gestured them over. "Damn. I'm a pig. Sorry for hogging the table."

The tallest of the girls, a brunette with legs so muscular she likely bench-pressed more than he did, tilted a blinding smile. "No sorries necessary, hot stuff."

Dan threw a glance back before realizing she spoke to him. "Errr. Okay. I was just leaving. It's all yours."

Warrior Girl's friend, another brunette with a pixie haircut, smiled wider than her friend. "But we wanted the table because you came with it."

"Huh?" he returned. "What?"

She'd strutted up to his right. She had to see the scars. Surely they weren't the reason for the fascination in her gaze. "You heard me...hot stuff." Sure enough, she lifted a hand, directing it right toward his mottled skin. He jerked away on instinct, lungs slicing on breaths that suddenly felt like...fear. "Ssshhh, honey. It's okay. We just want to have fun. We're *all* freaks of the night here, right? Let me be the beauty to your beast, Quasimodo."

Dan grabbed her slender wrist. Heaved it away as fast as he could—but not as fast as the fear twisted into something worse. Something uglier than his face.

"Enjoy the table." He snarled it with enough venom to drain her smile and drop her hand. As soon as she did, Dan rose and bolted.

How much crazier could this night get?

He wanted to forget the question had ever crossed his mind.

He needed the one person who could help him do that.

Out in the club's lobby, he palmed his phone and took a deep breath. The space was a throwback to Vegas's early days, with a curved reception desk, velvet ottomans, and a chandelier out of a Ray Bradbury novel. Appropriate, given that he suddenly felt like Frankie Avalon, nervously calling his Annette Funicello for the fiftieth time.

He sat in a corner and punched in her number at once. If he was calling in a special from Lady Luck, might as well reach for the big brass ring.

One ring. Two. Three. Four.

Shit.

"Hey, stranger."

As her voice filled the line, he silently promised Lady

Luck a huge-ass kiss. "Hey!" His greeting sounded as awkward as the goat guy too. "I...uh...wasn't expecting you to pick up."

"I know." An apology threaded it. "I'm really sorry. I saw your calls and texts. It was just...a weird weekend."

He shoved up from the ottoman. Considering how her weekend had started off, alarm bells clanged in his blood. But Emerald had called him on Saturday, ensuring she'd waved goodbye to a peaceful and happy Tess. What the hell had happened since?

"Weird? How?"

"I..." She broke off with a flustered sigh. "I don't know where to start."

"*Ruby.*" It was a command, not an admonishment.

"Forget it," she snapped. "How are *you*? What's up?"

He attempted a laugh. *Textbook lame.* "Ohhh, no. I'm not chasing after *that* squirrel so easily. Why don't you just back up and try that answer again?"

She whooshed out a breath over the line. "Damn it. I have no secrets from you anymore, do I?"

*Not since I had you naked, clamped, and moaning beneath me, little girl.*

"You're evading."

"I'm *not* evading. I'm...thinking."

"About what?"

"'About what?'" she slung back. "What the hell kind of a counterattack is that?"

"One that needs an answer."

"I want some Colton sarcasm first."

"And I want an answer."

She huffed. The line scratched as if she'd angled the device away. "You all really *are* like hawks with their prey."

Warmth instantly bloomed through him. Unbelievably, it spread faster than the first time she'd uttered the accusation—in that zap of a moment, surrounded by the candlelight of Catacomb, when her spirit reached out and wrapped around his, intoxicating him, making him want more.

A lot more.

Fuck.

*Might as well come clean, man.*

*You haven't shaken a goddamn thing about her.*

Dominating Tess, and fucking her on top of it, had accomplished exactly the opposite. Just hearing her voice again confirmed it. The vibrations of it, smart and sexy and sassy, torched his blood, ignited his mind, sent shock waves up his cock...

Until her sob burst across the line.

"Tess?"

Silence. Too long and too thick.

Shit, shit, shit.

*Don't jump to conclusions. It's been almost three days. Anything could've happened in that time. A weekend emergency at work. The toilet broke at her place again. Bad hair day. That time of the month.*

"*Tess.*"

"I'm here."

"Was that meant to reassure me?"

"I'm sorry." A scuffle filled the line, like she'd picked up a Kleenex and tried to suck up her emotions. "God. I'm really sorry. This is stupid. I mean, it's been three days. I need to get over this!"

He held his own phone away. Swallowed hard.

So it wasn't her time of the month.

*Shit.*

"Three days?" He went for vaguely confused. Came out more like constipated angst. "Since what?"

She sighed. Well, tried to. Three seconds in, it broke into another string of tears.

"Sweetheart," Dan grated. "Talk to me."

She snuffled. Took a deep breath. "I...it's...hard."

"It's *me.*"

"That's why it's hard."

"Why?" He really *was* confused. Unless she suspected anything about his duplicity on Friday. In that case, he was fucked anyway, so why not go down doing the right thing? Whatever the hell that was anymore.

"I'll...I'll let you go. Let's talk later."

"You're not letting me go." *Because I'm not letting* you *go. Not now. Not like this.* The mask was off. He could do this. The care and tenderness he couldn't give her as a Dom was all his to give as a friend.

She snuffled again. "You didn't sign up for this."

"Sweetheart, I don't even know what *this* is." The ruse came easier now—which should have scared him more than it did. Right now, all that mattered was doing whatever it took to banish that melancholy in her voice. What the *hell* had he done to her?

"I'm being stupid anyway." She whimpered as if cutting off another sob. "*God.* So stupid."

"Tess. What the hell—"

"I understand a lot more now." She went on as if he hadn't spoken. "And why you said what you did at lunch last week."

His lips pressed together. "What part of what I said?"

"It makes sense. Your reaction when I suggested that you

be my Dom. All of this...it's much messier than I thought."

She started laughing at herself, but the sound was lost, despondent. It scared the shit out of him. "All right, that's it," he rumbled.

"That's what?"

"I'm coming over."

"*No.*"

"Yes."

"Damn it, Dan. I'm a big girl, in case you haven't noticed."

"You're also hurting, in case *you* haven't noticed."

"Hate to break it to you, buddy, but it's not the first time."

"First time on *my* watch."

In more ways than one. At least for now. He'd caused the last three days of her life to be a sub drop hell, and now he was going to fix it—as best he could.

"So?" she retorted. "What the hell does that mean?"

"That I'll be there in fifteen minutes."

★ ★ ★ ★ ★

Karma sure as hell got the last laugh in on his noble-minded ass.

Of course she was wearing her pink-and-purple *My Little Pony* PJ bottoms—and the tank top that went with them, dipping low enough to reveal she wasn't wearing a bra beneath. *And* a pair of the fuzzy socks she loved. *And* the matching pink bunchy thing in her hair, freeing cute cherry-red wisps along her neck. By the time it all added up, the little-girl-soft crossed with touch-me-please sex confused the shit out of how his body wanted to respond. While his brain pounded that he was *just* here for aftercare in disguise, his dick didn't get the memo.

His erection filled even more, ramming his fly in the zone between "you're so screwed" and "torture central."

It was a nippy winter desert night outside, but her apartment was heated and cozy, glowing with its warm, modern décor. She didn't invite him farther than the entryway. Instead, she spread out a hand, crossed her ankles, and leaned against the door. "Okay, here I am, all in one piece. Happy now?"

Dan grunted. Grabbed her chin between two fingers. Tugged up. "Are *you* happy now?"

Her breath snagged. Something equally primal crashed into Dan, clutching his own breath. His nostrils flared from the force. Fuck, she smelled good. Her normal rose and cinnamon were joined by a hint of fragrant smoke, likely from one of the scented candles she was so fond of.

He released her only when her eyes narrowed, their light-green flecks darkening with concern. "You look like shit."

He arched a brow. "Thanks. So do you."

"Now that we've cleared *that* up..."

"Why haven't you been sleeping?" he growled.

Her concern flashed into anger. "You putting up pinholes in my crib in your spare time, Colton?"

He scowled. That she looked halfway serious about the accusation was infuriating. He took a step in and kicked the door shut. "You think I need fiber-optic cameras, Lesange?" He reached up again, cupping the valley between her nape and jaw this time. "Those shadows under your eyes are my hard evidence, sweetheart. And the strain around your mouth. And the giant bag of corn chips on your table."

"I like corn chips."

"And you never indulge unless we're at Mundo." He leaned in, sniffing her more deeply, seizing his chance to push closer. "Did you just eat a Twinkie too?"

She jerked back. Well, she tried. Dan tightened his hold. A fire curled through him, protectiveness raging like he'd never known, penetrating every layer of his bone and muscle. *You're not getting away yet, little rose. No fucking way.*

"Tess." He didn't filter any rough note of it. "Little Ruby. What the hell's going on?"

The words were for formality's sake. In his deepest gut, even before she sagged against him once more, he already knew what the answer was.

"Damn it," she whimpered. "I'm such an idiot."

"And you can hit that delete key right this fucking second." He spread his fingers across her scalp, tugging her closer.

"I'll let you hit *yours* after you hear what I did."

He huffed softly. "You do remember some of the mission covers I've had, right?"

"Of course. Though I've tried brain bleaching the goat herder one."

"You and me both." He smiled. "That being said, you know not a lot can faze me anymore."

As he'd hoped, that brought her face up, and a faint smile tugged at her lips. Holy fuck, he loved that smile. *Any* of her smiles. Only downside? Those little movements of her mouth zapped more lightning into his cock.

"Come on." She pulled away, though she kept one of his hands latched in hers. After she went to the couch and pulled him down to sit, she kicked up a knee so she fully faced him. "Have you...ever heard of...Catacomb? The club?"

He forced his features into neutrality. "Of course." Probably best to let her settle on that through a few beats. "Might have even been there." A few more. "Have *you*?"

She wet her lips. Pinged him with a furtive glance. "Might have."

"Recently?"

She traced the purple pony on her knee with a fingertip. "Maybe. Possibly. Maybe, like...on Friday night."

He took advantage of the chance to angle up a knee in return. "Well, is that so?"

Tess scrunched her nose. "Don't make it sound like that."

"Like what?"

"All gooey and illicit."

"I was going for interested." And *shit*, was he interested. She wanted to talk about idiots? How about the guy in the room who'd had one of the most intense sessions of his life with a subbie and then gotten plopped into the rarest opportunity of them all: to hear *her* uncensored side of the story?

Tess dipped her head, her lips twisting with contemplation. "Maybe gooey and illicit fit better anyway."

"Is *that* so?"

His snark didn't yield any in return this time. She twisted enough to look up—and give him the full slam of her tear-filled eyes. "Maybe magical is better," she whispered. "And perfect."

His lips parted. His throat went dry. As his gaze twined with hers, an awful thought crashed in. *She knows. She* knows *it was me.* What else could explain how she didn't look *at* him anymore but right through him?

"Tess," he grated. *Let me explain. You have to understand. I looked at you and couldn't let anyone else have you. I had to make it good for you, Ruby. I had to make it* better *than good.*

He'd just never expected her to return the favor.

The best damn trip he'd ever taken to the kinky tea party.

Making him wonder if he'd ever dunk his bags in another

cup again.

"Want to know the really shitty thing?" she asked before he could get anything else out. "I...I didn't even learn his name."

It took a surreal second for her statement to sink in. "What?"

"Don't judge." She twisted a hand into the lapel of his leather jacket. "Please don't judge, okay? I really need to talk this out with someone."

Relief crashed in so fast, he had no choice but to smile. Fortunately, it seemed to translate as something close to understanding. "Well, I'm damn glad I can be that someone." He tucked his head over, favoring her with the unmarred side of his face. "No judging. I sure as hell don't have that right."

It didn't surprise him when she let go of his lapel to jab his shoulder. She always did it when he hid his scars, but he sure as hell wasn't going to stop. He'd come to like the pummels anyway. They meant more than she likely realized. Others saw his scars and "accepted" them or gawked at them. But Tess truly didn't see them, as if her mind was stuck on a surveillance loop of him from a year and a half ago. She'd carried a schoolgirl torch for him back then, and he caught her gazing with those same star-filled eyes even now. It was warped. He'd told her as much. She'd always scowled—then socked his shoulder.

"So here's me, not judging," he drawled. "But for the sake of the discussion, do I get to pick a nickname for this bastard who's messed you up? *Ow.*" He glared as she dropped her fist from his shoulder to his sternum.

"He's not—he *wasn't*—a bastard." She curled that hand against her chest, as if clutching a secret into her heart. The action grabbed him between the ribs, too. "He was... amazing. Commanding. A little arrogant. A *lot* mysterious.

And relentless. And beautiful. And ohhh, Dan..." Her throat convulsed on a gorgeous little rasp. "Sexy," she finally finished. "So, so, *so*...no. More than that. The things he said, and the way he said them...as if he already knew what my body needed, you know? Like he just...*got me* somehow..."

"Whoa." He wasn't stunned to hear his authentic amazement. That she'd gotten all that and really appreciated it... He was a little floored. A lot humbled.

And *a lot* turned on.

"Whoa is right." She shook her head, giving him a glimpse of her glossy eyes before they slid shut. "And his body..."

"Not sure I need to hear this part," he teased.

"Too late. I'm officially the president of his drool squad." She rolled her head back. "It was perfect. So perfect. I didn't know a man could move that way. Lunge his hips like that. Get thrusts in that deep..."

"Okay. TMI threshold is officially reached."

She blushed and giggled. "You're right. But seriously, if you only knew—"

"I'm good with the omission, sweetheart. All fine here." *Liar.* He yearned to hear every last, breathtaking syllable of what he'd done to her. But it wasn't going to happen. Couldn't ever happen. Wasn't that the hateful little bitch of things? The inside scoop for which he'd just been so thrilled flipped a Linda Blair on him, becoming demon more than dream—only worsening as her words stirred all *his* erotic memories from Friday night. And now, learning how deeply she'd enjoyed it... how she'd really wanted everything he'd done...

His dick surged to the point of pain. He shifted, readjusting as subtly as he could. Christ. Had he nearly pulled the crazy scheme off, only to have his erection betray him?

The next moment, it didn't matter. A new onslaught of tears hit Tess. As if her laughter had merely been the latch of a gate, the waterworks hit twice as hard as before. While the behavior was damn typical for sub drop, the logic didn't halt a shred of detonation in his heart. She was crashing hard, probably had been for three days, and had done so alone.

*You're an ass.*

"I'm sorry." Her tears slushed the words together as he yanked her over, swinging her leg across his hip to pull them tighter together. "Oh, sheez. I'm so—"

"*Hush.*" He pressed his lips into her hairline. "You make with that apology shit again, and I'll take you over my own knee."

"Promise?" she gibed tearfully.

*If you only knew what I'd trade to make that happen, red.* He looked to the ceiling, bargaining with the Big Celestial Guy. *You know the very hairs on my head, man—so go ahead and take whichever nut you want the most. Just let me help her hurt less.* Please *let me help her.*

"I did it wrong, didn't I?" she finally rasped.

He clutched her harder, scratching fingers along her spine. "What the hell are you talking about?"

"With the griffin," she explained.

"Who?" Mental fist bump. It really sounded confused this time.

"Sir Bastard," she explained.

"Oh. Him. The griffin?"

"I had to call him something. And it fit."

He quirked a half smile because he could. "Because he was so 'mysterious' and 'beautiful'?"

"And arrogant," she prompted. "And relentless."

"Oh, right." He slid the smirk wider. "Forgot about those."

"He sure as hell made sure *I* didn't."

"Sounds like my kind of guy."

She cleared her throat. "Funny you said that."

"Why?"

"Because he actually—"

"What?" he pushed when she self-interrupted. *Moron.* Pushing the subject was *not* a good idea—or so he thought until she tilted her head, whipping him an adorable little glance.

"He actually reminded me a lot of you."

He let out half a smile but nothing else. So much for the neutrality being a cinch to maintain. Just how extremely had he flirted with fate on Friday night? Despite the mask, the scruff, and the voice-alteration disk, had she connected the griffin to him at all?

The fact that she had, even a little, should've petrified him. Instead, he was giddier—and hornier—than before.

*Damn it.* His brain couldn't afford another withdrawal from his libido. The universe didn't provide overdraft protection for stupidity. If he bankrupted his vault and fucked this up, the price he'd pay was his relationship with the woman in his arms.

He was a Colton. He had an empire's worth of money. But his closeness to Tess was a jewel he couldn't—and wouldn't—give up. Ever.

If anything solidified that conclusion, it was coming here tonight and holding her through these tears. What would happen if she found out he was really the Dom who was responsible for this—the guy who'd supposedly left town for "business" on Friday instead of staying to even help her back into her clothes that night?

"Me? Well, wow. Was that before or after you decided he was arrogant?"

She smiled. "You forgot ruthless."

"Ohhh, right. And ruthless."

The smile bubbled into a laugh. "Dan Colton, you are so full of shit sometimes."

Her eyes twinkled like fairy dust again. The tears were gone, thank God, and he held her through a pause of easy silence. If she was onto him, even a little, he was pretty certain he'd know. Firsthand, he'd witnessed the woman turn into a sabertooth over the *idea* of deception. Granted, the fuck-up in question was usually a bunch of traitors on the other side of the world, but to Tess, it made no difference. Her drive for the truth wasn't just the nucleus of her nickname at the Agency. It was woven into the center of her character. Façades didn't come easily for her, even in the name of gaining greater truths, such as adopting a cover story for a mission—or donning a mask for her first visit to a kink club. It was why she wasn't interested in field ops and probably why she'd yanked off her mask so fast after they "met" at Catacomb. And yeah, as much as she'd respected his right to keep his cover on, she'd still tried to sneak a peek at him, too. Thank fuck he'd nipped that little temptation in the bud—

A lucky break he wouldn't be getting again.

He harbored no illusions about that—or about how close to the cliff he'd truly danced on Friday. While he'd gladly do it all over again, it was now another secret to be buried for the rest of his life. There'd be no "having one too many" with Tess and letting it slip past a booze haze. Not another "moment of weakness" when they got together for bad action movies and ended up spilling their guts to each other on the couch instead.

And for fuck's sake, there'd be no letting his dick, his pride, and his possessiveness collaborate on making a decision for him again. About *anything.*

She broke their silence by pulling him into another heartfelt embrace. "I'm glad you're here. Thanks for coming over."

He wound his arms around her, too. "You're welcome, Ruby Girl."

She lifted a hand, playing with the hairs along his nape. He tunneled fingers under her brilliant curls, doing the same.

"This feels good," she murmured.

"You're right," he replied. "As usual."

As she chuckled against his neck, a thought occurred. Maybe he'd been enduring a little drop of his own. It happened to Doms all the time too, not that he'd ever dealt with it himself—but he'd always had a high-octane job waiting.

He'd also never had a scene like the one he'd shared with Tess.

The connection. The heat. Her body. Her bravery.

Magic.

She was, he decided, extraordinary. More so than he'd ever given her credit for.

She sniffed. It was softer than the sobs, tamped again when she swallowed hard. "I'm still such a mess," she moaned. "I'm so sorry."

He twined fingers deeper in her hair and chastised, "No. *I'm* sorry, sweetheart."

"What? Why?"

Well, wasn't this little resolve for secrecy going well already? "Because...I'm a guy." *Lame. Ass.* "And guys do dumb things. Even Dom guys who are—how'd you say it..."

"Amazing? Commanding? Mysterious? Sexy?"

"Yeah." He laughed. "Even Dom guys who are all that."

"But he's not the dumb one here." A few new tears threaded her confession. "*I* am."

He huffed. "Tess—"

"I fucked it up, okay?" She was really clinging to this one—another nonsurprise, considering how doggedly she pursued everything from domestic terrorist cells to her new CrossFit classes. "This isn't his issue. It's mine. Somewhere along the line, I didn't just blur the line. I stomped right over it. So just tell me. Be honest, Colton. That's why I'm going through this now, right? I did this to myself. *Damn it.*"

"Okay, red light." He pushed her back enough in order to get a straight-on view of her face. "What the hell are you talking about?"

She responded with a dutiful, deep breath—perhaps one of the most gorgeous sights he'd ever seen—though a week ago, it would've flown right over his head as the truth it really was. Her strength and talent at work had blinded him to a truth that was there all along: Tess Lesange really was submissive.

Stunningly, perfectly so.

"I tripped up," she began again. "On the expectations side of things. Does that make sense?"

"Not entirely. Go on." He said it after a long moment of studying her. He'd always noticed the obvious things about her beauty: her collector doll eyes, vibrant hair, and of course, those plush, pouty lips. Why had he never looked further? Observed how her eyes turned velvety when she talked of naughty things? Noticed how her cheeks flushed dark pink... and her back straightened, trying to relieve the pressure that built in her aroused areolas? Of course, he was rarely treated to the view he had now, with those puckered peaks stabbing at her tank top, making him harder by the second...

"We—the griffin and I—walked into that play room with open eyes," she explained. "I wasn't expecting hearts and roses and collars afterward, and neither was he." The rose hue took over more of her cheeks. "This may sound weird, but...I think it made me more relaxed. Like I was a different person in that room, you know? No worries about what I'd say during the afterglow, or how awkward our goodbye would be. I just focused on each moment as it happened."

"Yeah. I get it." He reached for one of her hands and squeezed. "And no, it's not weird."

It occurred to him that the last time he'd done this, they'd been at lunch at Mundo. Like then, a palpable current zipped between them, sizzling with connection. To Tess, little had changed about that fun, friendly spark. To him, everything had changed. In seconds, all his mind's eye could see was her nude beauty, spread and bound and clamped beneath him. Then her eyes, dilated and dark. Then her chest, rising and falling, as she waited for him to feed his cock into her wet readiness...

*Damn.*

*Just get through this, and everything will get easier. She'll move on, you'll move on, and so will the memories.*

"So..." She sucked in a rickety breath. "What the hell's wrong with me, Dan?" When he pulled a little, wanting to just get her close again, she climbed all the way into his lap. "What the *hell* is wrong with me?"

He wound his arms around her, hating himself for her tears but, with disgusting selfishness, welcoming them—at least now. He'd been off-balance since Friday too—and only now did he realize the reason why. He craved the darker edges of D/s, which meant the balance of lavishing his subbies with his softer side too. He'd never skipped on aftercare with a submissive—until Friday.

*Dumbass.*

Maybe now he could right the axis again. For both of them.

"Tess. Sweetheart." He buried his lips against her hair, savoring the citrus of the product she lavished on it. "There's nothing wrong with you."

"Which is why I can't stop blubbering?"

He stroked fingers up and down her spine. "You know damn well what's going on. Say it for me, Ruby. Let me know you understand."

She swallowed hard but uttered, "Sub drop?"

"Good girl."

"But it's been three days." She angled a little to raise her face toward him. Her irises were full of dark-green tumult. "Three *days*, Dan. Typically, a submissive will display signs of sub drop for only a day or two after the dynamic with their Dom, especially after a scene of just an hour."

He snorted and wasn't shy about it. "Which textbook did that one come from?"

"All of them."

"Then all of them don't know shit."

"Excuse me?"

He embraced the excuse to press a palm to the side of her face. "For starters, you picked Catacomb for this little stunt of yours. Since that place isn't listed in the tourist guides or on the lifestyle directories, I assume you researched the choice— meaning you know *it* isn't textbook either."

Her lips compressed. "It wasn't a 'stunt.'"

His gaze descended. Tense or not, he loved looking at her

dark-strawberry mouth. It was his personal fetish, making him clench all over, battling the new surge of his erection. Fuck, how he longed to kiss his apology into her. Hard.

Instead, he settled for muttering, "Sorry. Bad choice of words. But I stand by the intent."

"I know." Her response was equally soft, staying in the cocoon sealed by his hold. *Shit.* When she got all raspy and trusting like this, all he wanted to do was turn into her real cocoon, never letting anything or anyone hurt her—a thought that opened the way for other conjectures. Troubling ones.

What really would've happened if he hadn't been there at Catacomb?

A Friday night, at the dungeon known for allowing its players to walk on the harder edges of BDSM. Some Dom *would* have noticed her and taken her submissiveness as permission—for anything. Screw the limits, let alone a safe word. Who knew better than him that dickheads could find their way past any barrier, even a screening process like Max's?

"Tess." No use holding back the intensity of his anxiety. "Why *did* you pick Catacomb?"

His desperate tone seemed to puzzle her. "Are you pissed that I picked it or that I didn't tell you?"

"Both." At least he could give her this truth. "And I'm not pissed. I'm—"

"Yes, you are."

"Tess! God*damn.*" He constricted his grip. "I'm... I'm scared, okay?"

*That* got her attention. Should have. Fear wasn't his default mode. It was the rare gear, and he hated indulging it. But this time, it had gotten the jump on him. Bitten him so hard, his throat turned his next words into sandpaper.

"You could've been sitting here dealing with a lot worse than sub drop," he accused. "*A lot* worse."

She sighed. Looked tempted to roll her eyes. Neither helped his tension. "You want to give me some credit here? In case you've forgotten, I peg lying assholes for a living."

"Through surveillance footage and radio chatter," he rebutted. She fumed a little and tried to pull away. He yanked her back in, purposely letting her chest press to his. "Things are a lot different in a dungeon, and you know it. When the light is dark, the air smells like leather, and a Dom is looking at you like he wants to take you to heaven and back"—he paused, savoring the catch in her breath and the dilation of her eyes—"the bad guys aren't so easy to discern, are they?"

Shit. Why hadn't he taken off his jacket? Her nipples were probably tighter now, incessant buttons that would stab past her shirt *and* his, teasing his skin with their erect heat...

"You know what?" He drew her in even tighter, molding her thigh along his. "Even *I* could be a bad guy."

Her breath snagged again. So did his. When they inhaled again, they also did it together. One rhythm. One energy. Just another couple of inches, and he could turn it into one kiss too. One taste...

Her lips parted. *Fuck*, her lips.

"How bad?"

He pulled on her. Another inch gone. Her whisper still vibrated the air. He could practically taste her now. The salt of her tears. The thickness of her desire. The promise of how good both would be, swirled together on her tongue...and his...

What could one kiss hurt?

With a groan, he jerked back.

Everything. It could hurt absolutely everything.

What would she taste on *his* tongue? Would she recognize the flavors of her griffin once her eyes were closed, her other senses opened? What then? Even if she didn't make the immediate connection, what would such a move do to her— processing the kiss from one man while dealing with the fallout from being dominated by another? Why the hell did he even consider fucking up her brain that way? Had he gone insane?

In disgust, he faced the inexorable answer to that.

Yes.

When it came to thinking about anyone hurting even a hair on Tess Lesange's head, *his* head rammed into the socket marked *insane*.

"Bad enough," he finally answered her. "Which you should take as another lesson, damn it."

Tess sat up a little more. "All right." She parted the air with outward sweeps of her hands. "All right. I get it. Yes, Sir."

Every word of it, even the last two, was sweetly compliant— raising every red flag in his brain again. There was only one reason she'd capitulate so fast about this.

"You're going to go back." He didn't hold back the brutality of the snarl. "To that place. Aren't you?"

She bolted to her feet. Folded her arms. "'That place'?" she retorted. "It's not the middle of Bogotá, okay?"

"You'd be safer in Bogotá. At least you'd be conscious of the danger you're facing."

"I don't need a chaperone."

"Right." He angled back, also crossing his arms. "Because you did so well handling everything from your first visit. Those shadows under your eyes are just my imagination. The corn chips on the counter *and* that empty ice cream bowl in the sink, same thing."

"Stop it," she seethed.

"No," he snapped. "You've holed up in here like a hormonal teenager, Tess—for three days. Ignored calls and texts. Sleeping patterns off. Is this the behavior of a submissive who's acting in her best mental and physical welfare?"

He made damn good points—but as the words spewed out, they felt and sounded all wrong. He was channeling his inner griffin, including the arrogant and ruthless knobs cranked to eleven.

Tess's furious flush confirmed it.

"Get out." She arrowed a stiff arm toward the door.

He didn't blame her. He also wasn't going to heed her. "All right, all right. Wrong choice of words again. But—"

"No," she spat. "No wrong words. Wrong *concept*." Before he could react, she turned one of the throw pillows into a *throw* pillow. It smacked his head with a *whump*. "You know what? Go screw yourself, Colton. Seems to be what you're hell-bent on doing anyway, so don't come in here and grandstand about my precious *submissive safety* when I offered it to *you* in the first place." A new wince crumpled her features. "Thanks for that new tune in the key of humiliation, by the way."

He fell into one of her big leather easy chairs. "Jesus, Tess. I never meant—"

"I know, I know. It's why you're even sitting here." She refolded her arms and toed the throw rug. "Let's move on."

"Right," he rejoined. "As in, me screwing myself."

She sank to the floor next to the chair. Dan almost groaned from the irony of it. Since stepping through the door, he'd done nothing but fight images of her submissive perfection. Fate wasn't going to let him have the win. His fingers ached in their fight not to reach out, press her head against his thigh, and whisper how much he loved seeing her like this, perfectly lowered on her knees. Yeah, even with the sassy smirk that wiggled at her lips.

"As interesting as that would be to watch," she said with equal sarcasm, "you know that I respect and value you, wherever you're at in your life. That includes the boundaries—or whatever the hell they are—of your journey as a Dom. But as the guy who keeps saying how much he respects me in return, you have to support where I'm at with my submissiveness too."

She might as well have lobbed an anchor down his gullet. "You're right. And I'm sorry."

He flattened his hand atop hers. She bent her head, briefly pressing her cheek to his knuckles. Her fiery hair brushed his skin as she raised back up, searing him for another breathtaking second, before she pulled back completely.

"It's not a matter of right or wrong," she murmured. "It's about being real. It's hard for me to do that sometimes." A breath wobbled in and out of her. "It's hard for me to do that *most* of the time." She looked to the darkness beyond the window. "Perfection isn't perfection if you've had to lie to everyone, even yourself, to get it. But I want this—*need* this—part of my life to be the real deal."

Though her gaze was still averted, Dan lifted one side of his mouth, hoping she felt the energy behind it. "'This part of my life'," he reiterated. "Because the other parts aren't real?"

She shrugged. "It's not important right now."

He almost growled. Just like he almost took advantage of her submissive position to push her for a truth she'd never trusted him with. He knew parts of it, simply from relentless observations over the last year. Her parents were tangled in it, as well as a pair of sisters. She spoke kindly of them from time to time but never *to* them. No phone calls on her birthday. No fond "when I was little" family memories. How did it all figure into her bigger picture? She knew affection, of course, but craved intimacy and honesty. That explained why she'd never defined him by his wealth and why his scars didn't matter to her either. It was also a clear explanation of why the BDSM dynamic drew her in so deeply.

And why she could never learn that the friend who'd refused to be her Dom had turned into the Dom who'd rocked her world.

And in doing so had gotten his world rocked just as hard.

Shit.

There it was.

*His* reality.

As explainable as it all was—he hadn't been with a subbie in a year; her first-time eagerness was a blowtorch of a turn-on—it was, in every incredible *and* disgusting sense, a gigantic truth. For now, and probably forever, a small part of him would always think of himself as her Dom.

Which transformed into another intractable truth.

Her happiness was now his ultimate goal—at whatever price he had to pay.

He glanced upward. *Hey, Big Guy. Bet you didn't expect to hear from me so soon. But here I am, ugly as ever, putting you on notice. You ready to forgive this black soul for a few more sins?*

He sure as fuck hoped so.

# CHAPTER EIGHT

On Tuesday morning, Tess sucked it up enough to stuff her sore breasts into a bra and report to work. By then, the lingering discomfort in her nipples was eclipsed by the enduring ache in her spirit, and chasing down terrorist assholes was the best therapy she could think of.

Returning to the routine of life—the banter of the morning-show DJs, the latte in her cup holder, the morning sun glinting off the hotels along the Strip—helped toward setting Friday night in perspective. It had been a dream come true, but it was still only a dream.

And the griffin?

He still occupied every other thought she had, a force powerful enough to sway her at times. His sensual fingers, his growl of a voice, his branding iron of domination... She'd been changed in so many ways by that hour beneath his control, as if he'd been sent by fate to be her perfect fantasy lover. She even saw the purpose behind the mask that had irritated her so much in the beginning. Without his anonymity, she wasn't sure she'd have flown so high into their intimacy.

*So* high...

It was crazy, wasn't it, that a stranger could actually set her truth free the most? Yet it made the most sense of all. Since he was still a stranger, the pangs of remembering him didn't cut so deep.

So she tried to tell herself.

Constantly.

The battle wasn't eased by the thoughts that took up space between the hot memories. Every one of them had only one face in them.

Dan.

Sleek as his leather jacket. Rugged as his faded jeans. Dark as the night that had brought him...when he'd filled her world with sun again.

Like she'd ever needed an excuse to let him in her brain.

Still, these thoughts felt...different. *He'd* been different that night, all intense and touchy and pensive, after inviting himself in with the subtlety of an ogre. She'd been mortified, of course, that he had—not that he'd never seen her Pony PJs and bedhead hair before. And not that any of it mattered anyway, now that they were going to stick to the friend zone.

It was the other shit she couldn't bear for him to see.

The tears. The aching. The *weakness*—over a man she couldn't name, much less identify, even if he'd shown up at the door right alongside Dan.

But Commander Colton, for all his pushy protectiveness, had understood. Held her, consoled her, even washed away her fears that three days of sub drop wasn't more freak-worthy than zombie Ebola. He'd told her she'd get through. He'd talked her back into stumbling one step in front of the other until she could run again.

Now, as she left the conference room after the morning staff briefing, she was pretty sure she'd have to *Freaky Friday* that shit back at him. In a number of huge ways.

He'd done the stumbling thing before. He could do it again now. He'd get back up again too, stronger than before, because that was what Dan Colton did better than anyone else she knew. She'd be here to help him do it, too—exactly as he'd been there for her.

The confidence bolstered her a little—a *little*—as she marched to the break room, hoping somebody had set the coffee maker to "Molasses" this morning. Nothing like a little overcaffeination to help a girl call her best friend and tell him one of his archenemies was on the short list for a huge presidential favor.

Right, right. Technically, they were still labeling Newport's compromise as "house arrest," but she wondered how many noses across DC were growing longer at this very second. Nobody halfway close to the situation was in the dark about the backdoor bullshit Newport would start once he'd showered off the prison stink. Perhaps before that.

She fell into one of the break room's steel chairs, along with the new java she'd poured into her travel mug. The liquid was hot and strong and *bad*. Juuuust perfect. The bitterness on her tongue was a perfect match for the seething emotions in her heart.

"Bloody good thing you really don't have laser capabilities." The jest came from the guy who'd just appeared in the doorway, finger-combing his rambunctious curls as he closed the space to the tea station. "I wager that report would be ashes by now."

She glanced over as Alex Kenyon filled a cup with hot water and then dunked in a bag of Earl Grey. The analyst was a fresh transport to the CIA by way of five years at MI6 and had already broken a swath of hearts Stateside with his dry British charm and soccer-player body. He was too smooth for Tess's tastes, but objectively she understood the appeal. And right now, smooth was what her roiling stomach needed.

"This isn't pretty," she muttered.

Alex settled into the next chair over. "Neither is the escalating tension with the Russians." He blew on his tea and met her gaze with the blue clarity of his own. His eyes were several shades lighter than Dan's, but she couldn't help using them as a jumping point for wondering how Dan's gaze would change once he knew Kirk Newport's demands were a signature away from being approved. Depending on how busy the president's day was, the former four-star general could be kicking up his heels—still dripping with the blood and guts of the innocents he'd walked over—in front of his fireplace by dinner hour.

"How the hell am I going to break this to him?"

Alex rubbed her forearm in reassurance. He knew the "him" to whom she referred. Ever since those weeks she'd spent nearly every day by Dan's side in the burn unit, everyone had known.

"You'll find the words," Alex assured. "You always do." He sipped his tea and arched both brows, teasing a little. "We're all just glad it'll be you and not any of us."

Tess glared at the report again—and now really wished she could laser the damn thing too. "This is fucking unfair."

"War is hell, buttercup."

"This isn't war, damn it!" She bolted back to her feet. "This is a stupid pissing match that could be handled with a closed-door meeting over a large bottle of vodka. Newport knows the exact same thing, but he's leveraging his 'sacred advice' about these bastards for everything he's worth—which isn't much, now that he's been disgraced like the cockroach that he is."

Alex thrust out his lower lip. "Mr. Wonderful, indeed."

She dumped her coffee down the drain with a violent

thrust. "I can't consider what Newport will be capable of. That report only scrapes the surface."

She dropped her head into her hands as her mind jumped back a year, remembering the frenzy around here once everyone realized that one of the country's biggest, most horrific biomedical experiments had been conducted for years right beneath everyone's noses, in a secure building at Area 51—because of Kirk Newport's collusion.

"I've seen enough of the paperwork to have a good idea," Alex declared. "The Big Idea project, turned into a cover-up under the Verge Pharmaceutical umbrella. Splicing human and animal DNA. *Bollocks.*" He peered back up at her. "Wasn't one of Dan's friends one of those poor souls?"

Tess nodded. "Shay Bommer. He gave himself up to Stock, Newport, and the brains guy, a whack job named Homer Adler, to save a bunch more of the test subjects. His friends tried to intervene, but the mission went really sideways. One of the guys took a bullet in his leg, and a couple of nurses died in a massive structure fire. It would've been *three* nurses if not for Dan."

"And that was how he got burned." Alex grimaced. After Tess nodded again, he asserted, "Bastard's a bloody hero."

She swallowed against the sharp sting behind her eyes. "Yeah. He is."

"Well, then." The guy rose, clearing his throat. "Good move, dumping the coffee. Just move on to the vodka, duck."

"Not a bad idea."

She scooped up her copy of the brief and made her way back down the utilitarian halls to her desk, with all its familiar piles of prioritized cases. Normally she'd be eager to turn on the laser and get to work, but today she plopped into her chair and gloomily eyed the stacks.

Maybe she could turn them into a little forest and hide out from making the inevitable phone call to Dan. Just thinking about Newport again, with a dozen canaries in his fat-cat belly, made her crave a punch—or ten—at the wall.

Her cell phone rang to life. Incoming call. Generic ringtone. The source number wasn't one she recognized, making the hairs on her neck prickle.

"Get a grip," she rebuked. "Telemarketers find their ways."

Two more rings. She lifted her thumb, eager to shoo the call straight into voice mail, but a rebellious grin caught her lips. Telling off a pushy asshat might be just what the doctor ordered for her craptastic morning.

"They're your data minutes. Start talking. And make it good."

"Little rose."

Shit.

*Shit.*

Time stood still. Jolted ahead. Froze again. Then broke free, racing to catch up with the electrons she'd once called a body, now splintered into a thousand tiny sparks that both fought and resisted the confines of her body. As if she had a choice in what they did now. She was a prisoner of the voice that still reverberated in her ear, its technically altered tone as low and sensual and beautiful as she remembered. The sound curled through her, taking over cell by cell, awakening her on every visceral level once more.

"Are you there?"

"I'm here." She tightened her grip on the phone so hard, it tumbled to the desk and slid beneath her file rack. "Crap, crap, crap, crap!" When she resettled it against her ear, his chuckle rumbled the line. "I... Sorry. I'm here. Really."

"And truly?" he teased.

She whooshed out a breath. "It's...you."

"Really. And truly."

"Shut up," she lobbed. But when he complied with that, she didn't know what to fill the silence with. "I...I just..." *Had never expected to talk to you again. Had never* hoped *to.* "How'd you get my number?" Because of her national-security clearance, her name never showed up on her personal line, but the fact that he had it was a little weird. Which should've been unnerving—if her nerves would calm down long enough to be undone.

"I asked Max for it." Even his weighted pause brought a new round of *Where's Waldo* for her heartbeat. "But that might depend on your definition of *ask*."

"Oh." While she hoped his innuendo didn't mean he'd literally forced the answer out of Max, his revelation clutched at her lower belly.

"So...how are you? Are you all right?"

"Of course I'm all right." She brushed fingertips along her hair, having gone glam pin curls with her style in honor of actually facing the world again. "Why wouldn't I be?"

"Because I haven't been."

She swallowed and tried to breathe. Then again. *He's only checking on you. Stop reading a thousand meanings into his words.* Of course, the tight growl he finished with, along with the voice-alteration device, didn't help things by a damn bit.

"I'm sorry," she finally managed. "Are you not feeling well?" That had to be it. He'd come down with something over the weekend and assumed he might have already been contagious on Friday night, so he was calling to warn her about it. "Did you catch something yucky?"

"Yeah. I caught something." The words fortified the lead lump in her stomach, but his tone was all off. A man newly felled by cold or flu rarely sounded so victorious about it.

"Damn," she murmured to be polite. "What do you have?"

"A craving for you again."

Forget trying to catch her breath this time. "Oh."

"Oh?"

"I'm...uh..." She grabbed a curl and twisted it around a finger. *Think you could add* any *more clichés to this?* She ducked her head like a shy teenager—*guess the answer to that is yes*—and murmured, "I've missed you too."

A rumble emanated from him, confirming his thoughts had ventured at least halfway down the same path as hers. Damn. That voice enhancer, especially over the phone, turned him into something dark, wicked, and barely tamed, making her very skin ache from yearning to be his prey once more.

"Missed me." His echo was a challenge. "A little or a lot?"

She twisted her hair tighter. *Damn it.* Talk about a case of rock and hard place. If she said a little, he was going to detect the lie. If she said a lot, then she became the picture of desperate and horny. Okay, she *was* desperate and horny, but that was none of his business.

"A...a lot."

On the other hand, maybe it was fully his business.

Take forehead. Drop to palm. *Could you be any more of a dork?* But was she supposed to have played it differently, when just the sound of his voice disconnected her mind from her body, except to acknowledge the fire in her blood, the tingling in her breasts, the exquisite pressure in her sex? It was as if part of her had been sleeping for the last four days and now

ANGEL PAYNE

received its perfect, Dominant wake-up call.

"Good." He said it like he expected it but still rejoiced in it. The sound was verbal sun, warming her enough to lift a cautious smile.

"Well, now that we have *that* established..."

"Meet me again."

The room spun once more. "You," she stammered. "I mean *me*. Well, and you." *Been forming coherent speech for long there, sister?* "You want to...meet me again? Where? You're not even here anymore. You had to leave—"

"And it tore my fucking gut out to do so."

"So I heard." She winced. *Well, there's the coherency— along with its new best friend, snarky bitch.* She added in a hurry, "But it was all okay. Honestly."

"The fuck it was."

His vicious tone was not to be debated—so she didn't. Probably a blessing in disguise. She might've blurted things she shouldn't, like, *How the hell do you just know what I went through with the sub drop? And why the hell are you so furious about it?*

"Well, it's not going to happen again." His voice mellowed a little. A *little*. "I changed my workload around to get more done from my Vegas office this week. This time, you're going to be pampered...*after* I tame every part of you again."

She gulped before managing, "That...that sounds pretty nice."

A savoring growl answered her. "Oh, it'll be nice."

Dilemma. Follow him down the path of yummy, dark, verbal debauchery he offered or seize the *other* opportunity too good to resist: the chance to possibly learn more about the man behind the mask?

"Your 'Vegas office,' hmmm? As opposed to the other office...where?"

No more than two seconds passed before his blunt reply. "I want to see you again, Odette. The sooner, the better."

Well, that was the last time she let curiosity win out over horny. "I...really think I'd like that."

"Good."

"Errrm...anyplace in mind, then? Are you a let's-do-coffee guy? Or is happy hour and bar mix more your speed?"

Another significant pause. Then, with low-toned care: "Was our time at Catacomb that awful for you?"

"Our time was heaven for me," she answered without thinking. She shrugged, despite knowing he couldn't see her. "I just didn't want you thinking that was all I wanted."

His chuckle filled more than just the digital line between them. It plowed through every cell in her body. He wasn't a man who laughed often. She had no idea how she knew that, but it was a fact as certain as the sky was blue and Nutella was nectar from the gods.

"Isn't that supposed to be my line?"

"Why?"

She could hear the gravity descend over him again. "Oh, little beauty." He exhaled at length. "You truly don't realize what kind of a gift you gave me on Friday, do you?"

Heart, meet moon. Fighting the stars cascading over her spirit from the impact, she rasped, "Just as you don't see what *you* gave to *me*."

"Hmmm." There was a creaking, as if he leaned back on expensive leather. Lots of it. Did he work in a corporate environment? If so, did he have his own office with one of those palatial chairs? What would it be like to kneel for him there, be ordered to pleasure him while he took a phone call from another powerful businessman?

So much for fighting off the ache between her thighs—which spread even deeper as he concluded, gravel thick in his voice, "It sounds like we're at somewhat of an impasse."

She sniffed delicately. "Respectfully speaking, Sir, it's only an impasse if both parties aren't determined to move beyond it."

"Hmmm."

That hum again. *Why* did he keep doing that? At this rate, he'd be making her come right here from the force of the syllable alone.

"Is that what we are, little red?" he murmured. "Two determined parties?"

She threw out a flippant laugh—which probably sounded more like a dying seal. "I'm in if you are, honey."

His sharp hiss would've been a complete excuse to giggle again—until he followed it with a growl that grabbed the middle of her clit. "Let me tell you what I'm determined about, sweet one. I'm determined about seeing you again. *All* of you. Bared to me. Naked for me. Once you've peeled off every thread of clothing, revealing every inch of your incredible skin, I'm determined to take that breathtaking body and turn it into a thing of ecstasy. I'm determined to push its limits, learn its fears, and then explode it past them all, until you're flying so high, you don't remember—or care—which direction the ether takes you."

She undoubtedly sounded like a creepy bitch by now, breathing as hard as she did—but she was beyond caring. "Y-Yes, please."

His gruff huff filled the line. "So fast to agree—when you

have no idea what I want to do to you."

She shifted again in her seat. It was the only way to assuage the pressure, continuing to take over new parts of her pussy. "If it's anything like last Friday, then do away."

His pause was a torture of silence. His reply was even more ominous. "I'm not going to play you easy this time, rose. Not by a fucking long shot."

And delicious.

And breath-stealing.

"Was Friday your idea of *easy*?"

*And has Tess ever heard of a filter?*

"Friday was my idea of heaven." The line sounded so much better with his resonance applied. At this moment, she didn't care that it was artificial. "But there are so many depths you haven't explored yet."

"Depths?" she repeated. "In heaven? You mean heights, don't you?"

"All depends on what you consider 'heaven,' dear one."

*Dear one.* Oh, that was by far her favorite. Her eyes closed from the impact. Her head dipped. She longed to keep going, to crumble to her knees for him even now. "I want to go to heaven, Sir."

"I can hear that." His comeback was threaded with the same brutal desire pounding her bloodstream. "But now... plead it to me."

Deep gulp. Her head dipped lower, along with her voice. "Please, Sir. Take me to heaven."

"Gorgeous," he praised. "Now...from your knees."

Her eyes flew open. "My...what?"

"You heard me, Odette. Do it. Say the words from your knees. I'll wait."

Tess snapped up her head. Peered around. Her normal workday view awaited. Filing cabinets. Supply closet. Pen cups. Staplers. Sticky note holders. Everything was the same— but it wasn't. "I'm at work," she whispered.

"At your desk?" he persisted.

"Yes. But—"

"Then be creative. Did you drop something, perhaps? Looking for something in your purse?" A knowing pause. "See, little one? Masquerade *can* be fun."

"Don't be a smartass."

"And don't talk back to your Dom."

"You're not my—"

"Right now, I most certainly am. But you still have a safe out. Just hang up, and we can be done at this point. No harm, no foul. You'll be on your way, I'll be on mine, and—"

"*No.*" She hated the desperation in her voice.

"Then you know what's required, rose. Lower to your knees...and imagine how good it will feel to do that in our own room at Catacomb. Imagine my hand against your cheek as you say the words to me in person."

*Ohhhh, shit.* The man was like a damn drug. His voice rendered her so woozy, the whole knees-on-the-floor thing might happen in spite of her reticence. "You won't even know if I'm really doing it or not," she groused. But lying to him was a seriously shitty choice. Trust was a two-way street, especially in the world of D/s.

"I'll know." He constructed a wall of command around each word. No option to do anything but believe him.

After one last little grunt as salvage for her dignity, she pushed her ass off the chair and slid her knees to the floor.

The second they hit, something crazy happened.

Crazy and wonderful.

She forgot all about her dignity. And remembered every tingling detail about the little preview Sir Sexy had just provided. His hand against her face. His approving growls in the air. His body in front of her, proud and hard and majestic, making her feel small yet sheltered...and so thoroughly a woman.

"Please, Sir...I want to go to heaven. Led by you."

The words brimmed from her in whispers, as natural as mist off a lake at dawn, pierced by the sun that was him. His response drove into her with the same power, thorough and primal and unalterable.

"Tomorrow night. Ten o'clock. Catacomb. I'll meet you at the door."

★ ★ ★ ★ ★

For the first time in her life, she hated herself for being obsessively punctual. Fifteen minutes had never felt more like fifteen hours—especially when every passing moment brought the chance to think more deeply about the strangeness of this moment.

The last time she'd sat here in her car, listening to the brush of the wind and staring at Catacomb's double entrance doors, she was damn certain she wouldn't ever do it again. Her quest for fulfilling her D/s dream seemed like it would only ever *be* a dream. Now, there was no question mark over the rabbit hole. She was diving straight into the darkness, led by a creature with a filthy rock god's voice mashed with a kinky king's arrogance. Both sides were like sexual crack to her— except for the part about having to choose which side of herself to access as a Dom-pleasing complement.

*What about choosing your true self?*

Shocking, how she didn't automatically attach Dan's voice to that. She had no doubt about his influence over it, though—a paradox she couldn't ignore. For a guy who spent most of his time hiding himself from the world, he loved riding *her* about the let-your-light-shine thing.

He hadn't always been the ashamed ogre under the bridge. She smiled a little, remembering the "Hot-lanta cowboy" of just last year, stealing hearts and slinging hokey one-liners everywhere he went. She missed the crap out of that guy sometimes—but that Dan Colton probably never would've grown into the man who'd become her closest, dearest friend.

A frown set in. She still hadn't told Dan about the development with Newport and felt like shit about it, despite her practical reasons for the delay. Someone way above her pay grade had Newport's deal snagged in red tape, hoping the tensions with Russia would die to a dull roar by the time the paperwork got as high as the Oval Office. If they didn't need Newport as much, his outrageous demands would have to be altered—if they were lucky, even revoked.

In the meantime, she maintained a lie of omission with Dan. She'd even met him for drinks, gushing about how much she was looking forward to this new experience with Sir Sexy, selfishly accepting his "Domly" advice without dropping a clue about the potential shit to hit the fan from the Newport deal.

But what if it didn't? She'd be torqueing Dan for no good reason. His not-so-little "adventure" with Stock, a stunt he got away with only because he wasn't on active duty with the Agency, might be just the right juice for the rockets he'd aim Newport's way. And even if he chilled on that shit this time around, did he deserve the agony of knowing the asshole was sleeping on silk and dining on filet every night instead of rotting in a jail cell? He'd been through enough pain because of Newport's corruption.

"It's better this way." She nodded, decision firmly made. Her head was on board with the message. She just wished her heart would get its act together.

Right now, she needed to get her own shit together, period. Why was she stressing over one man when only minutes away from meeting with another? Even if "meeting" wasn't the most accurate term...

A gulp sliced down her throat.

A thrill raced through her stomach.

A tremor claimed her whole body.

No. "Meeting" wasn't the right word at all.

Giving. Taking. Servicing. Submitting.

Only ten minutes now, and the griffin would be sliding his huge hand against hers once more. Lifting that slow, knowing smile. Speaking those deep, perfect commands. Taking over her body before one stitch of clothing came off...

Who was she kidding? He'd started taking over from the moment she picked up the phone yesterday.

When she thought of what she'd done for him, in the middle of the office, based on the power of his voice alone...

Another shiver. Deeper this time. Spiraling through her blood, taking over her marrow, pounding into her ears...

She could barely wait another moment.

Just knowing he was probably inside the club already, maybe at the bar nursing a drink, perhaps even watching the door for her...

"*Eccckkk.*" She rolled her eyes at her reflection while

sliding on some lipstick. "He's *not* watching the damn doorway for you, dork." As Mom was so fond of reminding her, *devoted princes exist only in worlds where girls have birds, mice, raccoons, and other disease-bearing animals as best friends.*

At least her makeup was being cooperative. Her lipstick was a shade called "Slaying the Enigma," designed by the new cosmetics division of Stone Global. Thank God Killian Stone's wife was a redhead, because this stuff looked great with her own coloring too. It was a perfect match for the dress she'd bought on her lunch hour today at an "alternative" boutique downtown: a bolder choice than the last time she'd been here.

*Much* bolder.

The crimson leather and vinyl one-piece, featuring a sweetheart neckline kept together by corset-style ties, tapered into a flared skirt that barely covered all the important stuff— the reason why she'd also purchased a pair of flattering red panties to go with it, topped with black lace and tied at the sides with dainty black bows. The sales clerk had helped her finish off the ensemble with a pair of black gladiator-style heels. Overall, the look gave her a little more cleavage, a lot more leg, and a bit more confidence.

She took a deep breath and checked the time again.

"Five minutes." Okay, *now* she could go in. Five minutes didn't make her desperate. It just made her punctual. The griffin would appreciate that. He was a Dominant who paid attention to the details, meaning timeliness was likely a hot button for him.

When she walked in and peered around, she indeed found him eyeing "details"—on a petite little thing with a Tinkerbell haircut and an eye-popping rack, dressed in a top and skirt that looked more like fancy-wrapped duct tape. In short, a show girl with curves that could fascinate a man for days.

And yeah, the man looked fascinated.

Insecurity swooped in, making Tess back against the wall. Her heart lodged in her throat. While she was certain the man wouldn't back out on their "appointment," would he consider the time merely an obligation now, to be filled on his way back to the duct-tape fairy? She wasn't certain about the answer even as he looked up, locked on to her with his mesmerizing stare...

And lifting the most wicked, wanton grin she'd ever seen.

She was suddenly grateful for the wall. Holy shit, how he could emulsify her in a matter of seconds. Even with the mask, which now just seemed a part of him, instead of something that frustrated the crap out of her. He'd developed lots of other ways to do that anyway. The way he stepped forward—leaving the pixie stuttering in midsentence—to get a better view of her. The way he stopped as soon as he did, sharply pulling in air, eyes glittering with lust. The way he squared his shoulders before restarting his approach, boots pounding the stone floor, leather pants and vest gleaming with every graceful move of his tawny muscles.

Frustration was her friend and enemy now. It took over as she watched him, hardening her breasts and pooling between her thighs, deepening with every powerful step he took. He wasn't moving fast enough. *Closer. Need you closer. Now.*

Her breath was a freight train by the time he finally got there.

He crashed his mouth over hers with the same force.

It was the last thing she expected. The only thing she wanted. She mewled as he pushed in, letting him dominate her tongue as he slammed against her body. The rugged aroma of his leathers and the earthy scent of his skin spooled their way through her senses, heating her blood to fevered intensity. If he demanded she strip and kneel for him right there, she doubted she could refuse.

*Even with the duct-tape fairy watching?*

The thought gave her the will to pull away. It didn't sit well with the man still pinned against her. "I'm not done with this part yet," he growled.

"Even with your new *friend* taking notes?" A fast glance confirmed that the blond pixie had indeed tracked his every move since leaving her, even this one.

The griffin huffed. "She can compare info with them." A jog of his head made Tess look the other direction, across the room, to where a pair of men stood with Scotches in their hands and gazes fixed on her. They were both attractive and commanding but had to be utter nutcases, since they raised their glasses and smiled as if conveying, *if things don't work out with the guy nailing you to the wall with his crotch...*

She couldn't help but laugh. "Well, damn."

"Sounds about right." His rougher timbre matched the new texture in his energy. His jaw was a crag beneath his dark-gold stubble. His biceps rippled as he splayed hands against her hips. "*Damn*, red. I'm the luckiest fucker here tonight."

He took her lips again, though he did it with a shocking sweep of tenderness. Though his tongue was just as hot as ever, he rolled it with hers like a sensual stream instead of a pounding wave, teasing her passion higher by calculated increments. That all changed when she freed a moan into his mouth, unable to hold back anymore. As if she'd pulled the pin on his dam, his passion surged. He groaned and dragged her thighs around his waist, never once breaking the pressure of his mouth.

He only broke the kiss after working a hand against her slit, exploring her from behind—before piercing her with a hard scowl. "You're wearing underwear."

"Duh." Mouthy? Yes. But accurate? That would also be a yes. "Have you looked at this thing?" She nodded downward. "More precisely, at the length of this thing?"

"From the second you walked in the door." His eyes glittered brighter, so gorgeous and blue, behind the mask.

"Really?" It was even mouthier, but at the moment, she needed the sarcasm. "Could've sworn you were a little preoccupied when I walked in the door."

His lips flattened. "You going to keep bringing that up?"

"That all depends. Did *she* 'bring you up'?"

"Fuck."

His disappointed mutter made her squirm. Damn it. She'd wanted to be perfect for him tonight, his sexy little subbie, not this ball of petty jealousy. Certainly not the girl who created drama over him simply standing next to another woman—and her barely wrapped boobs and booty. But for anything to work between them, tonight or any other night, he also required her truth—even copping to the claw of insecurity that dug into her because of duct-tape girl.

So, she could be perfect, or she could be authentic. One was impossible, the other disgraceful. At least right now.

She let her head drop.

Sexy didn't try to lift it back up.

He even lowered her legs, purposely setting their bodies a foot back from each other.

Shit. *Shit.*

The happy flips in her stomach were now taunting

clowns—all wearing Band-Aid dresses. She wanted to vomit. Then run out the door.

Then he spoke again. A command. In the deepest, gruffest tone she'd heard from him yet.

"Take them off."

Her stare jerked back up. Searched the eyes behind the mask for confirmation of his meaning. Sure enough, his irises had gone from sun-glowed cobalt to dark midnight smoke.

"You know what I mean," he pressed, reading the question on her face. "Take the panties off, rose. Then present them to me in your hands, palms up, with your feet in attention pose. Is that clear?"

She was vaguely aware of the long moment she took before answering. How had the rest of the room turned into mere fuzz and background noise, in the space of but three sentences from him? And why did she even care? All of it—the eyes she felt suddenly turned to them, the whispers flying through the air— were a semblance of irrelevance to what really mattered here.

Obeying him.

But actually doing it? Oh, yeah. *That* part. Though the club wasn't busy tonight, there was no ignoring the task being asked—commanded—of her. Stripping the covering over her most intimate parts, in front of strangers. Offering the evidence to her Sir in a formal position of submission, minus the kneeling. She should be grateful for that, at least.

*The dirty work doesn't get done by itself.*

It was one of Dan's favorite phrases, which she used to steady her hands while reaching beneath the little skirt and tucking her thumbs under the band of the panties she'd spent half an hour picking out. At least her efforts wouldn't be for naught. Everyone was going to get a nice view of them now.

With her eyes lowered—looking up meant gaping at one or more parts of his anatomy, and she *had* to stay focused—she let the panties drop to her ankles. As she leaned down, retrieving them off the heel of one sandal, her throat felt as dry as the wind whipping outside. And the cruel plot twist? Her pussy had never been wetter, responding at once to its naked freedom—and the griffin's growling prompt.

"Now present them."

With cheeks aflame and arms trembling, she gathered the red silk in both hands and extended it. Why she wasn't adding an incensed glare, she couldn't fathom. This was humiliating. Unnerving.

And totally arousing.

Sexy stepped back toward her. Another step, even closer, to the point that he pushed her elbows against her sides, hands just below her breasts. Dipped his head in, pausing a moment to draw in a breath of the bundle in her palms. Then tucked his lips against her neck, abrading her jaw with the fitted leather of his mask.

As he bit down into her flesh, he cupped a hand over her naked mound.

"*This* is all I desire tonight." His fingers curled in, taunting her moist layers like steeled hooks. "This is mine to rule. To use. To possess." He shifted his lips to her ear, infusing her with his torrid breath before sinking his teeth into the tender shell. "To fulfill."

Tess moaned. Her head fell back. Her eyes slid shut. Heat cascaded through her body like stars on fire, her fingers clenching around the fabric in her palms. A sigh erupted past her lips. Or at least she thought so. Nothing was clear. She didn't give a damn. Not one.

"Now tell me too, little red. Say it for me."

There was no confusion about what he directed. She knew what he wanted; somehow she just knew. "I am yours to rule tonight."

"And...?"

"And to use. And to possess."

"And...?"

"And to fulfill."

His tongue was like honey down the column of her neck. "Yessss..."

As he suckled at the juncture of her neck and shoulder, he shifted one finger up, into her throbbing channel. Then another. Tess bit her lip to keep from yelping. "Oh, my God. Oh...my...God."

The bastard unfurled a low laugh. Tangled the fingers of his free hand into hers, capturing her panties between them. "If you were still wearing these right now, would they be wet, babe?"

"Soaked," she sighed. "Drenched."

He twisted his hand, working a third finger into her clenched tunnel. "How about now?"

"Shit!" She dug her nails into the back of his hand. "If you don't stop, I'm going to—"

He halted her with a brutal kiss. When he tore away, her skin was abraded from the burn from his beard. "I empathize," he grated.

That much was blatant. Sheathed only in his soft leathers, his erection hammered at her stomach. His whole body was bound by the tension unique to sexual denial, every muscle quivering, every breath dense.

His hand unwrapped from hers. Grabbed the wad of her

panties. Lobbed it off to the side, swooshing it into a stone trashcan carved with hieroglyphics. Great. She'd hooked up with a Dom who could really take it to the net—with her brand-new panties.

No time to bitch about it now. Her go-to guy already hiked both her legs around his waist again. He wrapped his arms to her back, enfolding her torso against him now. She ducked her head into his chest, trying to ignore the visibility of her ass now that the panties were officially ditched, but that was silly. It'd only be an issue if he turned around—

Just like he did now.

Damn.

She should've known Sexy would feel her ripple of tension—and counter it with another infusion of his velvet voice as he carried her across the living room. "Hang on tight, kink monkey. I have plans that don't involve anyone looking at you but me."

"There are other people here?"

She meant it. Every word. Just like before, he'd read her mind, her needs, and her fantasies and then knew what she needed to hear in order to forget the world beyond their bubble once again. Right now, she didn't care if there were five people watching them or five thousand. She'd be just as oblivious to what they saw or didn't see, felt or didn't feel.

For now, all that mattered was the man who'd rearranged a week of his life for her. Who ducked his head close, making her feel protected and precious as he carried her past the conversations of the living rooms, toward the world she'd come here to discover once again—a world that terrified her as much as tantalized her. Where she was told she wouldn't be played easy this time. Where her limits would be stretched. Where her body would be tested, stretched, and marked—before he made her forget that body altogether.

She trembled just from the thought. The *impossible* thought. Sub space. It was the kink magical unicorn, mostly a dream more than reality. To believe the mastery of a Dom could really infuse a submissive with enough awesome biochemical juju to take their mind to another plane of consciousness...it seemed like a scene out of *Twilight Zone*. Or *Naked Lunch*.

It didn't matter. In so many senses, she was already flying. The knowledge of what she'd already shared with this man, along with his promise that everything tonight would be even more intense, already had her pulse speeding, her heart thundering, her body trembling. None of it was relieved when Sexy made a turn and the clamor of the common social areas was replaced by the muted dimness of the hallway to the private playrooms.

She clung to him tighter. In response, he gave an approving rumble for her ears alone. A low-key EDM soundtrack emanated from ceiling speakers, barely masking the smacks, cracks, screams, and moans filtering from Catacomb's already-occupied rooms. The sounds gripped Tess more viscerally than they had on Friday night, reminding her of what agony *and* ecstasy awaited her. Hiding their effects on her body was impossible; the griffin still had her legs fully parted, her naked cleft pressed against his expensive leathers. She was floating...

And then maybe not.

He stopped in front of the door engraved with a rearing cobra. *Shit.* She remembered this one from Friday night and was happy they'd bypassed it. A shiver claimed her as he lowered her and then pulled the key out of his pocket. The tremor was just the start. "Fight or flight" morphed into "submit or sprint." She honestly didn't know what to do. What lay beyond the door, and what she'd experience there, were as unfathomable as the cobra's black irises—*not* a position she was used to being in. She liked plans. Structure. Knowing the path ahead and preparing herself for it.

Preparedness?

So *not* happening right now.

And she'd rarely been more scared because of it.

Or felt more alive.

*Embrace that part. Concentrate on* that *part.*

The masked demigod next to her didn't make the task easy. She looked up to find Sexy right there, studying her with steady cobalt eyes. She quaked all over again as he tilted his head, almost as if taking inventory of her—with a blatant overlay of sexual intent.

An electrical charge. That was what his focus felt like. She sizzled from the jolt of it, burning up from the inside out. Her breaths came faster. Her pussy dripped wetter.

All before he leaned in and kissed her again.

Ohhhh...*damn.*

If his mouth was the devil's own tool when he took her hard and fast, it was hell's calling card with this slow and sensual shit. The electricity in her veins turned to pure lightning bolts, driving her hands to his nape, trying to pull his mouth in deeper. The maddening man just grabbed her wrists and pushed them around to her back, locking them there as he took his sweet, slow time with every inch of her moaning, sighing mouth.

When he finally dragged away, there was a little grin on his face. Tess yearned to slap the expression off him but couldn't. He was so damn sexy, all Dommed-out in arrogance and swagger, seeming to know just how desperately she'd dreamed of a man who'd adore her snark but push past it to the other person waiting underneath. The submissive Odette, still so unsure of her value as a female. The blank space who craved to be filled...the hungry desire in search of service.

He got it. All of it. He just...did. She knew it, even if she wasn't able to gaze into his shadowed eyes and see it there. It was more than what she could just observe in him anyway. It was what she felt from him—and yeah, even that cocky grin was part of it. So the guy could keep it—for now.

*Like he's going to let you have any choice in that, sister.*

Like she even *wanted* to have a choice...

He tugged her face a little higher by cupping both her cheeks. "You are so goddamn beautiful like this."

She crunched her brows. "As opposed to what?"

He blinked, seeming flustered for a moment, before stammering, "Well..."

"Wait." Comprehension set in. She rolled her eyes. "Oh, come *on*. The skirt from Friday wasn't *that* bad."

Why did he look relieved instead of peeved? "Fine. I'll let you hang on to that one, red."

He kept smirking. She kept scowling. That'd been too easy. What was going on? What kind of a mind fuck was he setting her up for?

She slanted a knowing smile. Maybe she should get ahead on this one. "But you like this skirt better."

"Won't argue with you on that one, either."

So much for getting ahead. He tumbled her back into aroused mush with his gruffer take on that, the disk turning his growl into a verbal vibrator. Tess bit her lip, trying to regulate her shaky breath, along with the new flow of arousal in her core. The effort was fruitless once he skated his hands down to her waist again—by way of a direct route over her breasts.

"You know...it's because of you, right?" she rasped.

"Me?"

"The reason I'm 'so damn beautiful.'" She air-quoted for emphasis. "*You*...make me this way. Here"—she gestured at the walls—"I can become a different person. A person I really like. And you helped her to be free." She dropped her arms behind her back, turning her face fully back up to him. "She likes you too, Sir. She likes what *you* like to do to her."

He swallowed hard. His jaw clenched. "Does she remember what I said on the phone yesterday? About what I want to do to her tonight?"

She nodded with slow solemnity. "You're not going to play easy. You're going to push."

He pulled in a long breath through his nose. "That is so fucking right."

Before she blinked again, he yanked her body in tighter than ever. His heat engulfed her like the blue flames in his eyes. She swayed a little, but he caught her with a fierce grip. She had no doubt he'd do it again, even if she was tumbling over the side of a cliff.

"Oh," she sighed.

The griffin responded with a low growl. "Tell me you want this, little rose."

"Yes." She gasped. "Oh yes, Sir."

"Tell me you understand that I'm going to push your limits, but that if you even whisper your safe word, everything stops and we talk."

"Yes. Ohhh!" She dug her teeth into her lip, coinciding with how the man pushed his thigh forward, making her damn near ride it here in the hallway. She forced herself to keep looking at him, even as her sex swelled and her thighs trembled.

"I... I... *Yes*," she finally got out. "I understand. I say the safe word and you stop." *But dear God, don't stop now...*

"So you're ready?"

"Fuck!" she snapped, glad that he didn't turn his little smile into a laugh. The sexy bite he gave his own lower lip was tantalizing enough. "Damn it. *Yes.* I'm ready, okay?"

"Good." So damn calm. So in control. So silken smooth as he slid a step back from her. That still gave him plenty of access for his next action: reaching to yank hard at the ends of the laces on her bodice, making her dress pop open enough to bare her breasts. His urbane demeanor did nothing to prepare her for the double pinches he gave her nipples, causing her to yelp and glare up again.

His grin was gone. His face was framed in lines that hadn't been there before. Strict angles. Inscrutable authority. Complete domination.

"Now you'll strip." His voice was low and firm, a man expecting to be heeded. "Leave your clothes out here. They'll be taken care of. Join me inside with your body fully naked, your mind fully clear—and your will ready to serve mine."

# CHAPTER NINE

How was this possible?

Dan did his best to figure out the anomaly without ruining it.

He wasn't supposed to walk *into* the dungeon feeling this good. Every one of his nerve endings wasn't supposed to feel like an earthquake had struck. Every drop of his blood wasn't supposed to be transformed into solar flares. Every muscle in his body wasn't supposed to be infused with magma, already threatening to blow the doors off his mind.

This was crazy. Unreal. Beautiful, yet disturbing. This was all shit for *after* the scene, the high he got after she got hers. Yeah, but he'd never *started* a session by making out with the most gorgeous subbie in the world, in the middle of a club's public room—then continued it with her in the play-room hall, where she stripped naked for him, so ready to be commanded to more.

*His* incredible girl, ready to bow to *his* orders.

If he'd harbored any doubt about doing this with her for a second time, it rapidly faded to nothing.

Then disappeared completely—as soon as he turned at the sound of her reentering the room.

Holy. Fuck.

He shoved his tongue against the roof of his mouth to keep the thing from falling on the floor. *You've seen her nude before, remember? Less than a week ago? Just down the hall?*

He grunted the inner voice into silence. Nothing, not even his own brain, was going to steal the power of this moment. The breath he held as she stepped through the portal, the light from the hallway silhouetting her sleek curves. The same breath, released in a hot rush as she closed the door, quickly licking her lips. Sucking the air back in as she approached on bare feet, toenails as pink as the flush across her skin, gaze darting over the equipment he could choose from to bind her body for his use tonight. Vertical stretch rack. Suspended fucking swing. Leather-bound whipping bench with an optional stockade. Full-body pin cage.

Her eyes flared while gazing at that last one. He hid his responding grin. Watching her get thrown off her game... It was a fucking turn-on, especially because he saw how aroused *she* got from it too. Such a contrast to the little laser beam he knew from the office.

Such a beautiful difference.

Such a perfect little subbie.

He was going to take her deep tonight. So much farther. Every gorgeous green glint in her eyes showed him how much she needed it. And fuck, did *he* need it.

Without a word, he unbuttoned his vest and then tossed it to a nearby chair. Christ, how he wanted to take off his pants too. Nothing made him happier than getting to be as free as his submissive while playing with her—but in this case, he'd be tempted to put the cart before the horse, fuck her before he took her senses to the realms he wanted to.

For now, he'd settle for having her fully bare—

And fully ready.

God*damn*, how beautiful she was. The light in her fiery hair. The strawberry tips of her erect breasts. The bumps of anticipation, pebbling all over the rest of her skin...

Dan slid a hand up, spreading four fingers along her nape and his thumb against her jaw. With a tug, he brought her face up, pulling her gaze into his. For a moment, he let himself get lost in her eyes. Damn. All the exotic lagoons of the world couldn't compare to the magic of those depths, which could've entranced him for hours—if his cock didn't have other plans. As the only part of him *not* sailing in sensory bliss yet, the aching fucker told him exactly what he could do with these moments of artistic mush.

*Fine. She's the most breathtaking thing on earth. In her smile, you find your home. In her kisses, you feel your soul. That's not getting you—or me—anywhere right now, asshole.*

No sense in fighting the point—since it made complete sense.

It was time to get this party started. They'd both waited too damn long already.

"Safe word?" he prompted.

Her lips quirked, but only for a second. "Taffy, Sir."

"Thank you, dear one." He stopped, curious, when his response visibly impacted her. "What?"

She released a laugh, clearly self-conscious. "Sorry. I didn't mean to... I'm being silly."

His own lips twisted. "Sometimes I like silly."

"Sure. And I like brussels sprouts."

"You hate brussels sprouts."

"My point exac—" She cocked her head. "How do *you* know that?"

God*damn.*

*You lose control of this charade now, while the woman is standing before you like Eve before the snake struck, and* you'll *be the serpent with its head cut off.*

"Everyone hates brussels sprouts." Wasn't hard to interject a menacing growl. "And if you want to keep dancing around the subject, red, we can just get back to it at the pin cage."

She gasped. Glowered. Then sighed. "Fine." She hitched a shoulder before murmuring, "'Dear one.' It's... Well, I like it."

He'd harbored no expectations of what she'd say. Even so, the confession stunned him—in a lot of wonderful ways. Warmth bathed him, enough to push a hard kiss on her forehead. "Go kneel on the mat in front of the whipping bench, *dear one.*"

A hum bubbled from her in response. Such a little sound, once more bringing a massive flood of heat. He should be burning up from it, but it didn't feel like enough. Why? Had his world been such a cold place before now, that even these tidbits of fun affected him so?

He refused to dissect that answer right now. Here, in this room, the only thing that mattered was the figure of nude perfection who lowered herself to the floor in the spot he'd designated. While she did that, Dan approached the armoire of toys, bondage aids, and discipline items. The closet had resembled a standing crypt in their room last Friday; tonight, he stepped over to a large wicker-looking case with wooden shelves inside. Items called to him from the inventory, matching exactly the thoughts in his head about what might please his little red tonight...but also what it would please him to watch her endure.

*Keep the beast leashed. At least for a little while longer.*

She remained still as he paced toward her with calm, sure steps. The new outbreak of little bumps on her skin told him another story about her state of mind, however—especially as he paused to lay out the toys on a nearby utility table. The pebbles grew more pronounced as he deliberately clattered the items, arranging them as he'd need them. He couldn't help another half smile when he caught her peeking over at the array. He had to adjust his cock when she licked her lips and fought to regulate her breaths.

And then there was the other observation he couldn't ignore. Like he'd want to.

"Damn it, little girl. If your tits get any harder, I'm going to hang a couple of carabiner hooks from them."

Her eyes popped wide before a glare took over. "Don't joke."

"Who says I'm joking?"

He made sure the light caught his face so she could see his wink. She squirmed, obviously still not sure whether to trust him. He chuckled.

"Ohhhh, little rose. This is going to be fun."

"Says the guy standing at the torture toy table?"

"Says the sadist who's found a little glutton for his brand of fun."

"I am *not*—" she stuttered when he raised a finger.

"Ssshhh." He selected a patent leather flogger from the table. "You have nothing to prove here. There's no *PC quota* to fill, nobody to check off the *approved* box—except me." He let his head drop, admiring all of her body again. She had legs like a gazelle, and they looked even better curled into the submissive kneel. "And believe me, I approve," he growled.

That gorgeous pink tint stole over her skin again. "I'm still not a glutton."

"For these?" he countered, holding up the flogger. "For

what they bring you...the pain *and* the pleasure?"

With a deft flick, he tapped the falls over the curve of her shoulder.

"Oh!" After her startled yelp, her body trembled and then melted. She leaned toward him, an intuitive plea for more.

Dan snarled softly. "My sweet rose...you crave this so much, you don't even know when you show it." He ran the shiny leather strands across her chest and then up her face. "Look at your nipples, hard as diamonds...and your eyes, so beautiful and alive... I'm certain if I ordered you to part your knees, your pussy would be wet and gleaming too." He paused, letting the leather caress the sensitive curves of her neck. "Tell me, rose. *Would* it be wet?"

She swallowed heavily before rasping, "Yes, Sir. It would be."

"Good girl."

His own voice was rough. He didn't mind exposing it to her. Wanted her to know exactly what kind of power *she* had over *him*, in equal measure to his dominance. This night would only be as good as the surrender she was willing to turn over, and right now, her face told him everything. She yearned to give it all.

With a weighted swallow of his own, Dan repositioned his stance. His cock, already engorged to the point of pain, bellowed at him for the move. As if he hadn't subjected the thing to enough torment already... But he was a billionaire who'd *chosen* to serve with the CIA. Under it all, he was as much a masochist as Tess.

"Kneel up," he instructed softly. She complied by rising off her heels, aligning her face with his crotch. "Now kiss me, rose." He wrapped his hand around her head and directed her succulent lips toward that taut ridge of leather. "Honor the passion of the Dominant you serve tonight."

She gazed up at him. Released a shuddering breath. Then closed her long lashes over those dark-green eyes and pressed her lips over his leathers.

Christ. He had to be out of his mind.

Or, God willing, soon would be.

"So good," he praised between the heated pumps of his lungs. "Thank you, rose. That's so damn good." He forced himself to set her back a few inches before sliding the flogger in front of her instead. "Now honor the first instrument of your submission."

With a serene sigh, she slid her mouth up and down the flogger's handle, then let the falls drift between her lips. Dan encouraged her with a feral sound that curled up from his balls, echoing through his whole being.

"Enough." He twisted his hand tighter in her hair to guide her toward the whipping bench. The furniture's red leather detailing proved itself the perfect match for what he wanted to do to her thighs, her ass, her sex. "Knees up on the pads," he ordered. "But this, we'll save for later." He unbuckled the stockade at the front of the bench and swung it away, letting her settle in, stomach down, over the main support. "Let your head drop, and rest your forearms here and here." He indicated two separate pads that were lower, near the floor, before drawling with deliberate wickedness, "Comfy?"

"Mmmmm." She whimpered it as he buckled her into the built-in ankle cuffs, matched by similar restraints for her wrists. "Yes, Sir. Thank you, Sir."

"Those are beautiful words to hear from your lips, little red. It's my mission to hear them over and over tonight."

"I've no doubt of it, S— *Ohhhh!*"

Her eruption was prompted by his first swat of the flogger, down the middle of her ass, delivered with decided impact.

"Have your attention now?"

He infused it with enough urbane snark to get her a little riled. Did he use his unfair advantage for it, also being the friend who observed how she hated the attitude in uppity waiters and Agency newbs? Absolutely. Would he do it again? The irked wiggle of her butt helped that answer along.

Abso-*fucking*-lutely.

"Rose?" he prodded. "I didn't hear you."

"Yes," she snapped. "Yes, all right? You have my— *Ahhhh!*" She shrieked it after he brought the falls down with equal impact, just below the stripes of the first. "What the *hell*?"

Dan wiped a hand over the perfect spheres of her ass, keeping his touch and his tone authoritative. "Tell me something. Did you come here tonight to submit to me, girl?"

She answered after a huff. "Yes, Sir."

"To entrust yourself to me and believe in my ability to make you feel good with this dynamic?"

Tight teeth dug into her next response. "Yes. Sir."

"Then do that." He lowered the leather again, but this time just brushed her skin, swooping back-and-forths he angled inward on purpose, letting the tips nip in at her pussy and clit. "Calm your tongue and open your senses. Breathe for me. Deeper, babe." He took his own advice as her body relaxed, her skin bloomed, and her ass lifted, unconsciously seeking the flogger's arousing touch. "Good. Better, isn't it?"

"Ummm. Yes, Sir." It slurred a little, telling him the stimulation had made its way to her mind. As the endorphins hit her, responsible Tess started shutting down. In her place was gorgeous, sensuous, submissive Odette.

The transformation was breathtaking.

Her skin wasn't the only thing that came alive beneath his strokes. Her energy flowed out to him differently, welcoming the flogger's kiss. Her body rolled and dipped as he channeled her power right back to her, starting their circle all over again. They were both buzzed on the elixir. Dan even smiled a little from it. Damn. Was his skin...tingling?

He didn't give a fuck.

He only wanted more. A lot more.

And knew she did too. In every sigh she released. Every breath she took. Every shiver of her skin...

So. Fucking. Incredible.

"Keep breathing, little one." He paused to rub her again, testing her flesh with broad sweeps of his hand. Heated and blushing, just the way it should be. "And buckle up. We're going to higher gears now."

She gave a little nod. "Mmmm. Okay...Sir."

He almost regretted bringing down the next swat, a blow twice as intense as the others. Almost.

"*Ahhhhh*," she cried again. "Oh, that was— *Ohhhh!* Damn!"

Dan leaned in, enforcing his intensity with a solid hand on her back. "Nothing changes about processing this, red. Give me your breaths. In, out. Give me your ass. Higher. *Higher*."

He rumbled his praise when she complied without hesitation. Something *was* getting through besides the stings, and it moved him to watch her reaching for the connection of that...the new bridge that spanned her pain to her arousal.

He swept the flogger again. Higher. Harder.

She yelped again. Longer. Louder.

But as her ass reddened, her screams lessened. Dan

established a steady rhythm, pumped on the power of her submission, coursing through every cell of his muscles. It was the best goddamn drug on the planet, and if he had a choice, he'd never yank the needle out.

"Fuck me, little one. You have no idea how gorgeous you are like this." He jammed the flogger into his back pocket for the privilege of dipping low to caress both sides of her ass directly with his lips. "I want to lick so much of this. You're so hot. So delicious. So perfect." He nipped at her lightly before licking at her abraded skin, whispering into it, "Thank you."

She blew out a long, contented sigh. "Thank *you*, Sir. It... it was amazing."

His head snapped up, and he frowned, confused—before making his way up her spine with teasing, wet kisses. "You sound like you think this is the end, babe."

As he expected, she tensed a little. "It...it isn't?"

Dan let a low, primal laugh vibrate into her nape. "Oh, my little rose...we're just getting started."

# CHAPTER TEN

What was the word for what his dark promise did to her body? *Shivers* was a laughable short change. *Tremors* made her think of a horror movie—and while she was scared, the next part of the show couldn't come fast enough. *Shock?* Closer perhaps, though it sounded like she'd been in a pile-up on the 15—and this was a collision more violent and twisted-metal awesome than anything she'd seen on the six o'clock news.

She wanted to be the wreckage now. *Needed* it. The sincerity in her moan, emitted as Sexy tugged her head back up, was real. So was the urgency in her sigh as he slid something against her lips again. Earthy but sensual. Steel beneath softness. The swell of his cock again, pulsing at her from beneath his leathers.

*Oh, yes...*

"Honor it again."

She eagerly obeyed, opening her mouth more, trying to stimulate as much of his length as she could. He was magnificent, even now. His penis was a solid, stiff rod, and all too clearly she remembered how perfectly it filled her body.

Too quickly, he pulled himself away. Once more, he presented her with an impact toy to worship in the same way. She cracked her eyes open to look—

And almost wished she hadn't.

The long, thin paddle was covered in hard leather on one side—and small steel studs on the other. She blinked, thinking maybe her lust-fogged vision was deceiving her, but as he passed that side of the instrument past her, the cold bumps were all too real against her lips and cheeks.

"Holy shit," she rasped.

The griffin stopped and turned. "Problem, little one?"

She winced and closed her eyes again. "No, Sir."

His hand pressed the top of her head. Skated down her spine. "Scared?"

Fume. He damn well knew the answer to that since her skin puckered and shivered beneath his touch, but no way in hell was he letting her get away with polite silence this time. "Yes, Sir," she uttered tightly. "A little." Maybe a lot, but he didn't need to know that.

"I like scared."

Or maybe he did need to know. If she could be promised more of that new burlap in his voice, wrapping every word in deep lust...then yeah, she was *scared*.

"Hang on tight, little girl."

Yep. Scared.

And turned way the hell on.

And wrapping her hands around the edges of the pads, determined to be brave about this—

Until a harsh *smack* snapped her head up—and set her ass on fire.

"Oh, my—"

Then another.

"Damn it!"

"Ssshhh." He backed it up by stroking her ass with the flip side of the paddle...as if the bastard knew how good those cool steel studs would feel on the burn across her cheeks. "Breathe deep. Take it in. Process it all—"

"Process *what?*" His Yoda-Dom Zen was the last thing she needed right now. "It hurts, damn you!"

"'Damn you' isn't your safe word."

"I *remember* my fucking safe— *Owwww!*"

That was one way of learning how fast he could play flip-and-spank with a paddle. He delivered another blow on top of that one, making her jerk against the restraints, struggling to process the inferno tearing its way across her poor backside and thighs.

"I can just as easily forget to flip this thing over, red."

His tone still resonated with humor, though it had gone dark and deliberate, a Dom-land mix of Loki and Batman.

"Now you really are trying to scare me."

"And it's working."

"Of course it is."

"And that makes me so goddamn hard." The rasp reentered his voice as the paddle returned to her ass. He just tapped at her now, a weird combination of both sides that brought more heat to her skin...but never quite enough. "How does that feel, sweet girl? To know what the awareness of your fear and the beauty of your skin do to me? To realize they're the most potent aphrodisiacs I've ever experienced, in all my years as a Dominant? To know I'm hurting as badly as you are right now, hypnotized by your red, gorgeous ass and all your aching, erotic screams?"

He increased the strength of the paddle, but only a little. Tess writhed, trying to shove her butt higher. *Not...enough. More. Need more.*

"I want to fuck you so badly right now," he growled. "But you're not ready yet, are you, babe?" He replaced the paddle with a hand, smoothing it over her skin, spreading the warmth...

everywhere. He verified as much by dipping fingers between her legs, exploring the wet lips of her sex, the quivering ridge of her clit. "No. Almost...but not quite."

Tess groaned, rolling her hips as he boldly touched her, explored her. But he was right. It wasn't enough. Somehow, she knew there was more. A level of this that she had yet to accept from him. Heights she had yet to ascend.

"Please." So strange. Her voice was a detached thing now, high and breathy, belonging to a creature she barely recognized. The phoenix of herself, taking flight into a new reality. A freedom like she'd never known.

But she wasn't...quite...there.

"Please," she repeated. "I need it. Now..."

When his leathers pressed into her face, she whined in heady relief. Caressed him once more, even biting at his erection through the fabric to express how much she craved him—

Even when the next item in front of her lips was long, cold, and lethally thin.

A fiberglass cane.

A quiver took over Tess's body. Damn it, it just figured. Yoda-Dom wanted to play with his scary lightsaber—and already knew that she wanted to let him. He'd deliberately ramped her higher with the paddling but then backed off, teasing her with the lighter sensation play, turning her into the wanton hussy she was now.

Wanton. And shameless. And needy.

God, *yes*...

"Are you ready, little one?" His voice, deep and rough, knifed to the heart of her trembling womb. Tess licked her lips. She could practically taste his desire on the air.

"Yes, Sir. Oh, yes."

A long moment passed. She parted her eyes open to look at him, sensing the weight of his new deliberation.

"No," he uttered, raking her with a thoughtful stare. "I don't think you *are* ready."

"What?" She scowled. "Why?"

Before her words were done, he leaned over to swing down the stockade part of the bench. As he locked down the panel, which had cutouts for her head and hands, Tess's breaths became razors in her chest. Her pulse throbbed in the center of her pussy. Shit, shit, shit. She'd been hoping the griffin would forget about the piece, because *she'd* been trying to.

Knowing how much it would freak her out.

Knowing how deeply she'd be aroused by all that helplessness.

While she wrestled with the psychobabble, her Dom unshackled her wrists. With wordless command, he placed them onto the padded holders, which would become full circles of bondage once he snapped the stockade's top piece into place. With her arms in position, there was only one place for her head to go: the larger hole in between.

Her whole body shook as Sexy lowered the stockade.

Her heart halted as he snapped the lock shut.

Her sex clenched as he released a carnal snarl.

"*Now* you're ready, dear one."

*Dear one.* He went there on purpose, as if knowing how much the endearment would ease her conflict. But *how* did he know? No Dom was David Blaine—every neuron of her brain knew that—but it didn't stop her heart from clinging to the reassurance that he somehow got it...that he felt every drop of the weirdness about loving this while hating it, asking herself why the most barbaric thing she'd ever consented to was also the source of the hottest sexual need she'd ever known.

Her inner battle raged on as he crouched down in front of her. At once, her vision was filled with that beautiful black mask. That inscrutable stare. Those lips, tilted in enigmatic mystery. That was only the beginning of the new magic. Oh yes, this position had its advantages. Greedily, she roamed her stare over the plateaus of his shoulders, his molded pecs and abs, and then the rigid guideposts of muscle that disappeared beneath his leathers...

She wet her lips. Holy God, the man was lick-worthy. Her entire body reacted to him with visceral force. Her nipples puckered and extended. Her thighs clenched, fighting their constraints. Her clit zinged and tingled, reacting to the honey that dripped from her aching, needy channel.

*Wow.*

How the hell had she gotten so lucky? To be with a Dom who knew her darkest desires, who read every inch of her mind, and was also *this* freaking hot?

Yeah. Wow.

Glimmers in his eyes made their way past his mask. Their intensity made her belly do new backflips as he shifted off his haunches, directly onto his knees. Tess gave him a soft smile as she watched his gaze flicker down to her lips, but he didn't move in for the expected kiss.

Instead, with their faces an inch apart, he murmured, "You're so fucking beautiful, red."

She almost sighed in relief. If he'd gone for *dear one* again, she wouldn't have guaranteed her composure. At least now, she could concoct something halfway witty in return. "Hmmpf. I bet you say that to all the girls in the stockade."

"Nope. Never."

"Ever?"

His lips firmed. "Are you trying to buy time with snark, little rose?"

"*Moi?*" A shuddery breath left her. Truth be known, he was right. The long rod in his hands terrified her as much as thrilled her. *I'm not going to play you easy, rose.* But what did that mean? What exactly was "not easy" for her? Where were her limits? How far was too far? And how would *he* know?

She was suddenly afraid to explore those answers.

*Really* afraid.

Finally, he touched her. Only once. A stroke of his knuckles, slow and sure, down the side of her face—before he spoke again. "This is going to happen, sweet subbie. And you're going to love it, I promise. Now tell me that you understand."

Tess squeezed her eyes shut again. "I...I understand, Sir."

"Now tell me that you trust me."

She jerked her way through a nod. "I trust you, Sir. I do."

"Such a good girl."

His hand rounded to the top of her head as he returned to his feet in one graceful sweep.

"Now tell me you crave my cane across your ass."

# CHAPTER ELEVEN

The words were a turn-on when he said them.

They were sexual speed when she did.

And, quite possibly, the beginning of his ruin.

Maybe it was because he didn't expect she'd really comply with him—at least not with this illicit order. Or if he did, that she wouldn't offer the words with such a husky whisper. Or that she'd lift her backside so exquisitely, presenting herself for him like the most eager of lifestyle slaves instead of a twice-in submissive with a day job often requiring her to play Domme to a whole crowd of people at once.

How the hell was he going to make this his last time in the dungeon with her?

*Why* the hell did he think he could?

*Not the issues to be hoisting on the table right now, bozo. You forget the item of kinky destruction in your hand right now—or the ways you can actually hurt her with it, if you're off in self-therapy la-la land?*

The rest of him wasn't going to argue. Not his soul, which had needed this moment since she'd agreed to meet him here again—and sure as hell not his body, resonating with energy he could only label as harmonic convergence, or some cosmic shit like that. He had no idea what else to call it, this huge window he seemed to have into *her* thoughts and feelings, but instead of standing here and analyzing it, he decided to simply be grateful—and give the woman what he knew she so clearly needed.

The perfect pain from this cane.

And the nirvana he was going to fly her to because of it.

He paced around her, skimming the cane's tip along her body. It was worth it to take his time, savoring the little tremors he created beneath her skin.

"Breathtaking."

Understatement in every way. Her new positioning in the stockade did incredible things for her lithe, long angles. Her breasts were stretched and taut, her spine graceful and sleek. And her ass...god*damn*. The beautiful globes were poised and ready, already an awesome landscape of dark pinks and brilliant reds. A masterpiece *he'd* created...hell, yes...

He traced the patterns with his free hand as he slid behind her again, growling low at the primal, possessive instinct coursing through him.

"Oh, little one...branding you like this could become an addiction."

She rolled her hips, trying to press deeper into his touch. "Addiction," she rasped. "That's a good word for it."

Conflict ripped into his reverie.

*What the hell are you saying? Promising?*

That *wasn't* a "good word for it." It couldn't be. Even being here tonight, he was pushing fate's favor. His caution was high, the voice disk was secure, and his mask was on tight, but none of that guaranteed he'd walk out the door before making the fatal slip that would reveal his masquerade to Tess. As remarkable as this connection was between them, how did he justify that he'd deceived her to have it—twice?

Those thoughts had no business in this moment. Focusing fully on her had to consume him right now. Taking a cane to a submissive on her second scene ever was a jump to the high wire, holding true to his promise that her limits would be stretched—but not dismissing his responsibility to her physical and emotional well-being.

He started with praise, underlined with intent about what she was in for next. "This ass is such a work of art. A bit more embellishment, babe, and it'll be absolutely perfect."

Her hips circled for him again, accompanied by her aroused moan. "Yes, Sir. Let's make it perfect."

She paved the way into a perfect response to that. "Dear, sweet red. Be careful what you wish for."

A little evil? Absolutely. But the twist of turn-on that she needed? *Absolutely.* Her quaking sigh told him just that—

Before his first two taps turned it into a high scream.

"Shit!" Tess finally exploded. "Did someone go double shots on the power smoothie today? What the hell?"

No sense in hiding his chuckle. "Barely threw weight into it, rose."

"Damn it," she spat. "Oh, damn it, damn it, dam— *Ohhhh!*"

One smack. With a decided notch up on the impact.

"Bastard!"

A crisscross this time. *Thap. Thap.*

"*Fucking* bastard!"

*Thap. Thap. Thap.* And because she shrieked so prettily as a result, two more. The deep red stripes across her buttocks and thighs were just as beautiful. "Christ," he uttered. "So perfect."

"No!" Tess protested. "*Not* perf— *Owwww!*"

*Thap. Thap. Thap.* Harder. Harder. Harder.

"Fucking rat-*ass* bastard!"

"With taffy?" he taunted.

"Shut *up.*"

"And do what?"

"And toss that thing out!"

"You can take this, rose."

"I can't."

"You *can.* For me. And for you." He caressed her skin with a full palm, making her jerk a little. "Do you trust me?"

She huffed. "Damn it, of course I do. But—"

"Then breathe." He stamped it with half a bellow this time. The twin blows he rained to finish were just as harsh. "And take it, damn it."

Breakthrough.

She didn't fling any anger or snark. Instead, her shoulders sagged. Her body softened. A desperate sob of surrender sliced from her.

As her resistance faded, her welts rose. Dan gazed at the wild, wonderful hashes across her flesh, while clenching his stomach against the fresh surge between his thighs. He cupped his crotch, struggling to convince the whole gang down there to get along, but wound up aggravating himself more. His dick was ready to be inside her, period. His balls yearned to be slapping her flesh as he screwed any remaining senses out of her head. Any alternate plan to that was futile.

Thank fuck that was the only futility happening here.

After another trio of smacks, easing off on the pressure now, he skirted around to view her face. As he'd hoped, her head lolled down. Her eyes were closed. Her lips were slightly parted, giving and receiving breath in unthinking little spurts.

He smiled.

*Control tower, the shuttle has reached sub space.*

He laid the cane on the table with the other toys,

exchanging it out for a new item. It was easy enough to strap the little vibe onto his right forefinger and have it out of the way as he unlatched the stockade. Tess moaned a little but didn't move. Fine with him. He clicked the vibe on and then took his time rolling it over her shoulders, down her arms, and to her wrists, even using it to gently massage her fingers. While it didn't stop his mind from clamoring for the vibe's ultimate use, every inch of his spirit was fed by the privilege of taking care of her this way.

"Mmmmm," she finally sighed. "Feels...good."

Dan let a low sound vibrate up his chest. With just a breath and three words, she'd sneaked her way into his soul too. He kissed the curves of both her shoulders, stroked his fingers through her hair, delighted in all the ways she melted even more for him. He could have done it for hours. Maybe he did. Time was a nuisance right now, mattering as much as dust, sifting past in the corners of his consciousness. Christ. Taking care of a subbie had never felt so damn good...

Because it had never meant so much?

*No. Damn it,* no.

*"Meanings" are for normal people, remember? People who have their heads screwed on straight. Who don't hire out whole teams of private mercenary crews just to chase bad guys across Mexico and are comfortable enough with their burn scars that they can function in public without pulling a fucking Batman.*

*"Meanings" are for the rest of the world, asshole. Not* you.

She moaned deeper as he trailed the vibe down the shallow valley of her back. By the time he returned to her ass, her wistful sighs had become full moans once more. The flesh beneath his hands undulated like dark-pink tides pulled by an unseen moon. There was no way for him to resist the sight. He leaned in, licking the lines of each bruise he'd given her.

"So beautiful," he whispered against her marks. "This ass is so fucking beautiful. And it's all mine tonight, isn't it?"

Tess visibly shivered. "*Yes. All yours.*"

He snarled softly once more while spreading her thighs, exposing the pathway to her deeper erotic treasures. "Even more stunning." He pushed the vibe back in, making tiny circles, teasing his way toward the sweetness of her pussy. "More red. More wet. Mine as well, sweet one?"

"*Ohhhh.*" Her head jacked up as her spine dipped, showing him exactly what effect the vibe had on her most tender flesh. "Damn. Don't stop...don't...oh..." She shrieked louder as he slid the vibe away. "God! *Please*, Sir Sexy!"

*That* was sure as fuck an attention-getter. "Pardon *me*?" he laughed out.

"On the back burner?" she begged. "As in, later? Please?"

He pushed the vibe near her slit again—but not any farther. "That depends."

"On...on what?"

"On your answer."

"My answer to *what*?"

He might have swatted her for the backtalk if her desire didn't drench each word. How could he discipline her, when she made every one of his wet dreams come to life from her lust alone?

"Is this all mine tonight too?"

She laughed too. The richness of the sound made its way far beyond his cock, burrowing into his soul like beautiful music or an inhalation of morning air. "If not, then they may have to cart me out of here on a stretcher."

Dan couldn't contain another chuckle. It prefaced the

lusty bite he sank into her shoulder. "That's the idea no matter what, little girl."

As he shoved her hair out of the way, repeating the invasion into the column of her neck, she rasped, "You don't say."

"I *do* say." He worked a finger into her hot, welcoming body—stretching out the vibe, starting to tap it at her clit. "I also say I'm going to fuck this. I'm going to do it as hard, as deep, and as long as I want. While I do it, you're going to come for me. Probably a few times. Only after that do we talk about the stretcher. Understood?" When she only nodded frantically, he bit her deeper. "I didn't hear you."

"Yes!" She exclaimed it while shifting her hands, pushing up to grip the curves of the stockade cutouts instead of being trapped by them. Dan looked on, not immune to the symbolism of the move. Though every inch of her was still submissive to him, she was glorious as a tigress, attacking the awareness— and acceptance—of her sexuality. "Yes. *Yes.* I understand. I do. Oh, please—damn it—just fuck me!"

Magnificent.

She was so goddamn magnificent.

Yeah, even when girl-growling at him.

Hell. He could no longer compose himself. He set himself free from his leathers, groaning in torment *and* delight while rasping the zipper down. His grip slipped a couple of times over his thick-veined flesh, now slick from precome, but he finally managed to free everything, including his throbbing balls. He wasted no time in digging into a back pocket and hauling out the square packet inside.

His tense moan mingled with Tess's urgent mewl.

"Hold on, sweet one," he promised. "Hold on, hold on."

He ripped the condom open with his teeth and yanked

the rubber out like a starving man with a T-bone. Rolling the fucker on over his swollen flesh was another thing altogether. His cock strained at the latex as she pushed her ass even higher, exposing her pink, sweet petals even more.

Dan took a step. Seized her waist with one hand. Guided his cock to her entrance with the other.

And was finally complete.

Her sheath pulled him in as if it had been months since he last fucked her, not days. "Damn," he growled. "*Damn.*"

She was snug and hot and soaked, her walls closing around him, forcing him to feel every constriction of her arousal. He leaned forward, strapping his arm all the way around her waist, forcing her body harder around him.

"Shit!" Tess exclaimed. "Oh, God...I'm...I'm..."

"I know," he grated. Her visit to sub space had already opened her so much. In seconds, he felt her climax stirring in her abdomen, quivering her ass against him, turning her hips into turbine pistons against his. "I know, little one."

He didn't want her to wait. Hell, *he* didn't want to wait. While plunging his cock deeper and deeper, he worked his other hand between her thighs again, stimulating her from the front. Her clit was waiting for his touch, erect and wet, making her buck harder as soon as he made contact—

Then flicked the vibrator on again.

"Oh!" Her whole body quaked. Her knuckles went white against the stockade pads. "That's...oh, that's...that's—"

"Your order to come." His own lust turned it into an animal's sound, raw and low, a few octaves short of being a full snarl. "Do it for me, rose. *Now!*"

Her sex clenched him tight, tighter, *tighter*, as the climax slammed her. A scream ripped from her throat. Her head fell back against his shoulder. Dan locked every tooth in his head to keep from following her over into the flames then and there, concentrating instead on the exquisite pressure up and down his dick.

*Squeeze it back. Save it up. Think of how good it's going to feel when you detonate deep inside her.*

"Oh. My. God." She dropped her head again, her shoulders heaving hard. "So good. Thank you, Sir. That... was..."

"Not over." He let the command resonate before changing his hold, clawing his hand to her hip, digging into the juncture between her hip and thigh. "Stay with me, red. It's going to be even better."

Her breath hitched. "Wh-What...do you...mean?"

"Stay." He raised his other hand into her hair. "With." Twisted hard. "Me."

"*Ahhhhh.*"

It curled off her pain-twisted lips. But the next second, another expression took hold of her gorgeous face. The agony gave way to ecstasy, brought on by a fresh recognition: he was screwing her in a new way. Clarification: *screwing* her. He focused on gyrating his hips in new angles, experimenting with a sole goal in mind. He watched every nuance of her body and face, needing to know when he reached just the right—

"Oh, my *God*!"

Target acquired.

He smirked in sensual triumph before angling in the exact same way. Then again. Again. Again. Every time, her scream proved he'd found the Holy Grail of Tess Lesange's sweet pussy—and he'd be damned not to dip his cock into that magical chalice as many times as he could.

"My— Holy— Wow— Gggaaahh—"

He grinned wider. It was official—the toughest part about seeing her again outside this place would be forgetting this moment and her adorable dive into the bathtub of speechlessness. And knowing that *he'd* thrown her there.

"You're going to come for me again, rose." He didn't leave a millimeter of opening for argument. His maddening little ruby tried, anyway.

"I... Please...I can't—"

"You can. You *will*." He braced his hips harder. Thrust in deeper. Started to hold position at the peak of each lunge, driving in his point with his *point*. "Feel that, babe? Do you feel *me*? That's the head of my cock, adoring your sweet little cunt from the inside out. That's how you're going to come for me, rose—from the inside out. Clench me now. Tighten it for me. Feel every inch of me, fucking you...needing you to come hard around me."

He watched her thighs clench. That caused a chain reaction through her buttocks, still painted in fiery tones from the wicked pleasure he'd given to them. In turn, her body clamped him harder, squeezing his dick...and all parts beyond.

The parts that weren't supposed to be getting involved in all this.

The parts that wouldn't slide out as fast as his cock or get tossed away as easily as the condom.

Shit. *Shit.*

Too late. *Too late.*

He needed this now.

He needed her.

He wound his hand tighter into her hair. His balls swelled to excruciating pressure. His chest worked to get air. His abdomen drew tight. His ass clenched and shuddered.

Heavier. Harder. Deeper. Fuller. His lust built and pounded, hammered and thundered, climbing as he read all the signs in Tess's frame too. Her coiled arms. Her high, hurting pants. The twin points of her nipples, hardened to the realm of fantasy-come-true.

Suddenly, she screamed without sound. Threw her head back with eyes squeezed shut, her body vibrating hard around him, milking the hot, mindless explosion up his cock and out of his body.

It flowed forever yet only an instant. Consumed him yet detached him. His senses rocketed but floated. Where was he? *Who* was he? What day was it? He seriously wondered if he'd ever be capable of linear logic again.

He seriously questioned if he ever wanted to be.

With that dream-within-a-dream-within-a-dream weirdness, a scythe of all-too-real horror swooshed in.

If *he* wasn't going to be the same after this, what had it all done to Tess?

What had *he* done to her?

And how the hell was he going to fix it—without completely ruining her?

# CHAPTER TWELVE

"Sir?"

"Hmmm?"

"I'm onto you, you know."

He halted his caresses on the curves of her shoulders, and sucked in a sharp breath. In most situations, Tess would gauge the reaction as alarm. This wasn't most situations. Not by a long shot.

"I'm...not sure I follow." His tone turned as stiff as his stature. Yeah, she could tell even with her eyes closed and her brain half-baked.

Guilt invaded her. It wasn't fair, turning him the texture of an icicle while she had become a ball of hot mush—because of him.

She came clean by teasing, "You think I don't know that aftercare isn't always like this?"

His tension drained. "Hush and eat your strawberry."

"Huh? *What* straw—" She was silenced by a mouthful of perfect sweetness. The berry tasted so good that she nibbled to get more, moaning in ecstasy. "Oh, wow," she finally mumbled. She didn't remember seeing any food when they first arrived, but half her brain was still back in the dungeon, lost in the tangle of sensations he'd rained on her in the scene.

She'd never, in her life, experienced anything like it.

Now, she just didn't know if that was a good thing or a bad thing.

"Another?" Sexy ran a second berry along her bottom lip. Tess opened and dutifully bit the fruit. She yearned to help him out, to at least pick up her own damn strawberries, but convincing her body it really wasn't a noodle? New tune altogether. Like her limbs could be blamed after he'd peeled her off the whipping bench, gathered her into his arms, and then refused to set her down until stepping into this opulent chamber, slipping her into the heated waters of this subterranean bathing pool. If she'd regained any rational thought in her head since her orgasms, it vanished as soon as the eucalyptus steam filled her senses and the lavender bubbles nipped at her body.

Doubling the whammy was the man himself, instructing her to lay tummy-down on the pool's seating shelf while he ran a natural sponge from her shoulders to her ankles. She damn near fell asleep on him like that but protested and sat back up—only to have him frame her from behind, leathered legs in the water to either side, as he flowed vanilla and rosemary leaves over her shoulders. And now, the hand-feeding with the fruit...

Paradise.

The Native Americans liked to say that it was captured in the small moments of life, often so tiny that they went missed. Tess closed her eyes and chewed, grateful she'd been looking closely enough to recognize this one. So perfect. So profound. So complete.

With a man she barely knew.

But had known forever.

*Of course.*

The concept crashed in, broadsiding her psyche—exploding her heart. The helpless thing didn't know what hit it, thrashing against her ribs.

*This is insane. Just a result of all the chemicals from the scene colliding in your brain. The high is going to bring you an even harder drop than last weekend—both so freaking worth it.*

*Maybe Mother and Father were always right. Maybe you're just a dreamer who simply wants perfection too damn much.*

But what if it was the only explanation that really made sense?

What if she *hadn't* just met Griffin by accident?

What if some crazy "higher power" had really brought him across the room to her that night—when others had had the chance for two nights before that? How else could she justify how instantly right it felt to be standing at his side? And following him to private dungeon space? And surrendering to him without fear or hesitation? How else had *he* known exactly what needs she had as a submissive...all the dark, wicked parts of herself that wanted to be tested, pushed, shattered?

And why else was she lingering in the warmth of this moment and the heat of him, instead of asking for her clothes and seeking the nearest exit back to the safety of reality?

Because reality didn't feel so safe anymore.

Because he began that dribbling water thing over her shoulders again.

Because it felt so damn good.

Because it felt safer to lean into the broad strength of his chest once again, challenging in a murmur, "You didn't answer my question."

This time, his fingers didn't stop. "Which one?"

She splashed him. His leathers were already drenched to the calves; a little more H2O wouldn't hurt. "How about the *only* one?"

"Wasn't that rhetorical?" After she sent more water flying

up, he chuckled. The sound, filtered by the voice disk, was as decadent as the kiss he lowered to her nape. "Shut it off, babe. Typical aftercare is for typical submissives. And you are far, far from typical."

Her lips parted to reply. No words brimmed. Not a syllable. Damn it, she needed just one go-to line, something coy and smooth and elegant. In the last couple of hours, she'd shown him more of herself than most people saw over years. It was more than just the steamy naked stuff. It was the baring of her soul—the parts of her that were womanly and vulnerable, a little scared yet yearning to break free from those limits too.

He had seen it all.

*But damn it,* he *couldn't have it all.* Nobody could. She'd divvied her life into clean compartments for a reason—a damn good one. If one of the sections collapsed, the others would remain intact. Nothing to get hurt. Everything safe, by the rules. That had even explained her initial fascination with BDSM and submission. She could dress pretty, follow the rules, obey the orders, and get a prize. Hell, the best prize of them all.

But now she knew the truth.

It was about so much more than that.

*Too* much.

The broadside hit again. Her senses rebelled, unable to process anything more. Sexy's indrawn breath told her that he noticed, too—deepening her panic. She couldn't let him get in the verbal kicker again. He'd say something magical and captivating, and then add a soft kiss or ten to ensure her bones were fully liquefied...

And she'd never get out of tonight without half her soul missing.

"I'm getting prune fingers in here," she blurted. "I'd better start thinking of—"

*going home.*

The words were ditched as soon as the man lifted her from the water, turned her in his arms, and swathed her in a huge towel. Moving with smooth confidence, he carried her to a wide chaise-style bed tucked into an alcove near the pool. A mountain of gold and blue pillows was arranged against the headboard. Near the foot, another ornate serving tray supported more food—correction, one of the best chocolate selections she'd ever seen—along with bottles of the flavored fitness water she liked so much.

As Sexy settled her against the pillows, patterns of light were reflected from the pool, dancing over his sculpted chest and biceps—boulders in shades of aqua and white. She absorbed the sight greedily, barely resisting the urge to join those lucky light rays and fondle every inch of him.

Barely.

Resisting.

He was so damn mesmerizing...

What harm would it be to trace the edge of just one perfect pectoral? Embrace the bulge of just one sinewy shoulder?

*Just one? And what alternate universe are you living in, Lesange, that you think you'll stop there?*

He became her knight in half-soaked leathers, saving her from herself by climbing in for the perfect spoon instead. Nestling her head into the crook of his shoulder, he curled up one hand to finger-comb her hair. His other hand sneaked beneath the towel, lightly stroking the curve of her thigh.

It was a textbook finish to quite possibly the best night of her life—doubling her guilt for letting a frustrated huff break free.

"Okay," the griffin murmured. "Talk to me." He synched up his touches, matching the massages of her scalp to his fingertips' spider act on her hip.

Here it was. Her open door of opportunity. She just hadn't expected it *that* wide. His insistence on the mask, on the voice alteration, on using nicknames for her most of the time, and even the burner phone he'd used to call her from yesterday—yeah, she'd checked in spite of herself—none of those factors were huge screams for the Great Tess Inquisition. In short, she'd come to this part of things completely unprepared.

*May I phone a friend, please?* She smiled in spite of herself, wondering exactly what Dan would say about all of this.

"Rose?"

She tilted her head, responding to his undertone of alarm, discernible despite the voice disk. "I'm just thinking."

"About what?"

"About how to broach the subject that I barely know you."

She didn't anticipate that would surprise him. Sure enough, neither of his hands faltered. He pressed closer behind her. "Do you really believe that?"

Every syllable he uttered was like a kiss of completion. Every breath he pushed against her neck was matched by one from her own lungs. Still, she persisted, "I don't even know your real name."

"And *I* know *yours*?"

He had a point—at least halfway. She tried to push away. He locked his arm around her waist. She capitulated, facing the futility of resistance. Okay, so there was the newness factor about feeling up an eight-pack with her ass. There had to be some scientific value to the world in that research. She was willing to take the step for humanity.

"I...I work for the government," she stated. "I have to be careful. I rely on the trust and respect of others to get my job accomplished. While my free-time choices should have no bearing on that—"

"It's not always the case," he finished for her in a deep mutter. "I understand."

Just like that, he'd cracked open his door a little more. "You do, don't you?" she returned.

Was *that* why he needed total anonymity? Was his day job just as intense as hers? Maybe more so? Was he a high-ranking officer from Nellis? An elected city official? A famous performer from one of the shows on the Strip? Even in Vegas, public perception was a huge quotient of acceptance. Kink was still "wrong" to so many. In short, one could sin in the City of Sin as long as they were nobody.

"I'm sorry," she offered. "This is just strange for me. Sharing what we've shared, twice now—"

"Which won't change in importance if we exchange birth-certificate details," Sexy interjected.

"You're right."

Obeying a sudden impulse, she tilted her head back, seeking his kiss. He obliged readily, forming his mouth to hers though keeping tongues totally out of the picture. Even so, her core awakened for him again. Her tunnel constricted in need. Unbelievably, it was one of the hottest kisses they'd ever shared.

When he finally pulled up, she gulped and then rasped, "*Damn.*"

"Yeah," he grated back. "Damn."

"That really didn't stop me from wanting to know

everything about you."

He chuckled as she rolled back over, letting his lips continue out along her shoulder. "Nor I you, sweet woman. Nor I you."

Another sigh escaped. This time, it was pushed by much different emotions. Fulfillment but longing. Satiation but thirst. Feeling complete yet utterly broken.

She swallowed. Clenched her teeth against the stings behind her eyes. When Sexy felt the change in her, accommodating by pulling her yet tighter, she fought the urge to elbow him in the gut for it.

"Don't," she begged. "Please. Don't..."

"Ssshhh."

"No." Damn it, now her voice cracked. "I don't want to *ssshhh*. I don't want to *have* to."

"I know." He scraped her hair a little harder. His arm cinched her waist tighter. "I know."

Screw it. She let the salty rush come, flowing over her cheeks. "This is it, isn't it?" she charged. "With us. With this. You're not going to call again or even come back to Catacomb again. That's the reason you arranged for the Cadillac aftercare. The pool, the fruit, the chocolate. We're not going to do this again."

She had a mental list of his possible reactions, but the little push it took to get her on her back, fully beneath him, wasn't one of them. As he braced himself over her on his elbows, Tess stared past the mask, into the intensity of his eyes.

Finally, he muttered, "Do you think that would be a good idea?"

She didn't speak the answer. She already knew it—and saw that he did too. Tonight's "play" session was horridly named.

None of it had been play for either of them. Every touch, word, command, and obeisance had been another drop of glue in an unmistakable bond. Even tonight, that glue had become part of her blood...that was thick in every tear on her cheeks now.

Tess wrapped her arms around his neck and pulled him down against her. "I don't want to say goodbye."

"No." Though he growled it before her final word was done, his throat clutched on the sound. He repeated it, just as broken, while hammering the opposite effect with the thrust of his hips between hers. "Not yet," he rasped.

"Not yet," she echoed, letting the towel fall free and her thighs spread open. The fly of his leathers was taut again, the button he'd left undone now a wonderful scratch against her abdomen. "Please."

"I'm here," he told her. The slash of his zipper was as perfect a sound as the pool's lapping waters. "I'm here."

And then he was.

Sliding on another condom and then moistening it with the juices from her needy folds. Making her shudder again as he teased the broad head along her erect clit—and then slid it deeper, deeper still, nudging her open more, *more*...

Then filling her as no one had before.

As, quite possibly, no one might ever again.

In ways she didn't even want to contemplate.

Not now.

Damn it...not ever.

# CHAPTER THIRTEEN

"Master?"

The little redhead who'd just entered Dan's living room directed the request over her shoulder at the tall, tawny-haired man with whom he'd just broken from a gruff guy hug.

"Yes, my beauty?" Levi called in his smooth Georgia accent, reminding Dan it had been too damn long since he'd been back home. Maybe it was because he realized that he'd soon be seeing more of Atlanta than he cared to. In another year, maybe two, Dad would be officially resigning the helm of Colton Steel—to him. This place, with the ranch-style layout and the desert colors he loved so much, would only be his vacation home.

His chest clenched. His gut twisted.

*Focus on the moment. Not the future, not the past. Just now, goddamnit, and how good it feels to just be living it.*

Seven years of fieldwork in the CIA had taught him to carve the mantra into his brain—especially after the mission that had changed his life.

Two nights of being inside Tess Lesange, and it was razed to nothing.

He'd start the engraving all over again tonight. At least he'd try, considering the circumstances. The resolve enforced the smile on his lips as little Bella Stratham turned to them, hands braced on her hips, exposing the green-and-gold tattoos that swirled up both her arms. The same colors were woven through her casual sweater dress, worn over heeled suede boots. She gave his buddy, Levi Cowell, a scowl of such domestic ire, nobody would've guessed they weren't wifie and hubbie or even brother and sister.

In many ways, their relationship went deeper than either. They were submissive and Dominant, one of his favorite couples from the Shadowlands club back home.

Okay, technically not *home* home, but Tampa wasn't a long hop in the company jet. Using the thing had always made him wince a little, until having a compelling reason to use it. He'd never thought that cause would arise until a couple of years ago, when taking a brief leave from the Agency to help Dad handle an issue with a Colton Steel ex-employee. Levi had been called in to supervise extra security measures for the Colton HQ buildings and became a friend Dan would value for the rest of his life. Bonded initially by their Georgia roots and mutual quest for the perfect slice of peach pie, the friendship moved deeper when they discovered another mutual interest: the BDSM dynamic. Levi introduced Dan to Dominants who helped him understand his attraction to the darker side of kink, as well as a few submissives who shared the same passions.

There'd been some extraordinary sessions with those wonderful women, times he'd never forget—but they, and those nights at the Shadowlands, were just memories now. None of it resonated in the core of him, the crater that had yet to be flooded with the fulfillment of bringing a woman every drop *she* needed from the beauty of Power Exchange too. He'd begun comparing himself to a loser Don Quixote, chasing a Dulcinea who simply didn't exist—until the session last Friday night that had changed everything.

*Focus. On. The. Moment.*

Isabelle—Bella to everyone except her parents and the IRS—certainly helped on that level, twisting her lips and blurting, "Didn't you tell me Dan wasn't seeing a woman right now?"

Dan scowled. "I'm not." He glanced at Levi, who gave an urbane shrug. "Why?"

Bella looked around the room again. "Oh, I get it. So you're seeing a man."

"Excuse the hell out of me?"

"There's nothing wrong with it, Dan."

"No shit. But why the hell do you think—"

"*Please.* Candles on the mantel? Fresh flowers everywhere? Napkin rings and bread plates on the table?"

She finished with a glower, emphasizing her own burn scar, a silvery path that disappeared down the left side of her neck. It reminded Dan why she could get away with this sass with him. He owed her. She'd reached out at one of the darkest times of his life, after the docs had told him much of the burn damage on his face would be permanent. While Tess had been there as a friend for his heart, Bella had been there for his head, coordinating with Tess through hours' worth of video chats. The woman's unique mix of sarcasm and pragmatism had been invaluable. Unlike others, she'd never made him feel like a victim, because he *wasn't* one. Nobody had forced him to run into that burning building. While he'd been on crisis autopilot, thinking only of getting those nurses out alive, he'd also been jacked on his typical idiotic swagger. He'd dodged bullets, escaped battle zones, and been catching the bad guys for years. What the hell was the issue with a burning building?

The answer to that had come the hard way. As every mirror on the planet reminded him, every single day.

Bella's huff yanked him back to the moment. "Don't play coy, Colton. Where is she?"

Levi cocked a brow at his woman. Though the guy had ditched his typical dark suit for a fitted blue sweater and black casual pants, he still looked ready to commandeer a tank if he had to. "Sugar, it *is* Thanksgiving."

"Thanksgiving *weekend*." She nodded toward the appetizer plates on the coffee table. "The Food Channel's already moved on to recipes with leftovers, but this guy has crackers arranged like a flower."

Levi stepped toward his subbie. Looked at the table. Raised a brow again. "She's right. You have a cracker flower."

Dan chuckled. Stretched a finger along his temple. "All right. You got me. Her name is Olga. I found her on Craigslist for a song. They have a new category there—Betty Crockers for Crabby Bachelors. She's been great. Doesn't exactly look like Betty Crocker, though. If you can ignore the wart on her chin and the hair in her ears—"

"Watch it, pal. You're on thin ice there."

He didn't have to worry about a good comeback for Tess's interruption. Bella's squeal handled the job fine. She nearly tackled Tess, making him damn glad his little rose had kicked off her own heels in favor of bare feet beneath her pink, retro-inspired jumpsuit. As the two redheads enjoyed their first in-person hug, Dan joined Levi in snaking a couple of "petals" from the cracker flower.

He stopped midchew when confronted by Bella's fresh glare.

"Damn it, Colton. You didn't tell me *she's* your secret weapon!"

"It's called a surprise, fireball." He winked while using the nickname he'd coined for her during his recovery—though this time, he was able to use it with affection instead of animosity. There were times when he'd been none too pleased about the camaraderie the little brat had formed with Tess, even via video chats, considering their "partnership" usually ended up in schemes for combating his dismal mood swings. But there was simply no way to tell a pair of determined women that his idea of "constructive therapy" didn't include a pedicure, a trip to the *Le Chat* Coffee Bar for coffee and kittens—literally—and then a stop at the chocolate shop on the way home. There'd been similar excursions, but that one had pretty much topped the emasculation scale.

Right now, every moment of the torture had been worth it.

Because right now, Tess needed Bella more than he did.

Thanks to the mental bullshit *he'd* subjected her to. For a second time.

*For the* last *time, asshole. You told her as much two nights ago—and you'll adhere to that word, no matter how agonizing it is to even be in the same room as her now.*

As in, the compulsions he fought against every single second. The twitches in his fingers to reach for her. The craving in his chest to have her smashed against it. The strain of his cock, still remembering the perfection of her hot pussy...

"Well, then, pour me a tall glass of awesomely surprised," Bella gushed, "and don't leave out the cute umbrella."

Levi wrapped an arm around his woman, kissing the top of her head. "Funny girl."

He didn't try to make the words public, though he certainly didn't keep them a secret. The man didn't fathom how his action turned Bella and him into the giant white elephants in the room, positioned there between Tess and Dan. With every syllable of the adoration, Tess's gaze glittered brighter, becoming the damn Northern Lights of pain. And Dan had no choice but to watch her, confronting the mess he'd made, choking down crackers to keep from calling himself a jackass out loud.

*Want to look at the positive here? At least she's not crying. Not yet.*

*But if she does, you'll be here this time.*

Because that was going to make up for lying to her? For giving her everything she'd ever dreamed of in a D/s dynamic and then ripping it away because of that same lie?

He hadn't deserved her before this whole stunt. He sure as hell didn't deserve her now.

He just wished like hell that his heart, soul, and spirit would get the message too.

While he indulged that mope, Levi stepped over and extended a hand toward Tess. "Since certain people have apparently turned into crackers, I'll do the honors. Good evening. I'm Levi Cowell."

A smile spread across Tess's lips, emphasizing the heart God must've patterned her face after. "You know that I already know that, right?"

"Irrelevant. Good manners are the door to beautiful opportunities." He kissed Bella's head as punctuation, indicating exactly what fit his definition of "beautiful."

"Very well, then." Tess laughed. "Lovely to meet you. Therese Lesange. But please call me Tess."

"As they say where I come from, whatever the lady wants."

Her grin widened, emphasizing the rosy hue spreading across her cheeks. Dan was damn near mesmerized by it. That same color filled her breasts when she was aroused in all the right ways, on the brink of begging for more. Dan wondered if they were flushing like that even now, even subconsciously, as a result of Levi's effortless charm.

*Fuck.*

The crackers turned in his stomach. He locked his teeth in time to prevent the acid from brimming into a snarl at his friend, before coming up with a better reprisal. "I believe what the lady really wants is a glass of good Merlot."

"Ooooo." Tess grabbed his forearm. "Yes, please."

Damn. *Damn.*

One touch. A tiny one, at that. Like his bloodstream knew the difference. Now that every platelet felt like a rocket, it was agony to fight off the craving to kiss her senseless. He settled for lifting her hand and playfully bussing the back. "As they say where *I* come from, whatever the lady *really* wants."

Levi tossed a wry glance. "Well played, asshat."

"Thanks, cock waffle."

Bella giggled. "Touché once more...asshat."

He answered that with narrowed eyes. "You know, I was just going to ask what *you'd* like from the bar too."

"Handled," Levi cut in. "*I* know what the lady likes in her deliveries."

"Oh, hell." Bella rolled her eyes. "Down, boys. There are enough trees in the park for everyone to pee on, okay?"

Dan cocked his head. "Your girl is begging for a very bright ass, Cowell."

"A matter upon which we finally agree," Levi replied.

Bella snorted at them both while linking arms with Tess. "Okay, honey. *Your* story has to be infinitely more interesting than this."

Dan could read a fireball set-up when he heard it but already forgave Bella, able to light up mirth in Tess that he'd sorely been missing. Still, she echoed, "Story? I don't understand."

Bella jerked her head toward Dan. "We called *yesterday* to tell this bozo we'd decided to extend the holiday weekend into a Vegas vay-cay. Even if he dialed your digits next, and I assume he did, that only gave you twenty-four hours to pull all this together. Sooooo..." Her eyes glowed like dark honey. "I'm thinking magic elves, a few shirtless slave boys, or a fairy godmother."

"*No* shirtless slaves." Levi's gaze changed as well—to the shade of ink.

"Magic elves might be just as dangerous," Dan rejoined.

"Fairy godmother it is," Tess quipped. "No complaints here. I'll sure as hell put her sparkly ass to work on a few miracles."

Levi and Bella burst with laughs. Dan didn't join them. Couldn't, not even in feigned form—not when Tess's breezy tone was already the lie here. Didn't his friends see it? The shadows of sadness in her eyes. The crimps at the corners of her smile. The yearning that gripped her whole posture with every stare she directed at the two of them...the girl who'd been taken to the party but abandoned by her date.

*Damn it.*

He'd been so thankful when Levi called about their impromptu visit, hoping that calling Tess for her help would keep her too busy for sub drop. It worked, at least for a little while. Tess had taken the afternoon off work, arriving just after lunch to take over the kitchen, chopping and boiling and cooking things she refused to let him see "until the perfect time." Now, he wondered if *she'd* make it to that moment.

Party. Girl in the corner. Still looking for her date.

Searching for *his* damn alter ego.

*Dickwad. Dickwad. Dickwad.*

"Well, shit," Bella muttered. She also wasn't fooled by Tess's façade. The woman pulled her into one of those "side hugs" only a girlfriend or a gay bestie could get away with. "Does that Merlot need a chaser of girl talk, sweetie?"

Tess's pause gave Dan ample opportunity to envy Bella for where she stood and he didn't. He'd steered clear of anything remotely physical with Tess today, acknowledging the tightrope his own composure already treaded. Hands on Lesange? It'd be only the beginning of his ready and willing fall from that height. The woman's fingertips on his forearm were the impulse for half a hard-on; God only knew what a whole hug would tempt him toward. And if his lips touched hers again, even as Dan, there'd be no holding back the words that would spill from him along with the passion. *My sweet rose. My hot, sweet subbie. My dear one...*

Right. And *that* would go over *so well* right now.

"Can I just trade the Merlot for the godmother and the miracle?" she finally mumbled to Bella. The wobble in her voice drove a fist to Dan's middle. He cleared his throat to conceal the reaction.

Bella wasn't so subtle about hers.

"Yikes on a stick, Li'l T. What happ—" She stopped short after brushing Tess's hair off her face. Then gasped, pulling back the hair more—to expose the bite marks on Tess's neck to them all.

"Whoa," Levi uttered.

"Hell," Tess rasped.

Dan coughed again. No way to avoid the memories now—all the images that replayed exactly how she'd come by those bruises.

Thank fuck for Levi, who cocked his head and stared at the bruises with something nearing admiration. "What an interesting icebreaker."

Bella rolled her eyes but quipped, "I hope to hell you got those the fun way, girlfriend."

To his relief, Tess smiled—sort of. Her lips tilted enough to be convincing now, as she offered, "If 'fun' is part of describing the best night of one's life, then I guess it was fun."

Bella hauled her into another hug. "Ohhhh, sweetie, that's awesome! Errr, that's...awesome? Tess?"

She asked it as Tess returned the embrace with fierce force, turning the air into a soup of I'm-about-to-bawl tension. Bella pushed her purse off onto Levi before yanking her friend in tighter.

*Shit. Hell. Fuck.*

With the words a cloud bank on his chest, Dan stared toward Levi, who was clearly thinking the same thing—with the I-have-no-idea-what's-happening-but-now-I'm-holding-a-purse modification.

"Sweetie," Bella crooned. "Oh, *sweetie*, what is it? What's wrong? If it was the best night of your life—" Tess's first sob cut her short. "Ohhhh, dear. Well gosh, did he feel the same way? Surely he did, right?"

"I...I don't know." Her face stole his heart—and then broke it. With lips twisted, nose pink, and gaze filled with agony, she was still every one of his dreams come to life, followed by every nightmare he dreaded inducing. His hand lifted toward her, drawn by a force beyond his control, needing to comfort her.

At the last second, he ripped it back, fingers curling into a fist. *Outstanding.* The woman of his dreams was falling apart before his eyes, and he was brushing up for a melodrama audition. Trouble was, he had the wrong script. The unredeemable villain was the mustache twirler, not the fist-in-the-air Dudley Do-Right. He'd given up all privileges to Dudley the second he walked up to her in that mask last Friday.

"You don't know?" Bella echoed. "Why? Didn't he tell you?"

Tess blushed. Yeah, right there, staring at her friend with the collar around her neck and the Master at her back—and it was fucking adorable. Dan had to fist his other hand.

"I guess he did," she finally replied. "In his own way, I suppose." She grabbed a strand of hair, which she was wearing straight and half up tonight, and nervously twirled it. "I met him...at a club."

"A club." Bella crunched a frown, almost making it a question.

"A *club*?"

Somehow, Levi's emphasis clarified it. "Oh!" Bella exclaimed. "A *club*. Holy shit, Tess. Really?"

"Really." She wobbled out a laugh. "I've been...curious... about something more intense for a while now. And Dan's been awesome about answering my questions, helping me learn. I also read a lot of books."

Levi's jaw tightened. "Which ones?"

Dan snorted and filled in, "All of them."

"Damn it."

"No kidding."

Bella rolled her eyes again. "Can you two chill? She's not taking the LSAT of BDSM. Be *happy*. Our Li'l T met a Dom—

and likes him!"

Tess shook her head, eyes pooling with heavier tears. "And doesn't even know him, sweetie."

"Huh?"

"Shit," she muttered, lips trembling. She looked over at Dan, face pleading with him for strength. Talk about a new definition of conflict. While his spirit was a skyscraper of joy at being her go-to for the fortitude, his soul was a tenement of shame.

"I'm right here, Ruby. It's okay." His nod of encouragement was easy, but adding an assuring smile—well, attempting to—logged him back into stupidity mode. Not the biggest commercial for credibility, if he correctly read the quirks at the edges of Levi's stare.

*Damn it.* How much of this shit could he realistically keep holding back? It was torture not to touch her...not to rip her from Bella's embrace, clutch her tight to his chest, and whisper *his* words of tenderness to her. To hear her sighs of surrender as she took them in, absorbing his comfort...

*Comfort she needs because of* you, *asswipe. Remember that part?*

Tess turned back to Bella. Closed her eyes through a deep breath. "It just happened, I guess," she confessed. "Okay, maybe it didn't just *happen*. I mean, I *wanted* it to but just never thought it would be so..." She sighed in a way Dan hadn't seen in months, since the night she'd forced him to watch some animated "masterpiece" with a princess swooning over some Dudley on a horse as big as a house. "It was so perfect," she finally whispered. "And intense. And magical. And wonderful."

"Ohhhh." Bella sighed too. "Yes!"

"And safe?" Levi made the demand work despite

the bright-blue handbag dangling off his elbow. "Sane? Consensual?"

*Of course it was.*

Before Dan knew it, he was snarling, too. *Fuck.* He rushed to amend, "You think I'd advise her otherwise?"

"He followed all the essentials," Tess assured them— before a wistful smile sneaked across her lips. "Went by the books. *All* of them. As for everything beyond that..."

Bella grabbed both her hands. "Yeah? Don't leave a girlfriend hanging!"

Tess cocked her head. "Maybe it was just the allure of the mask."

"The *mask*? You're serious, aren't you?"

"Not even my imagination is that good." She let her head fall fully back. "And ohhh God, Bel...it was *good.* No. Better than that. There were times...when I couldn't see the color in his eyes at all, just these glittering lights from behind the mask...and then just knew exactly how wicked he was going to be with me..." She glanced at Dan and Levi like a teen busted for breaking curfew. "Errr...TMI?"

"A little," Levi growled.

"Just," Dan concurred—or at least appeared to. Truth? Her moments of "TMI" were the few respites of heaven in this hell of living with the greatest lie he'd ever told. It became bearable when he watched the memories take over her face, saw the bliss wind through her body, heard the joy of submissiveness in her voice. Another Dom would now be the one taking care of her—he had no doubt she'd be quickly collared as the treasure she was—but he'd find solace in knowing he'd set her off in the right direction. It was his only choice.

"Sorry," Tess offered to all of them. "But it *was* incredible."

She slipped her hands from Bella's grip. "No matter what you must be thinking right now."

The little fireball shot a dark frown. "What I must be thinking? Hmmm. You know the score that well, do you?"

"Come *on*," Tess countered. "Bella, I didn't even know his name. Granted, he came with high credentials, but I took to calling him *Sir Sexy*. And he wore a damn *mask*."

Her friend smirked. "All sounds pretty hot to me. 'Sir Sexy,' huh? Did he earn it?"

"Are you listening to me?" Tess leaned over, furiously whispering, "I let him get kinky with me, Bel. I mean, *really* kinky. *Twice*."

"And were you safe about it? Condoms? Lube where necessary?"

Tess's new blush was her most gorgeous of all. "Of course."

"So what's the issue?"

"I...well..."

Bella wiggled her shoulders and flashed an impish grin. "Just tell me when you're scheduled for a three-peat so I can vid-call your ass afterward."

"We're not."

"What? Why?"

"Not meant to be, I guess."

Every syllable of it was soaked in how deeply she disbelieved it—and how it crushed her to say it. Dan braced himself for the impact to his own gut. Plummeting from heaven to hell in less than ten seconds; *there* was something he could cross off the bucket list. Now he just had to add the burning fires of his own stupid mistakes. The new weight in Tess's eyes told him the ordeal wasn't far off.

"The mask," she went on. "I think there was a distinct

reason for it. He has secrets, and they aren't easy ones. I saw that much. I mean, I guess I did." She kicked at the floor and waved a dismissive hand. "Whatever, right? It was amazing, and I'm thankful my first experience was so awesome, but it's time to move on." Her lips flattened, betraying how she fought like hell against more tears. "Then again, maybe that's easier said than done."

Bella twisted their fingers together again. "Oh, Li'l T. I'm sorry. This sucks."

Tess dipped her head, trying to snuffle discreetly. "Now you understand why I'm such a huge mess."

"*Stop*," Bella ordered. "We're *all* messes, girl. Now figuring out the best cleanser for your chaos...*that's* the tricky part." She pulled back far enough to throw a telling glance at Dan and Levi. "In this instance, maybe we'll start with some good Merlot."

If the cue was any clearer, it'd be a pair of tattoos on their foreheads. Dan let his friend nod the confirmation first. "Lead the way, superspook." Levi swept out an arm and bowed, full of Rhett Butler flash once more. As Dan led the way to the small den around the corner that held the bar, he debated between calling the guy a dandy douche or just a lame suck-up.

His ringing doorbell took the place of making a final choice.

Before he took two steps toward the front door, it rang again. Then again. A trio of thumps on the portal followed right after.

"Christ, Colton," Levi grumbled. "Have you been out making trouble for the world again? Or did you just invite a circus troupe to dinner as well?"

"Why not?" he retorted. "You'd look good in some tights,

Cowell. Balancing on an elephant, yeah?"

"That leaves the high wire and tutu for you, pretty boy."

Once Dan opened the door, he really did wish it was the circus.

"John?" He clasped hands with the half-Samoan giant who filled his portal, outfitted differently than the black-and-gray club gear in which Dan had seen him a few nights ago. Franzen actually looked more daunting in his camouflage uniform and heavy boots, the stripes on his shoulder denoting him as Captain, the beret on his head adorned with the yellow flash of the First Special Forces Group.

"Dan," he responded—another incentive for his neck hairs to jolt up. *Dan.* Not "shithead" or "spook man" or "buddy." The last time Franz had gone with "Dan," they'd been gripping hands in the back of an air transport, a journey Dan barely remembered because half his face had just been fried off. Even so, his scars flared with phantom pain.

He clenched his jaw to battle the ghosts as Franz invited himself into the foyer, followed by an equally tall guy with a jaw that matched his boxy crew cut. A shorter figure was behind them, outfitted in the black suit and white shirt of the Secret Service. Though that "uniform" was meant to make its wearers as "invisible" as possible, there was no way Dan ever dismissed it—

Just in case it was filled by the feisty female who grinned at him now.

With a moan of joy, he rushed her like a linebacker and embraced her like a favorite pillow. His chest burst. His throat constricted. "Hey, you little shit."

She laughed against his shoulder. "Hey, you big shit."

A not-so-discreet cough brought the world rushing back.

Reluctantly, he stepped back—colliding with Tess as he did. With his brain already spinning, it was too huge an effort to hold himself back from the most natural action in the world: wrapping an arm around her waist to steady them both. Too bad the haters were right about best-laid plans. The moment his hand pressed to the curve of her body, he wanted her closer—in about a hundred other places.

"Ruby." He dipped his voice on the endearment, needing her to feel her preferred status. "I'm honored to introduce—"

"Shut. Up." Tess shoved away from him to rush forward as he had. "Like you don't have a baby sister photo shrine in the den." She went in for one of her signature Tess hugs, brief but brutal, before greeting, "Hi, Devyn. It's awesome to meet you. I'm—"

"Shut. Up." Devyn's eyes sparkled, bright blue and sassy, as she turned the tables on Tess. "I know exactly who you are too. It's great to meet you, despite the shitty circumstances."

More neck hairs on high alert. "What's going on?" he charged. "It's not Dad, is it?" It was his best guess, though Franz's camos and the presence of the cube-head didn't bear it out.

"Dad's fine." The only assuring thing about Devyn's statement were the words themselves. Her fidgeting fingers told a different story. Franz's jumpy gaze only deepened the impression.

*What the hell?*

Devyn tugged on his elbow. "We're here about something else, Dan."

"You don't say," he drawled.

"Can we come in?" she pressed. "And talk someplace... quiet?" The glance she tossed at Levi and Bella all but bullhorned her subtext. *Quiet*, as in *private*.

"Maybe a rain check is in order." Levi wound a hand into Bella's and then scooted around everyone with surprising grace, given his size. From the open doorway, he called, "Yo, asshat? We'll be in town until Wednesday, at the Wynn. Call if you can."

"Sure, man."

After waving goodbye to the couple, he shut the door and returned to the living room, where everyone was filling in the blanks on the missing introductions. Since he had the advantage of knowing everyone but the cube-head, he cut to the chase and riveted his attention on the guy. It didn't take Cary Grant too long to approach, hand extended. "Hi there. Caspar Menken. FBI."

"Pleasure." He didn't mean either syllable. A glance to Tess for commiseration was worth the effort. It wasn't that they absolutely hated teaming with the feds on cases; it just wasn't their preferred method of tackling issues. Red tape and hoops were bad enough when *one* group of spies was involved. Doubling the manpower didn't always equate to doubling effectiveness.

Franz stomped forward, clearly determined to be Switzerland. "Okay, everyone play nice, boys and girls. This stack of bang sticks is too hot for us to fuck up."

Dan glared. "What are you talking about?"

Menken braced a hand to John's shoulder. When the huge warrior didn't bite it off, a chill gripped Dan's chest.

This *was* serious shit.

"Kirk Newport has been relegated to house arrest," the fed explained.

Screw the ice. Fury detonated through Dan in a hundred

different ways. Make that a thousand.

"What. The. Fuck?" He surged toward Menken—only to be stopped cold by his sister, ramming a hand against the center of his chest.

"Sit the hell down, sparky."

He twisted away from her. Hurled a new glower at Franz. "You said a sentence *downgrade*, John. House arrest isn't a fucking downgrade!"

"Sit." Devyn again. Shoving him this time. "*Down.*"

He stumbled back and fell to the couch. At the same time, Tess lowered to a chair on the other side of the coffee table. Her tongue flicked nervously over her lips. "So the president signed the papers."

Dan redirected his glare at her. His ire dripped, heavy and hot, right over the fucking cracker flower. "*You* knew this might happen?"

She paled—and he wished that didn't look as gorgeous as any of her blushes. Menken saved her from having to answer by stepping stiffly forward. "Shit's going down with Moscow. They need Newport on board," he explained. "Nichols signed everything about forty-eight hours ago. It was discreet. Nobody was supposed to find out."

"But somebody did." The whole right side of Dan's face was a bath of fire, signaling his psyche's security alert system was in perfect working order. *Rage level high. Evacuate all but necessary instincts for survival.* "Didn't they?" he demanded, digging his fingers into the couch cushion. "And now the shit's hit the goddamn fan."

Menken's composure was damn near irritating. "Well, thanks to your sister, we're not dodging as many fecal Frisbees as we first anticipated."

Franzen snarled. "No time for walking cocky yet, G-man. This is far from over."

"What's going on?" Tess focused on Devyn. Her evasion was so obvious, he wondered why she didn't just flash a neon sign. *Officially avoiding Dan.*

It hurt. Deeply. How long had she known the full plan for Newport? And why hadn't she breathed a word of it to him?

"After they settled Newport in at his house, the vice president went to visit him," Devyn explained. She lifted her gaze to Dan for a second. It was pointless to hide his conflict from her. The connection they shared was difficult to explain to anyone. They weren't twins or best buddies or even raised in adversity. They were just...close. Over the miles, through the years, beyond the crazy job demands for them both—nothing changed the fact that she was one of his coolest blessings and biggest curses. Right now, it was tough to decide which, especially after she stated, "Daniel, I know you're sideways about this—"

"Sideways." He barked it on a bitter laugh. "Oh, sister. You have no fucking idea."

"But you don't see the entire picture. Nobody does. The Soviets are pulling some bullshit that could be pretty degrading for US security in Europe and the Middle East. To keep Americans safe, President Nichols had to strike a deal with the devil."

"The devil." Franz folded his arms. "*There's* a truth we can all get behind."

"No shit." Devyn's agreement turned his mood around a little. A *little.* Her continued tension kept his attention amped.

He wasn't the only one. Tess bolted from her seat with both hands balled. "What. Happened?"

Before Devyn answered, she pulled in a measured breath. "On a sweep during Madame Vice President's meeting with Newport, I found a cell phone hidden in a lead planter."

Tess sat right back down. "Damn."

"Yeah," Devyn snapped. "Damn. That bastard isn't allowed to have a cell, let alone a secret one. And what we found on it—" She cut herself short as her stare swung over, riveting on Dan.

It was a sledgehammer of a moment for him too. Never had he seen such a look on his little sister's face before. He stared over every inch of her, wondering where or how she'd been so violently stabbed. Surely there wasn't any other reason for the violent pain on her face—and the last-breath kind of love in her eyes.

"I wanted to kill him," she whispered after a long moment. "I *did*, Dan. When I saw what the bastard was capable of ordering, just punching it all into a damn cell phone like a takeout Chinese meal—" She inhaled and exhaled, shoulders shaking from the effort. "I could've taken out my SIG and blown his worthless head off. And damn it, I couldn't. I can't. I can't even give that cocksucker a paper cut because of his value to our national security." She spun and drove a fist into the wall. "Fuck!"

Tension fell over the room like a funeral knell—until Franz cocked his head in a wry glance at Dan. "Can't tell you two are related at *all*."

The urge to rise and pace was excruciating. Dan fought it, sensing whatever came next would make him want to turn the wall into a punching bag too. He leaned forward, parking his elbows on his knees before looking back up at his friend.

Softly, he asked, "What was on the phone?"

Franz dipped his head to one side and then the next, a cross between a shrug and a scowl. "Want to take a guess?"

Dan linked his fingers. The comeback was actually perfect. Franzen knew him well enough by now to discern he'd feel more empowered if he could slam together parts of the puzzle himself. "GPS locator pins on everyone involved with the mission that took him down—and their women and kids."

Franz straightened his head. "Very nice, Holmes. And what else?"

Dan swallowed hard. "Links back to other GPS coordinates. Real-time locations of the operatives for each hit. Probably statuses too."

Franz dinged an imaginary bell. "Give the man a prize."

Devyn swore again.

Menken turned, bracing both hands to the fireplace mantel.

Tess went eerily still.

And yeah...Dan noticed.

Every damn inch of her.

His gut gave his gaze no other alternative. His spirit gave his heart no other path. Yeah, even in his wrath at her. Maybe even because of it. Every thought in his head and sensation in his body was revved on high octane right now, even the recognition that, while he was pissed as hell at her, he was awed into paralysis by her.

How was this possible? How had she turned him into this mess?

Because she was unlike any woman he'd ever met—especially now. Others, even toughened field agents, would likely be shaking from head to toe after hearing the news Franz, Devyn, and Menken had brought—that as they spoke,

Kirk Newport had a different assassin headed for every dot on his secret cell phone. But Tess lifted her face with pride, dedication, and determination. She didn't stop focusing on Franz. Her lips mingled with her teeth and tongue as she processed thoughts, accessing her amazing laser beam of a mind for any knowledge she could bring to this makeshift war room of theirs, any new angle she could lend to thwarting Newport without killing him.

She floored him. Enraged him. Mesmerized him.

Tore him apart.

"Needless to say, we're working with Spec Ops in all the cities to take out the assassins before they get to us," Franz clarified. "But until that happens, we're arranging for fully supplied safe houses for all the families."

"Nichols gave us clearance for that much," Menken supplied.

"I didn't give the fucker much of a choice," Franz growled. "We saved his life last year, goddamnit."

"That op was one hell of a hat trick." Menken's voice was thick with fanboy admiration, referencing the insane mission Franz and his team had pulled off, that had saved the president as well as the entire US West Coast. Franz barely noticed the compliment. His sculpted Samoan features, normally set in the requisite Spec Ops mode of tough-guy arrogance, were much different tonight. They were an open book of fear for his men and their families.

"Z's fiancée Rayna, along with Sage and Racer Hawkins, are already tight in the Seattle location," he stated. "A few more Stateside members of the team, including Rhett Lange and Rebel Stafford, are with them. Can we use the new condo you secured in downtown LA for Ethan Archer's wife?"

"Of course," Dan answered before a scowl took over. "Hold on. Ethan wasn't even on the mission last year."

"You think Newport knows the difference?"

"Or cares?" Devyn added.

That flipped open another page of Franz's book. "We're already covered in Hawaii," he rushed on. "Luckily, Shay and Zoe are still there on honeymoon. They've been transported to the cottages on the Barking Sands Missile Base. Nobody's getting on that base without stripping to their skivvies and handing over five official forms of ID."

Dan nodded, approving the move. "Is there a chance Newport may still want Shay more alive than dead, though? And would he try to use Tait as bait for that?"

One more page peeled back across Franz's face. "That's why Tait, Kellan, and Lani are staying in the next cottage over. Lani's little brother, Leo, is with them."

He punctuated it by fully locking his gaze with Dan's— baring the full extent of his dread. The move reeled Dan through his third shock of the night. Fate had gotten in the first smack with Devyn appearing on his front doorstep, followed by her fist in his wall. Now, the exposure to this side of John Franzen he'd never seen. During the entire history of their friendship, the tough soldier had never allowed his composure to unravel so much.

"These men are my *ohana*, Colton," Franz told him. "My family. If even one of them or their loved ones are taken down by Newport's fucked-up rampage, the man will not live to see another sunrise—and I'll gladly tell the world in a court of law, including President Craig Nichols, that I was the one who rid it of that sonofabitch."

Another long pause weighted the room. This time,

Menken didn't attempt to calm the Samoan. The only person with those kinds of guts was, not surprisingly, Devyn. "Okay, big guy." She stroked his shoulder, her hand looking tiny on his bicep. "We're on a good roll here. Stay focused. One more safe house to secure, and then you can go out and track some bad-guy motherfuckers." She shook her head and pouted. "*Damn it.*" Added a pitiful whine. "I wanna go too, *mauna* man."

"*No.*"

Dan commanded it in unison with Franzen. He was about to embellish it with a rant about how playing roulette with safety got half of one's face burned off, but that was when all his thoughts of fire were totally doused—

By the glacier of horror that had taken the place of his chest.

Shit. *Shit.*

The last safe house would be Vegas. Because Devyn would be going in it.

Sure enough, Menken looked up from a smartpad he'd opened, declaring, "We've got a furnished place ready to go not too far from here, tucked into a gated community. Nice view of the lake and everything."

"Sounds charming," Devyn groused. "I can toodle around the water in my cute little paddleboat, getting blitzed on margaritas—or you can just send me to hell. Same diff."

Dan jolted to his feet. Paced all the way to the kitchen and back again. Then again. He had no idea what else to do with the terror now gripping *his* soul—the crazy what-ifs that bombarded him from all angles, shattering the glacier into shards that tumbled through every inch of his body, every drop of his blood.

*You want to talk about hell, baby sister?*

Hell was the certainty that Newport likely knew, with crystal clarity, what Tess had come to mean to him in the last year—and that if he'd been followed by any of the bastard's minions over the last week, especially to Catacomb, it wouldn't be an outrageous leap to assume they'd taken their relationship to new levels.

Hell was the certainty that if Newport even suspected Tess was Dan's sexual submissive, he'd take her to his own dungeon—where safe, sane, and consensual would be merely fancy words from a dictionary.

"Hey, king shit."

Devyn's shout jerked him around.

"What?" he snapped.

"I think that's my line," she rebutted. "Well, *our* line." She spread her hands. "What the hell? What're you doing?"

He took a second to breathe. To evaluate the accuracy of the shitstorm that had just plummeted over his logic—and still led to the only course of action, disgusting as it was, that he could take because of it.

*Fuck.*

He scraped a hand through his hair. When he lifted his head back up, he arrowed his stare straight at Tess.

"You have to go with her," he directed.

Tess's gaze widened. "What? Who? *Me?* Where?"

"To the safe house." He didn't falter any syllable. "With Devyn. You have to go with her, Tess. It's not negotiable."

She gawked like he'd just grown webbed feet and had quacked it at her. "You're smoking crack, Colton. If you send me, you'll have to send half the office too. We're all just your work friends. Trained CIA work friends who work in a damn secure building, at that."

"Damn it."

"Damn it what?" Her head slid back as if on a rail, spearing him with a full *what the hell*, as he started crossing the room toward her.

"You're going to make me do this the hard way, aren't you?"

"The hard way...*what*?" But when he didn't deter his gaze from her beautiful face for a second, her demeanor started to crack. She blinked hard, and he knew—*knew*—that for a moment, she didn't just see him. She felt him. She felt *them*. All the connection and perfection and power of what they'd shared in the middle of the desert, in the darkness of that dungeon, was just as real and brilliant here, as he knew it would be—as she shook her head against it, refusing to believe. Dan didn't blame her. Looking at the sun was hard enough, but being forced to hop in a space shuttle and then land on it?

Death was death, no matter how good the fire felt getting there.

When he was finally close enough, he lifted his hands to her shoulders but didn't grab them. Instead, with hands turned over, he trailed his knuckles along both those sweet curves, hoping she felt his longing, even now, to kiss them, shield them, hold them—

To protect her with his own damn life, if that was what this all came to.

"You're going to the safe house with my sister."

"No, I'm not."

"*Yes*...you are. I'm not going to let that asshole *or* his dipshits near you, Ruby."

A tremble ran the length of her body. An answering energy vibrated through him. Just like that, it all returned...

the threads, so spectral yet so strong, that bound their very chemistries. Undeniable. Unbreakable.

Tess jolted her stare up at him, stabbing daggers of jade confusion through dark-ginger lashes, sharpening as he shifted even closer. *Help*, he pleaded to heaven. *Help me to help* her *understand.* If at least her senses acknowledged the truth of who he was, she'd comply. She'd be safe, and so would his secret.

Not happening.

The next second, she made her chin follow her gaze. It jutted up as she huffed again at him. "Damn it, Dan. They're not going to come anywhere near me. Honestly, I don't think there's any need to—"

Desperate times. Desperate measures.

He flipped his hands over. Dug his fingers into the flesh of her arms and his stare into the deepest corners of hers. "We don't have time," he growled. "And you will *not* argue with me about this anymore. You're going to that house, little rose, and that's a goddamn order."

# CHAPTER FOURTEEN

"Tess."

She ignored him, tugging the blanket tighter around her shoulders. She'd found it in the window seat of the bedroom she'd claimed at the Summerlin safe house and then instantly wrapped herself in it, craving the symbolic refuge as much as the real.

Even so, she wished the thing would become a full invisibility cloak. That would mean she couldn't enjoy the view of the lake—Caspar had been right; it was awesome—not that she saw it, anyway. She was numb. Sealed off. Barriers up. Nothing in, nothing out. She couldn't drool over her luxurious surroundings or even laugh at the family of ducks on the patio below, shaking their backsides after a midnight dip in the water. She certainly couldn't risk a speck of fear for everyone, even herself, who had targets on their backs courtesy of that bastard, Kirk Newport.

Letting any of it in meant letting *all* of it in. That meant remembering the blast from two hours ago that had dropped her to her knees in the middle of Dan's living room. *Warp core breached, Captain.* She'd proved that by shivering through the most agonizing minute of her life, before letting Devyn yank her up and help her out the door.

Between there and here, everything had turned into a blur. It was for the best. Even slivers of memory made her ball up, knees to chest, checking the shields in her soul for full coverage.

The thing was, she wasn't sure they all still worked. The gears of her emotional defenses were rusty, *too* rusty, not having to be activated since the day after her eighteenth birthday, when she'd hauled the last of her moving boxes from home.

No. Not home. Just Mother and Father's house. That place had never been home.

A home was a place for feeling wanted. Accepted. Safe.

She'd found home after that—at least parts of it, here and there. At college, where classmates and professors helped her grow and flourish, and then at the Agency, where the days were challenging and the fulfillment was high, finally giving her the feeling that she'd gotten something right in her life.

Then there'd been Dan.

Meeting Dan. Knowing Dan. Trusting Dan.

*Home.* He'd been home. Or at least the closest she'd ever come to knowing it in her life.

Had all of that been a lie too?

Who the hell was he? Who was the man she'd entrusted with so many deep secrets? With whom she'd shared so many laughs—and tears? Who'd put up with her dorky princess cartoons, brought her cheesy balloons on her birthday, always let her have the chunkiest pieces of the guacamole, even the last spoonful on ice cream cheat night?

Who'd told her he could never dominate her—then went ahead and did it as another person. Then did it *again*—and put the cherry on that shit-fun sundae by telling her they could never meet like that again.

Why?

What the hell was wrong with *her* that he had to become

a different person to be intimate with her? What was wrong with Tess but right about Odette? Was it the whole coworker thing—though technically, right now, they weren't even that? And what had she gotten so wrong about submitting to him that he'd called it all off after their second amazing night?

*Amazing for you, maybe...*

Maybe it really was just her. Maybe all of this had just been written in the stars since the day she was born, and there wasn't a damn thing she could do to change it. She'd always be the middle one. The disposable one. Getting it all right still wasn't good enough, even for the lover who'd made her feel, at least for a week, that "good" was just the beginning of what she could accomplish.

Maybe it was pointless to even continue trying.

"*Tess.*"

"Go away, Daniel."

"No."

Despite the order, he maintained his position in the doorway. Tess didn't move. With her head turned, she was able to focus on every detail of his voice, all the things even the voice disk couldn't cloak. Why hadn't she picked up on it before? The core of baritone command. The subtle Atlanta accent. The husky word endings that wrapped their way around every nerve ending in her body, even now.

"I can't do this, Dan."

"I can't leave until you do."

"I'm reeling."

"I know."

The sky flashed over the lake. A thunderstorm was approaching, even as the moon sneaked from between the clouds to drench the landscape in silver. She winced, almost shutting it all out, feeling as if she peered into a mirror instead of a window—if mirrors could reflect the depths of souls too. Hers was an equal palette of darkness, fighting the bursts of memory that kept trying to take over, painfully hot and blinding. When they weren't, the electricity lingered on every particle of the air, razing her composure, singeing her nerves— all because he still stood there.

*Damn it.*

Even now, he could do this to her. Make her feel just like the lake outside, churning, waiting—needing the strike of his lightning to feel completely alive.

But what was lightning when it was a lie?

Just a cloud. Filled with ice. With nowhere to go.

"Tess."

"*No.* Daniel, please—just go away!"

Of course, he took two stomps into the room. Looked like he wanted to swear but didn't. Slammed out a breath through his nose. "Look...I—" An inhale now, sharp and angry. "I had no idea you'd be at Catacomb that night."

She huffed. "No shit."

"I—"

"Was just there with your handy mask and voice disguise, figuring you'd check out what was up in submissive tail for the night? Good on you, Dark Knight."

She grabbed her chance to lob an over-the-shoulder glare but instantly regretted it. Damn. He was so beautiful, it was torture to look. His gaze pierced her like sunlight through blue glass. His body, clad now in mission gear consisting of a black skintight T-shirt and cargo pants, was as perfect as a life-size GI Joe. Even with anguish possessing every inch of him, he was flawless.

*No. He's not in anguish. He's in pain. And shame. He hid himself from you and then came clean only because he had to. He shattered your trust, your friendship—*

*Your heart.*

"Hell," he gritted. "I was only there to visit, okay? Max Brickham is a friend. I had no intentions but to wish him the best with the club." He dared another step. "Then I turned around and saw you there..."

"And wasn't that convenient?" she spat.

"You think that was pleasant for me? In any fucking sense of the word?" He pounded closer. "Do you think I kicked up my heels at seeing you there, your skin spilling out of that corset, looking like a goddamn Dominant's dream?"

"But not yours." She flung the blanket off and pivoted to fully face him. "You told me you didn't want me. You told me to my damn face, that you wouldn't even think about stepping into a dungeon with me!"

"No." He leaned closer. "Not that I wouldn't think about it. That I *couldn't*. That I didn't want to fuck up what we had already." His hands spread, fingers jerking as if he wanted to reach for her, but he lowered them back into taut fists. "What I found with you, Tess...what we had...well, I've never done that with a woman before." He looked away, peering out as if he'd lost something out in the lake too. "It was so...real. And honest. And so damn good."

She gripped the edge of the window seat. Dipped her head to stave the tears. "Yeah. It was."

"So do you get it?" he pressed. "Now? Even a little? How we couldn't have turned off the D/s part of things? How it would have changed everything?"

Rain began to spatter the window. A thousand thoughts

were just as persistent, bringing a flood of understanding.

*Damn it.*

He was right. As much as she fought against the admission, it was true. Pieces of their first scene flowed back to her in longer ribbons of recall. The demands he'd made of her. The boundaries he'd pushed. The way he'd restrained her, filled her, been in complete control of her. She'd never have surrendered all that to Daniel Colton. With the griffin, she had nothing to lose. It had been the key to her complete freedom.

"But why didn't you tell me?" She jerked her gaze up. "After that first session? Why, Daniel?" As more memories pushed in, fury drove her to her feet. "You *left*. You said you had 'business out of town.' What the hell?"

He finally lifted a fist. Pushed it against the frame of the window seat. "*That* sucked. It was wrong."

"Damn straight it was."

"I'm sorry, Tess. So fucking sorry."

"Damn right you are."

But it still didn't provide her with an explanation. The jagged set of his face proclaimed he knew it too. "I...panicked," he finally uttered. "I know it's lame, but—"

"Lame doesn't come close to it."

"I thought it was the best for *you*."

Okay, *that* one was the lame kicker. But as Tess stood, debating *her* best choices for calling him on the bullshit, something equally outrageous occurred. Her stare locked once more with his—and she saw that he meant it. Every damn word.

"I panicked," he rushed on, "because everything we shared in the dungeon that night was..." He shoved out another breath. "Well, it was fucking amazing was what it was."

"You sound surprised by that."

A sheepish grin quirked his lips. "Surprised doesn't come close to it, dear one." As if using her own words *and* her favorite endearment weren't panty-dissolving enough, he swooped back in to fill her personal space, consuming her very air with his tall, graceful, not-an-inch-of-soft glory. Looking too damn much like he had when first approaching her at Catacomb—without his signature accessory. Without the mask, there were no shadows hiding the intensity of his eyes, or distract from the determined lines of his jaw. And there sure as hell was nothing diluting how her body still responded to him like a tigress in heat, brutal and raw and hot...

"So surprised is a bad thing?" She zeroed her focus in on the offense, just to keep the confrontation grounded. Fine, the man flipped every lust switch she had, especially now that she realized her best friend was also the hottest lover she'd ever had. That didn't change a damn thing about the *rest* of the truth he owed her.

"No," Dan replied. "Not a bad thing. But that night, it also wasn't a good thing."

She scowled. "Do I want to know why?"

He pushed in even closer. Raised a hand and stroked her cheek with the back of a hand. "I approached you in that living room because I couldn't bear to think of anyone else touching you. My concern wasn't *brotherly* or *friendly*, Tess. The second I saw you, my blood was on fire...and my cock turned to steel."

Her lips popped open. "That's...errrmm..." *Shit, shit, shit.* "Well. That's...uh...nice."

"That's *not* nice," he flung. "I had no business approaching you, not when I knew I couldn't give you anything lasting with this fucked-up psyche and this half-monster face, but I did it anyway. I did it because I was selfish. Because I didn't want any other man to be responsible for your first experience in that dungeon." His caress changed. He stretched his fingers along her jaw, curling the tips into her hairline. "No other man in that place knew you as well as me. Nobody else would have cared that everything about that night be as perfect as you'd dreamed."

As if controlled by another, her arm rose. Her hand flattened to his face, mirroring his touch. "And it was," she whispered. "Oh God, Daniel. You have no idea..."

"I have *every* idea." He slid in tighter, fitting the rest of his body against hers. Tess's breath left her in a quiver as each awareness struck her senses. Her breasts to his chest. His thighs around her hips. His cock notched to her cleft. "I have every idea because it was like that for me too." His breath warmed her forehead. "Getting to restrain you...hurt you... push you..." He tangled his hand in her hair, fisting the strands until she gasped. "Then getting to please you...arouse you... fuck you..."

"Heaven," Tess whispered.

"Heaven." His echo was thick and rough, resonating in the deepest parts of her spirit, not just her libido. *Shit. You're in trouble, girl.* Proof: she seriously played with ditching the vow about giving in to the lusties. Luckily, Dan resolved the challenge, pulling away enough to let her grab half a brain. "But it was a heaven I had to disconnect from," he went on. "I knew it as soon as I laid you down in that aftercare nook and watched you sleep in my arms. I knew that if I waited until you woke up, I'd be tempted to lay you flat, spread you wide, and bury myself inside you all over again. And *that*, I likely wouldn't have survived in anonymity."

"You watched me sleep?" Damn it, that wasn't supposed to *soften* her to what he'd done. Too late. Clear as if it happened now, she imagined him on the pallet in the dungeon, watching over her sleeping form with that midnight intensity in his eyes.

"For a long time," Dan confirmed. "That part, I was glad for. It firmed my resolve about not ever touching you as a Dominant again." His hand wound in her hair again. The other he gripped to her waist, fisting the red cotton T-shirt she'd changed into when arriving here. "Being with you like that...every damn moment of it...was a seismic rift to my soul. *Tess*"—he drew her in closer, cranking the heat between them again—"you were everything *everything*—I'd ever dreamed of in a submissive." A funny huff escaped him, tugging at his scars, signaling that he drew on thoughts that ran deep. "But I was damn sure that if I ever had you in a play room again, I wouldn't get so lucky about calling in favors from fate."

The revelation yanked twenty seconds of air from her. As soon as her lungs relented, she blurted, "But you dialed again anyway." Literally. Her heart tripped over itself, remembering how growly and impatient he'd been when calling her at the office. *I want to see you again, Odette. The sooner, the better.*

"Yeah." He actually smiled. "I dialed again. As fast as I could."

"I don't understand."

"Little intervention, courtesy of your sub drop."

"Oh."

"Yeah." His grin plummeted. "Oh. As in *oh*, hell *no* was I going to let that blister fester in your mind. You weren't going to go through another day of feeling like that if I could help it."

She wanted to let her chest do more backflips from that— his angry protectiveness spoke to so many of the parts inside that had never been sheltered by anyone—but her heart had a heckler. A nasty, frustrated one, bellowing loudly enough to make her speak its message out loud.

"Why didn't you just tell me the truth then?" she charged. "Why'd you let me continue in the dark, Daniel? Why'd you let me keep thinking I was a slut, an idiot, or both to keep aching for a Dom I didn't even know?"

"Didn't know?" He dipped his head, underlining the question. "Do you really mean that, rose?"

"*Don't* call me that."

"Why?" He planted both feet, raising his posture to a warrior-like stance, fully primed to claim back the space she'd just spread between them. "Because it'll make you remember everything else I called you...things that your body and your soul craved to hear, even from a *stranger*? Because it'll make you think too much about what you did with that *stranger*?" Sure enough, he moved forward and pulled at her elbows, banding the bottom borders of her tattoos. As he forced her forward, he dipped his head, making it impossible to escape his stare. "Because it'll make you realize that even if you'd never known me before we came together at Catacomb, you *knew* me...little rose?"

She breathed hard. Swallowed harder. Damn him! Every last syllable was the truth, but she'd confess to murder before admitting it—before she'd give him one single *clue* about how deeply he'd affected her.

About how thoroughly he'd taken over her heart.

Every tattered piece of it.

"Tess."

She didn't answer him.

"Odette."

Bastard. Bastard. Bastard.

"*What?*"

"Look at me."

Her head refused. Even her heart refused. But as lightning flared beyond the window again, the thunderheads in her soul roiled, summoned by the matching storm of his. Like air and water and wind, she was a helpless element, called to action by her Master.

She lifted her head.

And clenched back tears once more.

Unable to ignore the raw emotion on his face. The brick now embedded beneath his jaw. The contortions of his lips. The glass-sharp surfaces of his eyes, barely holding back the rain from *his* soul.

He twisted tighter into her arms. "You lied to me, too."

She choked out a laugh. "About the plans for Newport? Right. That was a whopper, wasn't it?"

"I had a right to know, damn it."

"I know, Dan. I know."

She tried to match him note for bitter note but couldn't. She was too heartsick. Too heart*broken*. Too chewed up about the dumb things they'd held back from each other, too quickly transformed into the bricks of the wall that rose between them.

Or maybe he'd been right all along. Maybe the sex *had* messed everything up. Maybe this was the big joke from the Big Guy upstairs. Mars and Venus really couldn't do it all with each other.

Why didn't they just put crystal balls in every damn BDSM play room?

She lifted both her arms. Dug one hand's fingers into his shirt. Pressed the palm of the other to the center of his chest.

For a moment, she simply reveled in the strong, bold beat beneath her hand.

*Home.*

Ever again?

Or never again?

"It's scary," she finally rasped.

"What?" Dan replied.

"The wall." She looked up, seeing that he got it already. "These are deep shadows, Colton."

His jaw stiffened. "Yeah."

"I can't see past them anymore."

She slid her hand to his face. This time, for the very first time, she ran her fingers directly over his silvery scars. He flinched. She yanked on his shirt. Persisting, persevering, forcing. Making him accept every inch of her soft exploration.

Making him accept her unspoken love.

"But you, Daniel..." she whispered, "you're still right at home in the shadows, aren't you?"

The heat behind her eyes, too unbearable, went to liquid—as the windows in his gaze shattered. She responded by pressing her whole hand to the waxy planes, letting his tears pool between her fingers, capturing every drop of the spirit he poured into her safekeeping.

"Come into the light with me, Daniel. Please." She leaned up, kissing his mottled skin, rasping her entreaty into his ear. *"Please."*

He didn't answer. She didn't care. She didn't know how long they'd stood there, crying into each other as the skies wept outside, but it was long enough for Franzen to yell up from the living room. "Spook man! Damn it! Sometime this year, yeah?"

Dan dropped his head and pulled away. He still didn't

speak a word. Tess still didn't care. His shoulders remained weighted, slinking from her in shame—until she yanked him up, forcing his reddened gaze to knot with hers again.

Forcing his lips to mesh with hers again.

She sucked at him. Bit at him. Slammed his mouth open so she could plunder him, lick him, taste him, adore him...love him. His stance turned as rigid as the Red Rock cliffs. She didn't relent. He moaned and grunted, sounds of agony and pain. She didn't give up. As an incredible Dom had once shown her, the most extreme pain was often what a person needed for the hugest breakthrough.

He shoved away, his chest pumping and his fists coiled. He looked to her—once—taking just enough time about it to show that there was no more glass left in his gaze.

He'd put up solid steel in its place.

Retreating to the shadows.

And as he spun from her and marched out of the room without another glance, she had no idea if she'd dragged him even one damn inch back toward the light.

★ ★ ★ ★ ★

"Ohhhh sister, I've got one wheel down and the axle's dragging."

She chuckled at the latest line of creative imagery to pop out of Devyn while walking across her living room to slide a glass of iced tea in front of the little blonde.

Just like her brother, Devyn couldn't simply declare she was pooped from an afternoon of hitting every store in Crystals and The Fashion Show. And just like she'd done a thousand times over the last ten days, Tess wouldn't let the observation go any deeper than that.

Ten days. Ten years. What was the difference?

She hadn't seen Dan since their intense embrace back at the safe house—and then the parting stare he'd given her, too intense and too brief, before leaving the place with Franzen. After that, she'd only spoken to him once. Two days into their imprisonment—errr, protective custody—he'd called to relay they'd identified the henchmen Newport had assigned to Vegas and were moving in on the assholes. The call had lasted all of three minutes, dominated by his all-business Jack Bauer gruff, ordering her and Devyn to stay inside in case the agents were looking at live satellite images.

For two more days, she and Devyn had lounged, read, eaten, and Hulu-binged while awaiting word about the manhunt. Devyn, thinking the if-you-can't-beat-'em-join-'em coping mechanism might be worth a try, suddenly decided she was in paradise.

Tess had damn near climbed the walls.

After two *more* torturous days, Caspar Menken had finally shown up again, disguised as the pool boy—not a bad choice, if Devyn's lusty looks at his tank and board shorts were an accurate gauge. But he'd come bearing more than just tanned biceps and formidable thighs. There were updates on Operation Sink Newport.

They'd learned the bastard's set-up: four different teams of two, hired independently of each other, to cover the kill order in each city. The pair in LA, likely wannabe action stars who'd lied to Newport about their credentials, were the easiest to catch and arrest. The hitmen assigned to Seattle were more elusive but finally taken down during a car chase ended by their Maserati flying into the Sound. The men were fished out and then booked. The car was fished out and then towed for scrap metal. *Ouch.*

In Honolulu, things had gotten stickier. A *lot* stickier. Newport had managed to bribe two guards at the Barking Sands base, who apparently possessed large *cojones.* Not only did they risk court martial for accepting Newport's bribe, but also their assignment wasn't just an easy kill. As Franz and Dan had suspected, they tried to snatch Zoe Bommer—and the baby in her belly—alive. She disappeared from the beach in front of their cottage when Shay ducked inside to pee, thrown into an SUV that only made it as far as the base's gate, where Shay somehow caught up to them. Caspar didn't communicate any details beyond how the scene ended, dropping Tess's and Devyn's jaws in the process. Both henchmen had needed an ambulance. The car needed two new doors.

While Tess had cringed at that story, nothing compared to her blood pressure spike when hearing of Dan and Franzen's bad-guy pursuit. After spotting the assassins on the South Strip, they'd given chase through the Trop, the MGM, and then across to the Monte Carlo, where things had ended in a shootout that was, in Caspar's words, "a goddamn bulletfest."

Her blood went icy all over again just from recalling the moment Caspar had relayed both men's damage. Franz had taken a nick across his upper right cheek, and the word was still out about the fate of his sight in that eye. And Dan? *Holy shit.* Though Caspar maintained it could've been much worse, a bullet to the back of the thigh was still a bullet to the back of the thigh. She'd crumpled to her knees for the second time in as many weeks...

Thank God for Devyn, who'd become an expert at spotting her descent into that misery. Her sharp whistle sliced in, jerking Tess's head up.

"Yo, sweetie. Front and center. Buh-bye, safe house. Hello, real life. Let's play in center court, okay?"

Tess managed another laugh. "I'm here, I'm here. Ready to play, coach."

Devyn tilted her head, openly scrutinizing. "You sure?"

"I'm *sure*." She rolled her eyes and sipped her own tea.

"You know he's going to be okay, don't you?" The woman pulled over one of her shopping bags, emblazoned with a logo that made them both sigh. As she turned the entwined *L* and *V* on their sides and reached in, Devyn groused, "Big shit even pulled the bullet out himself before they got to the hospital. Sure, *now* he doesn't mind a scar. But who's going to look at *his* sorry ass?" She jabbed a finger at Tess. "Don't answer that."

Tess didn't need to be told twice. It was a welcome change, considering Devyn had all but declared herself president of the Dan and Tess Reunion campaign lately. Because *that* made sense. A reunion of *what*? Would they be lovers again? Friends?

The answers didn't matter. Dan was resigned to living his life in the dark. To letting his scars stand for shame and anger, not courage and uniqueness. It went deeper than ducking his face against walls and doing his grocery shopping at five in the morning. It gave him an excuse to hide, to lie.

To lie to her.

She had to give up the illusion it would ever be any other way. That her love would somehow dissolve the mortar of his wall.

Yes, damn it...she'd fallen in love with him. She'd figured it out sometime between reading her eighth and ninth Misadventures novels—before reaching the conclusion that it didn't make a difference to anything anyway. Unlike the awesome endings for the daring fictional couples, she and Daniel weren't meant for a kiss, a sunset, and a breathtaking trip to the bedroom.

Or the dungeon.

The silence was broken by Devyn's blissful moan. Tess looked up to watch her friend stroking a pair of Pucci ankle boots. "Welcome home, girls," Devyn crooned into the russet suede. "We won't see each other for a while after I'm back at work, but you'll always be in my heart."

Tess joined her friend in a giggle. She let her smile linger for a few seconds, disguising a secret message brought on by Devyn's declaration.

*You'll always be in my heart.*

Did Dan know how often she sent the message to him too? How she still needed to keep him close, even if it was only in her most hidden thoughts and most secret desires? How she drew on his strength to get her through each day, even if it was only through memories? Could *his* heart hear anything hers said, or had his wall developed into a fortress? Could he hear her vow *anywhere* inside, perhaps in that deep place their souls had always connected?

"Helllooo, Miss Lesange? Main court? Remember?"

Tess tried to laugh. "Sorry."

Devyn sank back, cradling her boots like a kid with stuffed animals. "No, you're not."

Tess arched her brows. "Like the universe is listening to the girl who just talked dirty to her shoes?"

"Like the universe believes anything from the girl who wants to talk dirty to my brother?"

She tipped her glass of tea up to hide the heat invading her face—and, in true overachiever style, sloshed out more than she could take in. As the drink spilled over onto her white tee, Devyn snickered.

"It's okay, girlfriend," Devyn crooned. "Not as if it's a state secret. And for what it's worth"—she stabbed the heels of the boots in the air—"little sis gives you two boots up."

Tess stood. Glared down at her shirt. It was probably ruined, but a trip to the kitchen felt instinctive, to try the cold water and detergent dab thing. Along the way, she rejoined as lightly as she could, "Dan and I aren't going to happen, missy."

"*Pssshh.*" The woman rammed her shoes back into the box, betraying that her stake in this conversation went beyond a casual chat. "You throwing the baby out with the bathwater, Miss Lesange?"

Tess paused after retrieving the spot remover from under the sink. "He's no baby. As for the state of his bathwater—"

"Ew."

"*Now* you going to drop it?"

Devyn rose, too. Set her hands on her hips. The motion seemed to flip a switch, turning off snarky little sister and turning on no-nonsense Secret Service woman. The transformation was sudden—and startling. Though Dev still stood there in a flowered sundress and heeled espadrilles, Tess expected her to spin around any moment and Wonder Woman it into her black suit and work flats.

"Tess," she said, just as serious, "I've really never seen or heard him like this. It's because of you. I know it."

She averted her gaze again. Shook her head, fighting all of the longing and need and hope—again. "And he's...special... to me too." She pulled out a hand towel but instantly tossed it to the countertop. "No. *Special* isn't even in the same league as him."

Devyn paced closer. Leaned on the counter with both elbows. "You love him."

"Yeah," she whispered. "I love him."

"I think he loves you too." The woman's voice was almost reverent with it. "The way he asks about you..."

Well, that was worth a stunned stare. "He— He asks about me?"

"Oh, yeah." The snark sneaked back in on a little snort. "Only he *doesn't* ask, right? Sneaks it in so I'm not onto him." Devyn curled her upper lip. "Like he's freaking Swiper and I'm a clueless Dora. Does he think I don't see past the lame mask?"

Tess was suddenly glad her shirt was stained. Nothing like dabbing between one's boobs to disguise an even more awkward moment. *Well, I sure as hell didn't.*

"Men are such boneheads," Devyn grumbled on.

"Which explains why you want me to try again with your brother...why?"

Devyn rolled her eyes. "To debone him, of course." She let Tess spurt a laugh at that before resetting her tone to serious. "Listen, I don't know what happened between you guys—"

"And you don't want to."

"No duh. But that doesn't mean—"

"It *does* mean, Devyn." She stepped over to link their hands. "Look, things are...complicated...with your brother and me. Let's leave it at that and move on."

She should have known better. Instead of ending the handclasp, Devyn screwed her grip tighter. "Maybe I can help in some way."

Tess made no secret of her squirm. "I really don't think so." *Unless you want to hear about some sides of your brother that no ear or eye bleach will wash away.*

"Tess—"

"No."

"Why not?"

"*Aggghh.*" She siphoned off some frustration with a string of laughter. "What is it with you Coltons and the word *no*?"

Devyn smirked. "Besides being allergic to it?"

"You don't say."

"So is that a *yes*?"

She huffed. "Okay...bathwater?" she finally blurted. "And your brother? And the *ew* factor? Remember?"

"Well, damn it."

She laughed again. It felt better this time, prompted by real mirth. "Let's not dwell on this. You're leaving in two days. How about forgetting your silly brother with some Chinese and an *Outlander* binge?"

Devyn shook her head and laughed. "Because *that* goes together."

"That's the whole point." She laughed too, glad the air had eased again between them. "Go cue up episode one. I'll call Yen Chu and—"

She'd just turned and reached into the takeout menus drawer when a loud crash came from the living room. Devyn spiked her alarm higher with a yell worthy of a sailor. "Motherfucker!"

"What the—" Tess dropped the menus and raced back into the other room, expecting to find Devyn sprawled on the floor, bleeding from the eyes, or both. But the little blonde was upright and the scene gore-free, unless one counted the remains of the remote now lying in a few pieces on the coffee table between her and the TV—

Which was filled with her brother's face.

"Oh, my God," Tess stammered.

Revision. Her brother's stunning, heart-stopping, completely gorgeous face.

Okay, so Dan could drop Tess's jaw even in baggy shorts and a tattered T-shirt—and he had before—but hell, did the man slide into a tailored suit with shocking perfection. The pinstriped Tom Ford was like nothing Dan had worn to the office on the few occasions he'd been forced to report for what he liked calling "himbo duty."

He wasn't a himbo now. He was a straight-up, sexier-than-hell hunk in designer wear. The proud lines of his sculpted shoulders were enhanced to perfection by the tailored jacket, open to reveal a matching vest beneath. His luxurious white dress shirt was the ideal offset for a silk tie in Caribbean blue, which made his eyes all but sear her through the screen itself. Or was the real power of his gaze due to his haircut?

*Haircut?*

Technically the term fit, though the stuff on his head was more dark-gold fuzz than hair, leaving people little to look at on his face except the swath of his scars.

And the throng of reporters in front of him sure as hell looked.

And gawked.

And whispered.

And took *a lot* of pictures.

And he stood there...and let them.

In the full light of day. With a lot of flashing bulbs. Without a shadow to be seen.

Somehow, Tess stumbled into place next to Devyn. She had no idea how she'd moved from Point A to Point B. Her stare—and her heart and her gut and her soul—were tied into the man on the screen, standing at a podium that displayed the Colton Steel corporate logo. The same symbol was depicted in a massive steel-and-glass sculpture behind him, clearly an important showpiece in the building where he stood.

The building he didn't just belong in.

The building he commanded. The scene he controlled, despite the deep tension at the corners of his lips...and the way he *still* moved as stiff as a damn GI Joe doll...

And the somber veneer he'd kept in place across his gaze.

*Dan. What the hell are you doing?*

The news channel began scrolling information along the bottom of the screen, but it was wrong. It had to be.

*Surprise announcement from Colton Steel...Daniel Colton, CEO, speaks to reporters...*

"Motherfucker," Devyn repeated. A smile spread on her lips, but Tess couldn't tell if it meant she wanted to hug or murder her brother. "He's really going to do it."

"Do what?" She tugged at Devyn's arm. The other woman just kept grinning. *Not* the answer she needed, which was reassurance that her brother wasn't about to change his life in one of the most massive ways she could fathom. "Devyn, what the—"

"Good evening."

Dan's voice boomed out from the TV, silencing her—and the crowd on the screen with him. As he straightened his stance, lifted his head, and smiled, all her nerve endings melted. All the goo from them collected in her stomach, making her suddenly yearn to cry or throw up—or both. She'd never had time for teen-idol crushes when she was a kid. Now she understood why teen girls transformed into unthinking idiots when their favorite rock bands came to town.

Unthinking.

Idiot.

Yep. That about said it all.

"Thank you, everybody, for coming down at such short notice, to join me here at Colton Steel's corporate headquarters. I know there are a lot of other things you'd rather be doing tonight in Atlanta." Dan flashed a fast grin. "Since it looks ready to rain again outside, I wouldn't mind a Scotch, a fire, and my favorite fuzzy socks right about now."

The crowd warmed with a round of soft chuckles. Tess smiled, unable to resist his golden charm herself, until noticing a blond, long-legged reporter who started eyeing Daniel as if imagining him in those fuzzy socks and nothing else. *Don't go any further with that, darling...*

"I've called this gathering to make an official announcement to you all," he went on, attempting formality now. "In a few short hours, it will be December first, the official beginning of Colton Steel's next fiscal year. At that time, I am proud to say that I'll be taking over the reins of the company from my father, Aaron Colton."

As the room exploded with shouts and questions, he held up both hands, commanding them all back to silence. More of Tess's body turned the texture of gruel.

"I'll address the obvious first. Dad is in fine health. He's simply been at this since he was a kid and wants a break. I promise you and all of Colton Steel's employees that he'll be around plenty to drive us all up the walls—and probably across the ceilings too." He brought his hands down, still spread, to hold the outside edges of the podium. The movement alone made Tess's heartbeat speed and then stop. She held her breath, already sensing the importance of what he was about to say. Though she had no damn idea *what* he was about to say...

"On to the next elephant in the room," Dan stated. "Many of you know me well—or at least think you do. You've followed the company since I was a goofy kid and then when I grew up into a goofier kid. Since you followed my pranks and antics through high school and college, you simply assumed I'd run off afterward to expand my *Steel Gone Wild* video collection, tearing up a few ski slopes and nightclubs along the way. You probably think *this* impressive scenery is the product of a car stunt gone wrong or a bikini girl jumping out of my birthday cake too soon."

As he traced a finger along his scars, the room went abuzz again—though the reaction was more subdued this time. And uncomfortable. Tess could sense the uneasiness in the room even from where she stood.

"Well, I'm here to tell you now, you did a *great* job," Dan announced. He grinned wide as the press corps leaned in, subconsciously scenting the explosive scoop they were about to get. "You wrote exactly what I needed you to—and I'd like to thank you all for that."

A ballsy guy in the middle of the crowd shouted the conclusion he'd led them to. "So you *weren't* wrecking nightclubs?"

Dan's answering smirk was a mix of enigmatic and charismatic. Tess was sorely tempted to pause her TV and fixate on the image for another minute—or ninety. "Not in the way that you think," he replied.

"Which means...?"

"For the last six years, I've been an active field agent for the CIA."

Tess could've concluded that the room exploded again, but the term wouldn't do justice to the scene erupting on her TV screen. A few others did the job so much better anyway.

Pandemonium.

Bedlam.

Turmoil.

Feeding frenzy.

Which led to her further amazement—when blondie-with-the-legs managed to beat everyone else in shouting the next question. "So, Daniel...does that mean you were a spy?"

He smiled at her. Though Tess saw through the expression as the fake politeness that it was, she still longed to climb at him through the TV screen—and then drape herself across him as he answered the wench.

"That means I can't talk about a lot of my work, Nina—so don't ask."

Blondie tossed her waterfall of hair over the opposite shoulder, determined to land her juicy soundbite. "Then tell us if that's how you got so horribly disfigured."

Devyn looked ready to punch the wall again. "Bitch did *not* just go there!"

Tess was certain she could put a hole in the drywall right next to Dev's. The things she imagined doing to Nina the Brainless were even worse. But her mind didn't seize any of them. She didn't want to ruin this moment by dipping into useless anger...

When she knew that Dan clearly didn't.

Perhaps it was the expression that took over his face, filled with the serene swagger she hadn't seen in him for a year. Maybe it was the new lights that appeared in his eyes, piercing and brilliant and beautiful. She couldn't peg exactly what she saw or how she knew...but right now, across the miles, she just... knew him.

And always would.

He could wear a thousand more masks. Alter his voice in a million different tones, timbres, or accents. Dress for her in leather or denim or freaking chiffon. She didn't care. It didn't matter now. It never would.

She'd know him. She'd *know* him.

She'd love him.

And loved him even deeper as he continued to stand at that podium, cocking his head higher, damn certain that everyone in that room—and the millions of people watching via live feed—saw every wrinkle, bump, and trail in the waxy skin along the right side of his face.

The most beautiful he'd ever been to her.

"I'm not disfigured, Nina. I'm scarred. And yes, I sustained these burns while chasing some nasty assholes in the woods last year." He turned to the rest of the crowd with an apologetic shrug. "Oops. You all have your profanity delays turned on, yeah?"

"Who cares if we don't," a man yelled from the back of the crowd. "Keep going, Colton. This is awesome!"

The crowd sent up a cheer for that one. Dan grinned, basking in their support. As she watched him, Tess wrapped both arms around his sister.

"That fucker," Devyn mumbled past tears. "I'm so damn proud of him."

"Okay, let me tell you what's *really* awesome," he said to the throng. "It's..."

He stopped short, dropping his head. Tess held her breath

again, aching for him. "Go ahead," she rasped. "Say it, Sexy."

He raised his head again. "Awesome isn't what I did for the CIA, you guys. Awesome is what I *learned*. Sneaking around in costumes, playing with the techie gadgets, catching the bad guys... Yeah, that's all pretty dangerous and cool, but when you rely on the disguise to be your reality, you've lost the battle before you've begun. When you hide your truth in the shadows, then you've started the fall into weakness. That's where I was headed, friends. I really liked those shadows because they were easy. Because I didn't think I was strong enough to look at all this"—he ran a hand down his burns—"as a badge of honor instead of a mark of failure. But not anymore."

The crowd was silent as he lowered his hand.

"Not anymore," he repeated—while slipping that hand beneath the papers on the podium and pulling out a long-stemmed, bright-red rose.

Tess stepped away from Devyn.

And fell to her knees.

Devyn slid down with her, sliding hands back into hers, thankfully sharing her brother's strength for intuiting a situation. She sat silently, letting Tess stare at the screen, not saying a word as Tess's heart ached, soul burst, and lips pleaded.

"Don't let it go, Daniel. Please don't let it go!"

On the screen, Daniel still clutched the rose.

Lowered it toward the podium.

"No. *No*. Don't let me go!"

He leaned over once more so the microphones could pick up his closing statement. "There's nothing more at this time."

He turned and walked away, still clutching the rose...

Before tucking it into his jacket. Next to his heart.

For many long minutes, Tess remained on the floor. Afraid

to move. Afraid to think. What would happen if she did? Would she even be here, crouched next to Devyn? Or would she still be back in the kitchen, wondering whether to order cashew shrimp or chicken stir-fry for dinner? Would she forget the last fifteen minutes had happened?

"Tess?"

Devyn's whisper, husky with worry, sifted into her.

"Oh, my God. You're white as the sand in your backyard. Tess? Are you okay?"

She finally felt a breath spill out. Another. Another. She heaved the air back in just as fast. Again. Again. The actions made it easier to battle the tears raging up her throat. But they never got close to her eyes. Instead, they wadded up and pushed back down into her belly, pushing her into a crazy nether between nausea and paranoia.

"I'm...okay." She sat up. Then stood up. She peered into the woman's eyes, so clear and blue—just like his. She laughed in relief at Devyn's dimples, also just like his.

Also like her brother, she cocked a sardonic brow. "So you believe me *now* about how nuts that shithead is for you?"

Tess jabbed her chin up. "Only if you'll help me get my ass on the next possible plane to Atlanta."

Devyn threw her head back on a laugh. "*Now* you're talking, bitch!"

# CHAPTER FIFTEEN

"Thank you so much for the feedback, Mr. Colton."

Dan quirked a brow at Colton Steel's newest HR and Training intern. She had huge, twinkling eyes and a smile that could power Times Square with its wattage, but that didn't stop him from slicing a new glare at her.

"Well, you're welcome for the feedback, Maxi—wasn't much, since this new training program is already good stuff— but I swear if you call me 'Mr. Colton' one more time, I'm going to make you eat tuna fish sandwiches from the cafeteria every day next week."

Maxi's jaw popped open. "You wouldn't dare."

He grinned. "Try me."

She closed her mouth. Stood and started stacking her papers back into neat little piles. "You're having a lot of fun shaking shit up around here, aren't you?"

He leaned back in his chair at the head of the conference room table, hiding his grimace due to the bandages still taped over part of his ass. "You could say that."

She broke into an impish grin. "Well, *Dan*, I think it's kind of fun. Keep surprising us, okay?"

"Ten-four, little lady." He chuckled and waved as she hurried out. It was Friday afternoon. She probably had a hundred texts to send to as many friends, making plans on where they'd meet to kick off their weekend fun.

He wondered what Tess was doing tonight.

Then instantly fought the thought by punching a button embedded in what he'd come to call his "spaceship chair." The blinds on the picture windows rolled up, exposing the panoramic view of the city, the waters of the Chattahoochee sparkling in the distance.

If he had to spend most of his days with his ass parked in an office, at least the view helped.

He vowed to get out of here early today. Unpack some moving boxes at his new place, a condo over in The Wakefield. Hit the BeltLine for a long run, no matter how much it set his ass on fire. Clear his head. Free his mind. Flush out his soul. Untangle the tension in his body.

Items one and two? No problem.

But three and four?

He didn't delude himself. Running a fucking marathon wasn't going to lift those weights from him. Nor would burying himself in work—been there and bought the T-shirt for the last seventy-two hours—or even jumping on the jet down to the Shadowlands.

He had to accept that only two things would.

Tess.

Or time.

And since even his grand, flowery, *stupid* gesture at the press conference had failed to generate even a phone call from Ms. Lesange, he was going to have to make Time his new best friend.

This was going to suck.

Time wasn't a fun date. Time complained about everything. He never got it right with Time. He was either indulging it or cheating on it. And Time didn't laugh at his dumb jokes...or moan for him in the sweet little tone that drilled right to the center of his cock...or fall asleep in his arms, looking like an angel sent from heaven just for him...

He turned back around and growled at the empty room.

Okay, sure, he knew the platitudes about all of this. Had even tried a few on to see how they felt. He should've been proud of himself for stepping from the shadows, even without Tess waiting in the sun. The light was a good place to be, all by itself. The light was its own reward. He was living without shame or disguises, with a much easier haircut as a bonus. The light was right, even if he was in it alone...

Hell.

He glanced between his legs to make sure his balls were still there.

Just before his newly hired assistant, Mara, ducked her head in the doorway.

"Ah," he called out. "Mara, Mara, Mara. My *second* new best friend."

The woman struck him as a person born into the wrong century. With her classic, dark features and hair, he wouldn't be surprised if a past life regression turned up someone like Catherine of Aragon or Queen Isabella. She carried herself with equal regality, even when crumpling a confused frown at his greeting.

"Forget it." He waved a hand, bidding her to come closer. "Not important. What's still left that *is* important?"

"Just these three new shipping contracts to sign, with the revisions per your meetings this morning." Mara arranged the documents in front of him.

"Outstanding." He began scrawling his name near the fifty plastic flags she'd attached to each page. "Annnnd, I'm clear on the day pass after this, right?" When she didn't confirm that right away, he looked up and instantly scolded, "Maaarrraaa."

She twisted a little frown. "I'm sorry. She insisted."

"She?" For a second, hope fire-crackered through his chest. "She who?"

"Your sister."

He smiled anyway. The next-best thing to a visit from Tess was a visit from Devyn. "Did you let her wait in my office?"

"Of course." Mara's smile grew a little too. "I like her, Dan. Her hair is so...fiery."

"*Fiery?*" Well, this was going to be interesting. Dev was always too preoccupied with being a badass to ever think much about her hair. On the other hand, she'd developed a real accessory obsession lately. She'd also been with Tess nonstop for ten days. Lucky wench.

He entered his corner office, still decorated in Dad's old-school style of Tara-meets-Hogwarts, and frowned. "Yo, little shit?" he called. "You hiding out somewhere?"

A hand shot up from the big leather chair behind the desk, which was faced toward the window, letting in the lazy afternoon sun. The thing was a little less ostentatious than the Captain Kirk model back in the boardroom, but only a little.

The hand curled one finger at him, beckoning.

"Christ," he grumbled. "Really? Just because you colored your—"

His breath caught in his throat.

His *tongue* caught in his throat.

Devyn wasn't the one waiting for him.

Tess was.

A glorious, luminous, sun-drenched, sexy...

*Very naked...*

"Therese."

He said it with reverence and gratitude, with awe and amazement, as a prayer of thanks and a plea for confirmation—

Then again. Because he could. Because he needed to hear it for himself, if only to help drive in the certainty—the miracle—of her.

"Therese Odette Lesange."

It snarled out of him as he plummeted to his knees, hardly daring to touch her for fear she would vanish in a puff of his imagination. Instead, she sneaked teeth out over her bottom lip, hardening him at once with her sweet little pout, before she twisted a hand around his tie and yanked his mouth to her sweet strawberry lips.

At once, he was inside out. Upside down. Ripped apart and then put back together again. He drove his tongue inside her, unable to get enough of her taste, her scent, her softness, her passion.

"Fuck," he finally rasped, letting her drag his tie all the way off. "You're here." He gazed down, betraying his wonderment in no uncertain terms. And his joy. And his bursting, brilliant amazement. "Yeah...you're...*here*."

She bit her lip again, pushing her chest up in open invitation. Damn, how he missed those tits. The areolas were already drawn and puckered, her nipples punching up like perfect raspberries. "You're a tough man to surprise, Mr. Colton Steel top-of-the-food-chain. I really had to make my opportunity...stand out."

Unable to resist, he licked one of her nipples. Then the other. He blew across both of them, making them stand harder at attention. Tess mewled, arching higher for him. And goddamnit, bit into her lips *again*.

"You're definitely standing out."

"Even if I fudged the truth a little to accomplish it?"

He chuckled. "A *little*?"

"Maybe more than a little. But it was Devyn's idea."

"I'm sure it was." He reached in to pull a nipple between his thumb and forefinger. "But she won't be as much fun to punish."

"Punish?"

Oh.

Yes.

*That.*

The fear in her voice. The lust in her voice. The mix was so intoxicating, Dan almost laughed from the instant buzz to his spirit. Who needed booze when this woman was around?

Fuck it. He gave in to the laugh. But the second his gaze latched back onto hers, he sobered. Damn. Everything he'd dreamed of seeing in her eyes, and despaired of never seeing again, was there. The warmth of her friendship but the light of her adoration. The silk of her submission but the intense glimmer of her passion.

"I love you, Daniel Colton," she whispered.

"Not as much as I love you, my rose."

They kissed again, tenderly this time, before she smirked against his lips and murmured, "By the way, that was a slick move, Sir Sexy. With the rose, at the press conference."

He cocked a sideways grin. "Didn't want to be slick. Just wanted to be clear."

"How did you know I'd understand?"

"Because I've watched you a lot, darling subbie." He brushed bright-red silky strands from her face. "I've observed what makes you hotter, wetter, wilder...and how you enjoy the ideas of things just as much as doing them." He kissed her again, slowly but sensually wrapping his tongue around hers, until she softly moaned. "It's what makes commanding you so much fun."

"Hmmm." She contemplated him for a long moment, looking utterly sinful with her lipstick smeared and her hair sprawled against his chair. "So, what kinds of 'ideas' are making me hot and wet now, Carnac the Magnificent?"

"Carnac the Magnificent *Dom*."

"Ohhh, right. Sorry. Carnac the Magnificent *Dom*, just what is it that I'm loving the idea of right now?"

Before Dan answered her, he stood and leaned over his desk. Pressed the intercom for Mara's desk.

"Can I get you anything?" came her queenly voice over the speaker.

"Privacy," he barked. "Hold everything for the afternoon. My...sister...and I are discussing some things. We're bonding. Deeply."

"Yes, sir."

"Yes, *Sir*." Tess echoed it with a giggle as he closed the line with Mara. As soon as they were "alone" again, he spun the chair around so it faced the desk. With his cock now aligned at the level of her face, his answer to her query was all too easy to declare.

"Carnac the Magnificent says his subbie wants to wrap her sweet strawberry lips around the cock that's missed her so badly."

Tess broke into a smile. "Well, *Sir*, that sounds just about right."

She didn't waste time scooting forward in the chair and then putting her eager hands to work on his belt and fly. Just the flutters of her fingers over his clothes had to be one of the most erotic things Dan had ever felt. He locked his teeth, grinding down enamel while watching her reach inside his pants, exploring the hot bulge beneath with her uninhibited fingers.

He didn't want her to stop. He couldn't wait for her to get the hell on with it.

But the most breathtaking part of her service didn't come from anything she did to him physically. It was the glance she slid up to him, lips in a Mona Lisa smile, eyes twinkling with the bright-green excitement she always got when they were just hanging out as friends. The discovery of a movie they both liked. Her delight in spectacular sunsets. Her bliss at singing along to Fall Out Boy on the radio.

It was all still there. Thank *fuck*...all of it. All the joy and the good times and the friendship—but now better. Stronger.

And oh, yeah...a hell of a lot wilder.

A fact she emphasized by shifting her fingers down to cup his throbbing balls.

"Fuck!" He finished it in a long hiss. When her grin turned a little playful, he snaked a hand into her hair, tugging her head back enough to flare her eyes in new attention. "I like your opportunities, sweet rose," he told her, "as long as you remember who controls their destiny."

Her gaze softened. Her body slackened. "Yes, Sir," she whispered, soft as the angel he'd just compared her to. The angel he was about to defile with the shaft now hammering to escape his pants...

"On your knees, rose."

He aided her by yanking on her scalp, positioning her between the chair and his body. When she was in place, he slid his hand to her jaw, pushing gently to coax her open. With his other hand, he freed the length of his dick from the boxers she'd just been worshipping with her touch.

He touched the head of his cock to the warmth of her mouth. Groaned hard as her dark-red lips moved around him, pulling him in deeper...deeper...

"*Tess.* Sweet one. Take all of me. Yesssss..."

She matched his groan, especially after pushing his underwear aside to get her fingers on his balls again. As she massaged his aching sack, she worked his shaft with wet, hot strokes, surrounding him with the tight pull of her cheeks and the long licks of her tongue.

"Damn," he groaned. "This mouth is going to become my new favorite play toy."

His declaration made her wilder. She fucked him hard with her mouth, abandoning herself to bring him deep physical bliss. And she did. With every dip into her mouth, his cock was pure fire. With every withdrawal, it trembled in anticipation.

He had to give her the same thing.

No. It was more than that. He had to be inside her, a part of her. To seal himself to her. To mark her, body and mind and soul, as his. To fill her with nothing but his heat. To give himself to her as a lover, not just a Dom.

With another groan, he pulled himself out. She looked up at him, eyes glazed, lifting a woozy smile. Dan kissed her, savoring the taste of himself on her mouth, before lifting her back up into the chair and spreading her legs wide. With their next kiss, he brought a hand up to explore the soft pink wetness at the core of her body.

"Damn," he rasped once more. "You're so ready for me, aren't you?"

Tess shuddered beneath his touch, her clit trembling, her

slit clamping one of his fingers. Then two. Then three...

"Oh!" she cried. "Yes, Sir. Please..."

"No." Dan prompted her to look at him with a finger on her jaw. "Not Sir. Not *Sexy*. Not even the griffin. Let Daniel fuck you right now, babe." He took her lips again, working his way over her with slow but hungry desire. "Let Daniel love you."

She smiled, looking a little bashful about it, until he moved his fingers inside her again. Her walls clenched around him as her head fell back, arching her body up into the streaming sunlight.

"Holy fuck, Tess. You're the most beautiful thing I've ever seen."

"No," she whispered back. "*You're* beautiful, Daniel. Your love makes me this way. Your domination sets me free." She flashed him another of those lip-bitten smiles as she unbuttoned his shirt, exposing his chest for her eager licks, bites, sucklings, and kisses.

"So good," he murmured.

*So damn good...*

Until he couldn't take the pressure anymore. His erection throbbed like thunder. His heart churned in a downpour of need.

"My little rose," he grated into the hollow of her throat. "I need to be inside you."

"Yes," she whispered.

"Screwing you."

"Yes."

"Satisfying you."

She sighed, rocking him with another Tess buzz. While giving him another gorgeous smile, she reached into his right desk drawer, pulling out a perfect foil packet.

Dan laughed and then kissed her again. Her lips felt so good, all softness and surrender and love. Her mouth tasted so good, cinnamon and sex and woman. But best of all, her laugh sounded so good as he drawled, "My clever, clever little laser beam."

"Hmmm. You won't be able to live without me anymore."

He didn't miss a note of her saucy tone. Or an inch of her uncertain grin. That was why he kissed her twice as hard.

"That's the idea, Ruby."

Her insecurity faded. "So asking about a transfer to the Atlanta field office wasn't hasty?"

He growled while he rolled the condom on. "Not hasty enough."

Her eyes brimmed, liquid and gorgeous. "I love you so damn much."

"Ssshhh. No more talking. Spread your legs wider and let me get lost in you."

She did.

And *he* did.

At last, he was right where he was supposed to be. One with her. Buried in her. Uniting with her in the light only she'd been able to bring him to, with the perfection of her friendship, the courage of her honesty, the magic of her submission, the wildness of her love.

He only dared to ask fate for one more addition to his want list.

A lifetime to spend adoring her for it.

Continue the Honor Bound Series with Book Eight

# *Mastered*

**Coming Soon**
*Keep reading for an excerpt!*

# EXCERPT FROM *MASTERED*

## BOOK EIGHT IN THE HONOR BOUND SERIES

Time had dictated a lot of Brynn Monet's life. Watching it, abiding by it, dancing to it...and praying to it for better things to come.

This was one of the prayer moments.

*Lots* of prayer.

No one confirmed that better than Shay Bommer as he drove a fist into the living room wall of the suburban Las Vegas home he shared with his wife, Zoe—Brynn's best friend.

But Zoe wasn't here right now.

The emptiness was symbolized to sickening perfection by the gaping cavity left behind when Shay pulled his fist out of the wall and stepped back, snarling at everyone in the room like a cornered animal. It took a while. It was a full house tonight. Eight other people were in the room, five of them legitimately qualifying as humanized Mack Trucks. The men had dropped everything to fly here for the guy who'd once served side-by-side with them as part of the First Special Forces Group. Brynna stood nervously in an opposite corner with El Browning and Ryder Monroe, the friends she couldn't be without right now.

The hole Shay just created joined two he'd already made. Brynn doubted anyone would blink if he destroyed the whole wall.

Or maybe that was wishful thinking on her behalf.

Taking out a wall felt like a damn great idea right now.

Even better idea? Obliterating the bastards who'd kidnapped Zoe six hours ago.

"Shay." The word, hammered with command, was issued by the pirate hunk who stalked forward. Though Rebel Stafford didn't have an eye patch or a peg leg, the comparison fit in every other way. Those shoulder-length waves of jet-black hair. Those eyes, shot with Caribbean-blue specks. That accent, laced with earthy Creole. Those tattoos covering both arms—or so she assumed. The formfitting T-shirt he wore over his camouflage pants prevented final confirmation—not that her mind's eye hadn't already re-outfitted him in breeches, riding boots, a tricorn, and nothing else.

No time for the rest of that vision. Brynn would have been thankful for it if the reason for being here was anything other than this.

*Dear God. Why Zoe? Anyone but Zoe.*

Except no one but Zoe made sense.

A truth that ravaged every inch of Shay Bommer's face.

"What?" The man spun and glared at Rebel. "*What?* Have you come bearing any useful information about where the *fuck* my eight-months-pregnant wife is, Reb? If you haven't, then get the hell out of my sight."

A pulse ticked in Rebel's stubbled jaw. If she'd blinked she would've missed it, so formidable was the man's self-control. "Can't do that, man, and you know why."

"Fuck off."

"Not happening. You know I need to run through the details with you again."

Shay slumped against the wall. Brynn's heart broke for him. In this case, "the details" only meant one thing: the horrific sequence of events between his wife's bathroom break during their dinner date and the moment she'd screamed before being shoved into the back of a black van at the restaurant's rear exit. Shay had sprung to his feet, bursting into the alley in time to notice only two things about the van before it sped away. One, it had no plates of any kind. Two, the driver maneuvered the bulky thing like a seasoned pro.

"Damn it." Shay exposed locked teeth. "I've told you everything I know!"

"I know." Rebel squared his shoulders. "But I need you to sit down, take a shitload of deep breaths, and then tell me again. I need everything you can possibly remember."

Shay dropped his head and dragged both hands through his thick chestnut hair, choking back a broken breath. "I... can't."

"Yes, you can. We need more to go on. Something. *Anything.*"

By "we," Rebel included the guy right behind him, whom he was rarely seen without. Rhett Lange, call-sign Double-Oh, served as their battalion's tech and covert-identity specialist. This was a fancy way of saying that, on the team's most dangerous missions, his dependability was key. Nobody knew that more clearly than Rebel, who, as the "blow-shit-up guy," needed rock-solid intel at every turn of an op.

Brynn jerked her head, forcing the tangent away. Why the hell did she know all of that? Even worse, why did it give her the same adrenaline kick as her *Teen Scene* centerfolds wall from high school? Even right now. Especially right now.

*Focus, Monet. Focus on what* you *can do to help. Zo wasn't just your dance captain for three years. She was your rock through all the shitty times—and the days that were worse than that. You have to be there for her now. You have to do something.*

Another silent but desperate plea. She was going not-so-slowly insane, sitting here in helpless dread and disbelief...

A feeling she was no stranger to.

*Good afternoon, Brynna. I'm Officer Feld and this is Officer Smythe, Vegas PD. Sorry to pull you out of rehearsal, but I'm afraid we have some bad news. It's about your sister, Enya...*

She was saved from the memory in the nick of time by the man who stepped up and pulled her back to safety—mentally, at least. Rhett Lange's effect on her body wasn't so simple. The man matched his friend for sheer physical potency—with one difference. He wasn't a pirate. No other comparison worked for Rhett but *Viking*. Though no wild hair tumbled to his shoulders, the red tips of his short blond spikes lent an Icelandic flair. His eyes, the color of North Sea depths, were bracketed by rugged creases that deepened as he focused on Shay.

"Reb's straight up on this, Bommer. I can't do a thing with what you've given me. *Think.* You've been trained to do this. Close your eyes. Focus. Can you at least tell me which way the van turned at the end of the alley?"

Shay slid down the wall, *thunk*ed to his backside, and buried his head in his hands. "You mean as I watched them drive away with my helpless, screaming wife?"

The room fell silent—until a small sob stabbed the air to Brynn's left. She reached over, locking hands with El and Ryder. The woman who'd danced with her for as many years as Zoe and the male model who'd become the D'Artagnan to their Three Musketeers joined their desperate grips to hers.

The connection was comforting but didn't fill the void left by Zoe's absence. Nobody knew her as deeply as Zoe. Enya didn't count. Not anymore.

*Stay strong. You have to stay strong. Zo would do the same for you.*

She managed to keep from trembling—until a three a.m. breeze snuck in through the patio, threaded with enough of a March chill to thwart her effort. El began to shake too. Ry yanked them both against his chiseled chest—again, a huddle missing a key player.

"Zoe." El's sob was broken with grief. "Oh, my God...Zoe."

Her cry yanked Rhett's head around. As he took in their miserable clump, a grimace stabbed his soldier's veneer. "Fucking bollocks." The desperation in his voice, underlined by the accent clipped by both London and New York, reached into Brynn's heart. "We have to figure this fucker out."

Rebel stalked back across the room. "Damn it, Bommer. I get that this is hell for you—"

Shay surged up, a bestial sound bursting out. "You get it? Is that so? Then enlighten me, Moonstormer." The call-sign might as well have been hot oil on his tongue. "Tell me what the hell you *get*. You go through a different submissive each month. You flog 'em and fuck 'em, with aftercare barely over before you're eyeing the next skirt in line. Forgive me, asshole, if I have trouble believing how you *get* this."

Under other circumstances, the accusation would've earned Shay a black eye from Rebel, followed by the other guys in the room. Every one of them had dropped everything to be here for their buddy in his blackest moment. Rebel and Rhett had flown from Seattle with Garrett Hawkins and Zeke Hayes, where the four of them still served in Special Forces out of

Joint Base Lewis-McChord. Another former battalion-mate, Kellan Rush, had arrived an hour ago from Hawaii—an odd sight, since Tait Bommer wasn't with him. Shay's older brother was also Kell's best friend, damn near surgically attached to the man except for when he'd been hauled off for training in the middle of the ocean. Also taking part in that training were the battalion's captain, John Franzen, and language specialist Ethan Archer. While awaiting clearance for leave from the training, Franzen and Archer had joined Tait in calling every hour to check on Shay. The coincidence was very likely a blessing in disguise. Shay was already crumbling at the seams. Tait's presence would likely make that worse.

As if the assumption needed affirmation, Shay twisted back, trying to use his forehead on the wall. After three attempts, he gave up. The mountains of his shoulders heaved with his breaths.

Rebel filled in the other end of the composure spectrum. With barely a change to his stance, he calmly murmured, "Glad we got that covered. Do you want to talk about something that matters now?"

Shay's breaths stretched longer. "Left," he finally grated. "I think they turned left."

"That means they went south." Across the room, Rhett flashed a small smile. He'd clearly been hoping for that answer.

"Out of town, then?" Ryder queried. "To California? Or Arizona?"

"Not necessarily." El added her knowing gaze to Rhett's. Brynn looked on, hiding a bizarre bite of envy for their connection. Or *was* it that strange? El's mind worked like a hard drive, able to process a thousand pieces of information and spit out a conclusion in seconds. It was the key behind her impeccable dancing, why she always got audition callbacks before Brynn, who performed mostly from her gut. Two different routes to the same result—except when that outcome was impressing a man as incredible as Rhett Lange.

*Focus! This is your best friend's living room, not a damn cocktail bar. Phone numbers on napkins are not why you're here.*

Getting Zoe back. It was the only thing that mattered—no matter what it took from all of them to do so.

"The airport." El's hazel eyes favored dark green, betraying her anxiety. "Shit. They could have been headed for the airport, right?"

"Air*ports*," Rhett corrected. "Not just McCarran. In this case, Henderson Executive fits that bastard's MO better."

"MO?" Brynn looked from him to Rebel, who nodded grimly. "What bastard?"

"Yeah," Rebel muttered. "It does."

"*What* bastard?"

El twisted her lips. "Homer Adler."

**This story continues in**
**Mastered: *Honor Bound Book Eight!***

# ALSO BY ANGEL PAYNE

**The Misadventures Series:**
*Misadventures with a Super Hero*

**Honor Bound:**
*Saved*
*Cuffed*
*Seduced*
*Wild*
*Wet*
*Hot*
*Masked*
*Mastered (Coming Soon)*
*Conquered (Coming Soon)*
*Ruled (Coming Soon)*

**Secrets of Stone Series:**
*No Prince Charming*
*No More Masquerade*
*No Perfect Princess*
*No Magic Moment*
*No Lucky Number*
*No Simple Sacrifice*
*No Broken Bond*
*No White Knight*

**For a full list of Angel's other titles,
visit her at www.angelpayne.com**

# ABOUT ANGEL PAYNE

*USA Today* bestselling romance author Angel Payne loves to focus on high-heat romance starring memorable alpha men and the women who love them. She has numerous book series to her credit, including the Suited for Sin series, the Cimarron Saga, the Temptation Court series, the Secrets of Stone series, the Lords of Sin historicals, and the popular Honor Bound series, as well as several standalone titles.

Angel is a native Southern Californian, leading to her love of being in the outdoors, where she often reads and writes. She still lives in Southern California with her soul-mate husband and beautiful daughter, to whom she is a proud cosplay/culture con mom. Her passions also include whisky tasting, shoe shopping, and travel.

Visit her here:
www.angelpayne.com